A Desirable Arrangement

ALSO BY GWEN KIRKWOOD

SINCLAIR FAMILY SAGA SERIES
Book 1: Moorland Mist
Book 2: Moorend Farm
Book 3: Return To Bonnybrae
Book 4: A Scottish Destiny
Book 5: Love Has No Borders

MAXWELL FAMILY QUARTET
Book 1: An Orphan Of Scotland
Book 2: The Secrets That Bind Us
Book 3: Dreams Of The Valley
Book 4: Somewhere To Call Home

STANDALONES
Beyond Reason
A Desirable Arrangement

A Desirable Arrangement

GWEN KIRKWOOD

Joffe Books, London
www.joffebooks.com

First published in Great Britain in 2024

© Gwen Kirkwood 2024

This book is a work of fiction. Names, characters, businesses, organizations, places and events are either the product of the author's imagination or are used fictitiously. Any resemblance to actual persons, living or dead, events or locales is entirely coincidental. The spelling used is British English except where fidelity to the author's rendering of accent or dialect supersedes this. The right of Gwen Kirkwood to be identified as author of this work has been asserted in accordance with the Copyright, Designs and Patents Act 1988.

Cover art by Cover art by Jarmila Takač

ISBN: 978-1-83526-866-7

CHAPTER ONE

After celebrating Hogmanay and the dawn of 1977 with her father and Nessie at Rowandene Farm, her home in South West Scotland, Kim McLaren had set out to fly across the world to begin her lecture tour on animal breeding and genetics to groups of farmers. She knew she was fortunate to have been the person chosen by her own university, in collaboration with the universities in New Zealand, but wondered whether her audiences were prepared for a twenty-five-year-old woman — would they be expecting a man, possibly in his thirties or forties? She had been filled with both anticipation and trepidation.

Now, five months later, and nearing the end of her tour, Kim was filled with elation, knowing she had held the attention of her audiences and been made welcome everywhere. She had finished her lecture and was preparing to answer questions from the audience when the door at the back of the hall was flung open to admit a flustered-looking man carrying a note. He strode towards the front and handed a message to the chairman with a few brief words, then a glance in her direction. A sort of sixth sense told Kim that the missive concerned her, even before the chairman passed the note across to her with a look of concern. Taking the microphone, he addressed the audience, apologising for drawing the meeting to a hasty close. He explained there had been an urgent summons for Dr McLaren to return home, due to illness in the family.

The only family Kim had was her father, Ross McLaren, and Agnes, or Nessie, as she was known. Nessie was her father's sister, although she was closer in age to Kim herself. Nessie had been mother, aunt and dearest friend all rolled into one since Kim's mother died when she was nearly ten.

There were murmurs of sympathy and understanding from the audience as Kim hurried from the hall. The secretary of the agricultural organisation who had booked her appointments was already making enquiries about flights.

'What did the telephone message say exactly?' Kim asked.

'It was from a Miss Nessie McLaren, I think. The line was not very clear. She said she was telephoning from the hospital where they have taken your father, so you may not be able to contact her until she returns home. She was sure you would want to get back to Scotland as soon as possible.'

'Did she say if it was Dumfries hospital? I could phone there.'

'You don't have much time, Dr McLaren. You need to pack now if you want to catch the first available flight,' the chairman intervened anxiously. 'I will drive you to the airport myself.'

* * *

It seemed a lifetime to Kim before she reached London and caught the train to Carlisle. She felt utterly exhausted and desperate for the latest news about her father. She was searching for the platform number for the train to Dumfries, the last leg of her long journey, when Nessie came up and enveloped her in a warm hug.

'I thought I would spare you this last short train journey, Kim dear. You must be absolutely shattered, but I'm so relieved you're here.'

'Oh, Nessie, I am truly pleased to see you.' Kim felt unexpected tears spring to her eyes and blinked rapidly. She had learned to keep a tight control on her emotions ever since she'd walked behind her mother's coffin. Dear Nessie. The sight of her kind and familiar face was almost her undoing.

'How is my father? Please don't hide anything. I managed to put a brief call through to the hospital from Singapore, but they expressed the usual platitudes and told me barely anything.' Her voice trembled. 'He's only fifty-three. He has always been so fit, so healthy.'

'I know, dear. That's what Mr Sanders said. He is the consultant surgeon. He has been so kind and understanding and has promised to give Ross his best attention. Apparently he knows Ross because he has bought hay from him for his children's ponies. He lives in Ryankirk Village, or at least on the outskirts, the opposite end to Fairvale, actually.'

'I'm pleased he's getting good care.'

'I know. I was so distraught when we arrived at the hospital, but when Mr Sanders came, he was so calm and reassuring. The good news is Ross has regained consciousness as Mr Sanders had assured me he would. I visited earlier today and he was more alert than I had dared hope.'

'But what happened? Why is he in hospital at all?' Kim demanded sharply as they walked to Nessie's car. 'Oh Nessie, I'm so sorry. I have been so tense and wound up all the way home.'

'I know, and you must be tired out. I knew it would be a terrible journey for you. It was an awful thing to happen when you were so far away. Ross's leg is broken in two places. Mr Sanders insisted on operating on it himself because the leg had been twisted and we think he must have lain for several hours like that during the night. Joe found him outside the calving shed when he arrived for the morning milking. He was unconscious. We think he must have stumbled over the edge of the concrete ramp going up into the shed. We still don't know whether he knocked himself out when he fell or whether he lost consciousness due to the cold and wet. The young registrar who admitted him said the shock and the chill were enough to cause the pneumonia. I know it is lovely today, but we have had a really cold, wet spell, especially for May. Oh, there's my car over there. I couldn't get parked any closer,' Nessie said apologetically.

'But what was he doing outside during the night?' Kim asked.

'One of his imported heifers was calving. You know he likes to make sure they're not in difficulty, especially heifers, and he did pay a high price for the three Dutch ones. He must have gone out some time after midnight, I think. I went to bed about ten thirty and he said he was going to have a snooze in his chair then see how the heifer was doing. I don't know yet whether he remembers what happened.'

'I can't wait to see him for myself,' Kim said huskily.

'Here's my car,' Nessie said, opening the boot and helping Kim stow her luggage before she added, 'I don't think they will allow us to visit tonight, dear. I stayed with him all day and most of the first night, but the nurses like to keep to their routine and give the patients a good night's sleep. I told Ross this afternoon that you were on your way home. I-I think you'll find he's a bit emotional.'

'I feel a bit that way myself,' Kim admitted, climbing into the car beside Nessie. 'Do you think he's been working too hard? I should never have left him for so long!'

'Of course you should, Kim. It was a rare opportunity and Ross is so proud of you.' Nessie hesitated, then added slowly, 'He seems to have been pondering whether he ought to give up farming and retire, leaving you free to pursue your own future in the world of academia.'

'What? Retire from farming? But he loves Rowandene I love Rowandene! It's home! He lives for his animals, and if I'm honest, so do I. Besides, he's too young to retire.'

'I believe he could easily afford to retire, if it's money you're worried about, dear.'

'Of course it's not money. Farming the land, breeding good cattle — they're the breath of life to my father, and to me. He could have taught me everything I needed to know himself, but he was so insistent that I have an education because he'd promised my mother he'd ensure it.'

'But you did enjoy it, didn't you, Kim? I mean, you've done exceptionally well and I'm sure you couldn't have done that if you had hated it.'

'Oh I've never hated it, except when I first left home. Once I got over leaving you and Dad, and the animals and familiar faces, I quite enjoyed most of it, especially learning about genetics and breeding, and more recently the possibility of embryo transplants becoming more viable to breeders like my father. The researchers are always discovering something new.'

'Yes, that professor told Ross you could have a great future in research.'

'Professor Bradley? But how . . . ?'

'He came to Rowandene to see you, to offer you a job. He was disappointed to hear you were on the other side of the world. He stayed to lunch and had a long talk with your father. Ross said it sounded as though he was working on a new project, and missing your assistance.'

'Well, I'm home now and I vow I shall stay here and work beside Dad. It's where I belong. What's wrong, Nessie?' she asked. 'You look troubled. Is there something you're not telling me?'

Nessie concentrated on her driving for a few minutes while she considered how to tell Kim what had happened.

'You remember Sir Martin Newall died just before you left?'

'Of course I remember. I went with you and Dad to the funeral before I flew out. Ninety-six was a great age and he enjoyed a satisfying life. It was a huge funeral.'

'That's because he was such a kind and generous old man. He was always giving to the local fundraising in Ryankirk

— the village hall, the kirk, the school. He never turned down any worthwhile cause.'

'I know. He's never raised our rents either during the past fifteen years. I once heard him say to Father, "I have neither kith nor kin to benefit and I'd rather you use the money to make a comfortable home and improve Rowandene the way you need for modern twentieth-century farming." Dad and Mr Craig, at Burnhead, were his only remaining tenants — and he expected we would each buy our farms as sitting tenants. Mr Craig wasn't too keen on the idea because he's been talking about retirement for a while, but Dad's been looking forward to buying Rowandene. He's even considered buying Burnhead, too, if Mr Craig doesn't want it. He said we would discuss it all when I returned.'

'I'm afraid that's not going to happen now.'

'Because of this accident?'

'No, because the whole of Wedderburn Estate, including the Hall, Home Farm, the parks and acres and acres of woodland, have all been purchased by a newcomer to the area. Burnhead and Rowandene were included in the package, and the purchaser seems to have the impression he has bought the farms with vacant possession.'

'Vacant possession? But that's ridiculous!' Kim declared. 'Dad must be terribly disappointed not to have had the chance to buy Rowandene himself. I expect there might be a worry about future rent rises now — though I'm sure he'll accept any fair and reasonable change.'

'I wondered at first if news of the sale had caused him to have a mild stroke,' Nessie said in a subdued voice.

'Oh, surely not,' Kim said, horrified.

'No, Mr Sanders has reassured me on that. Ross asked me to look through the letters on his desk and arrange to pay any bills due. I found the letter from the new laird on top. Mr Daniel Nichol is his name and he clearly believes all the land has vacant possession, including Rowandene.'

'But he must realise Sir Martin had tenants! Mr Craig is ready to retire, but my father isn't. Or . . . or he wasn't . . .' Kim's voice trailed to a whisper. 'You think the letter upset him, Nessie?'

'I'll show it to you. Ross had left it open and it was as though he had read it more than once.'

'B-but we have security of tenure, if nothing else.'

'Your father does. But I'm not sure whether that would include you, Kim dear. According to the letter, it's as though this Mr Nichol believes Ross is an old man without any family.'

'But he has us!' Kim declared indignantly.

'He does. But I don't count in terms of the tenancy. I suppose technically Fairvale is my home, even though I do have tenants in at present. I have my accountancy business running from Rowandene — though that's something he won't be aware of yet. I have met Mr Nichol briefly. He probably thinks I'm a poor relation, housekeeping in return for a free home, rather than being part of the family,' Nessie said ruefully.

'Oh, Nessie. He doesn't know us at all! You and Dad have always been close. He once told me your arrival was a delight to everyone. Granny had had miscarriages after he was born and they didn't think they could have any more babies. Seventeen years later, there you were!'

'Thank you, dear, but this Mr Nichol is a stranger to the area. He won't know any of our history. Anyway, we can forget about him for now. We're nearly home,' she said thankfully, turning off the main road.

'Dad wrote in one of his letters that your accountancy business is growing so fast you've had to turn away clients.'

'That's true, and it's not something I like doing. Lots of tradespeople don't have time to keep accounts and send out their bills on time. That's the reason many of the young tradesmen fail when they set up on their own. I like to help them and see them get established, just as Ross and my father helped me.'

'Maybe you can take more of them on now that I'm back? It's time I took over the household and let you concentrate on your own business.'

'Oh, Kim, it has never been a chore to me, keeping house for Ross and you. You are all the family I have. My life would be worthless without you both.'

'But you have made sacrifices for us . . .'

'There will be two of us now. I'm looking forward to that. It will be lovely to do things together again, if you're home for good. I believe Ross feels the same. I know he was looking forward to discussing his plans with you — or at least he was until that letter arrived. I don't know what the future holds for any of us now.'

CHAPTER TWO

Kim was almost recovered from her exhausting journey home and the jet lag, and she was feeling more reassured that her father's health was improving since they had been allowed a proper visit and were able to speak with him.

'I shall keep a special eye on your new favourites, Dad,' she promised with a smile. 'I know you paid a high price to get the new bloodline you wanted.'

'Aye, well, I'm relieved they're in safe hands, lassie, now you're back.'

'I saw a big improvement in Ross's health today,' Nessie said as they drove home. 'You are the tonic he needed.'

The following morning, when Kim entered the calving shed, it was obvious to her that the Dutch heifer was going to need some assistance. She collected the calving jack and a clean bucket of hot water and soap, then climbed through the barrier between the feed passage and the calving pen. She murmured soothingly and stroked the flank of the quivering animal. There was no doubt she was restless and uneasy, no sooner lying down than she was on her feet again, giving low bellows of pain. Kim piled up some clean straw and hoped the heifer would lie down and settle long enough for her to feel if the calf was coming front feet first, as it should. Hopefully, all it needed was patience and a pull at the right time.

Eventually the heifer lay down and allowed Kim to ease the tight skin around the tiny ivory-coloured feet. It never ceased to amaze Kim how perfectly formed the little cloven hoofs were. She eased them further out until she could slip a rope around each of the calf's front legs, making sure she fixed them beyond the first joint before she tightened them and hooked the other end of the ropes to the calving jack, then she settled herself on the heap of fresh straw and prepared to wait patiently and pull each time the heifer was ready to push. Her father had always insisted that patience and instinct were more essential than brute strength — it was better to work with nature rather than wrench the calf out willy-nilly with a real risk of tearing the mother, and possibly even causing her to bleed to death. Kim cared too much for all animals to treat them ruthlessly. Slowly, bit by bit, she increased the tension on the calving jack as the calf's legs came further out with each push from the mother, but the crucial point was getting the head out and hoping the pain would not cause the heifer to scramble to her feet with the calf hanging out.

Some instinct caused Kim to glance sideways. She caught a glimpse of well-polished brown shoes and smart, sharply creased trousers.

'Can't you see I'm busy,' she muttered irritably, keeping her voice low.

'I'm not in a hurry,' a deep voice replied quietly.

'This is no time for salesmen. So please go away.'

'You may need my help.'

Kim wanted to yell that he would be no use dressed like a gentleman even if she did need help, but the calf's head was coming and she needed to concentrate. She eased the tight skin and cleared the mucus from the calf's nose and mouth as soon as she could reach. The heifer was panting and straining, but one more heave and the head was clear. Kim gave a sigh of relief, but it was vital the heifer should not get up at this point, or that the calf should be stuck with its hind legs and half its body still inside her. Out of the corner of her eye she saw the shoes move nearer.

'Go away!' she growled quietly, before murmuring soothingly to the distressed animal, willing her to stay lying down until the calf was fully out. The heifer settled again and Kim grabbed the legs, and with the next contraction she pulled with all her strength. The calf slithered out. Immediately the heifer struggled to her feet, but Kim continued rubbing the calf vigorously with handfuls of clean straw, drying and massaging it, urging it to breathe. It lifted its head slightly and gave a protesting little moo. Kim heaved another sigh of relief. The heifer moved closer and began licking vigorously with her rough tongue, massaging her offspring as nature intended. Kim lifted a hind leg to check if the calf was a heifer or a bull. A heifer! She grinned, knowing her father would be delighted. She pushed the calving jack through the rails of the barrier and out of the pen, then bent to squeeze between the bars herself. The material of her trousers was stretched taut, but she was oblivious to her unwelcome caller and his frank admiration of her neat behind.

She busied herself at the bucket of water, washing away the blood and mucus from her arms and cleaning the calving jack. Her father was meticulous about hygiene.

'I see you're still here,' she said, turning to face the stranger in exasperation, her mouth tightening. If he had been one of the regular salesmen he would have left when she asked him to. At five feet seven inches Kim was tall, but the man was a head taller. She saw a mixture of amusement and approval in his dark eyes, but before she could speak he held up a hand.

'I'm not selling anything. I was looking for Mr McLaren. I met a boy in the yard and he mumbled something about him being in hospital, but that I would find Miss Kimmery in the shed calving a heifer. Presumably you must be the local vet?'

Kim took a deep breath and gave him an exasperated look. 'If I was the local vet, I would probably have sworn at you when you refused to leave.'

'I thought you might need help.'

'You wouldn't have been much help all dressed up as you are.'

'I have wellingtons in the car and the trousers could always go to the cleaners. I would not have wanted to leave an animal in distress — or a lady, for that matter.' Kim's eyes flashed and she opened her mouth to protest, but he held up a placatory hand. 'As it is, I congratulate you. You managed that calving as well as any vet I've ever seen, male or female.'

'Maybe you've not seen many vets at work, Mr . . . ?' Kim spoke drily, though she was secretly pleased by his praise.

'That's not the case, Miss Kimmery. I trained as a vet myself.'

'You're a vet?' Kim's neat dark brows arched in surprise. 'You must be new to our local practice then, or at least you must have started in recent months, while I've been away in New Zealand. But why are you here? Did Joe phone for you?'

'Who is Joe?'

'Our dairyman, or cowman, you might call him, if you're English?' He didn't sound English, but not broad Scots either. 'He's in the parlour doing the milking right now, otherwise I expect he would have been here to help if I needed a hand.'

'Surely you would know whether I've joined the local veterinary practice, if you are one of them yourself?'

'I am not a vet. Nor is my name Miss Kimmery, and you've not told me who you are or why you are here.'

'My name is Daniel Nichol. I am new to the district.' He held out a hand in greeting. Kim's hand was still damp. She wiped it hastily on her trousers, but even as she held it out she was frowning. Nichol? Surely the name was familiar . . . ?

'So if you're not a local vet, and you are not Miss Kimmery, whom have I the pleasure of meeting?' His voice was deep and pleasant, his mouth curving upwards in a humorous quirk.

'Nichol! Of course! I should have remembered,' Kim said through gritted teeth. Her green eyes blazed.

Daniel stepped back in surprise, his brows raised.

'You are the new owner of Wedderburn Hall and the estate!' Her tone was almost accusing. 'I understand you are expecting to take over Rowandene with vacant possession, despite the legal tenancy agreement my father had with Sir Martin Newall. I suppose you think my father should meekly leave the land our family has farmed for four generations. I shall be the fifth.'

'Your father?' Daniel echoed. 'You are Mr McLaren's daughter? But I met Miss McLaren. Surely . . . ?' He stared in bewilderment.

'You may have met Miss Nessie McLaren, my father's sister? She is a chartered accountant. She has an apartment and her office here at Rowandene.' Kim lifted her small, determined chin and looked at him defiantly. 'The changes to the house were made with Sir Martin Newall's approval. My father paid for them himself.'

'Miss McLaren is your father's sister?' His surprise was evident.

'Nessie came to live with us when my mother died,' Kim said stiffly. 'She has a house of her own in the village called Fairvale. My grandparents left it to her, but she rented it out when my father needed her help.'

'I see.' He whistled through his teeth. 'So, your father cannot be such an old man as I thought then . . . unless . . .' He frowned. 'I understood from the solicitor there were no close relatives to take on the tenancy.'

'He has Nessie and myself,' Kim said indignantly. 'It is true he is a widower, but my mother was very young when she died.'

'The person I spoke to said I should find the boss in the calving shed. There must be some mistake.'

'My father is in hospital,' Kim said coldly. 'He had an accident and broke his leg.' She didn't mention it was a bad break in two places, nor that he had lain outside and suffered from concussion and pneumonia. 'Fortunately, he is making an excellent recovery.' She crossed her fingers behind her back and hoped that his recovery would continue apace.

'I see.' He frowned in confusion.

* * *

Daniel Nichol had only recently returned from Africa where he had spent several months working as a vet. He had not had anything to do with the purchase of the Wedderburn Estate, in Dumfriesshire, and therefore also Rowandene. Indeed, he had never even heard of it. Having been born and brought up in Aberdeenshire, he knew little of the south of Scotland.

Wedderburn had been bought as a gift for him by his great-uncle, Fergus Nichol, and the legalities had been handled from Aberdeenshire by Uncle Fergus's old friend and lawyer, Mr George Dodds.

When Daniel's parents had died, Fergus had taken Daniel in, given him a good home and education and generally regarded him as his foster son. Daniel loved Uncle Fergus and knew he owed him a debt he could never repay.

Yet Daniel had needed to escape. Before leaving for Africa, he had found himself in a ridiculous situation. Uncle Fergus's neighbour — and his neighbour's daughter — had become increasingly determined to have a say in Daniel's future, and their pressure for him to abandon his intended career as a vet had been overwhelming.

Daniel had sought some time out. He knew his decision to spend time working so far away in Africa had worried Uncle Fergus, but he promised he would return when he'd broadened his experience. Several months later Daniel was astonished to hear that Uncle Fergus had purchased and gifted him a small estate. It saddened him when he realised it was an inducement to get him to return to Britain. Yet when he arrived back in the UK Daniel had been dismayed at the deterioration in his uncle's health. After so many months away he saw that age and its effects were rendering his only relative a lonely old man. At the very least Daniel owed him his company and his loyalty, and with Uncle Fergus willing and eager to make his home in the south of Scotland with Daniel, he resolved to do his best to make his uncle and his housekeeper, Dolly Dunn, a comfortable home in part of the huge, rambling old building which was Wedderburn Hall.

* * *

Kim scuffed her feet in the silence, bringing Daniel's attention back to the reason for his visit to Rowandene. As he talked to Miss McLaren, and learned that her father was far from ready to retire and give up the tenancy, he wondered whether their solicitor could have been under a misapprehension about the farms having vacant possession. Vacant possession would have given the estate a higher value. It also meant more money for the solicitors handling the sale on behalf of the charity to which Sir Martin Newall had left it. As far as Daniel was concerned, it didn't really make any difference to him. He had no desire to farm the land himself. For as long as he could remember he had wanted to be a vet. His only concern was to have tenants who did a good job and paid their rents on time.

'So, if Mr McLaren is in hospital, who did the herdsman mean when he said I should speak to the boss?'

'You're looking at her,' Kim said, daring him to challenge her authority. 'Father made me a partner in the business as soon as I finished university. Probably whoever you spoke to also assumed you were a salesman.'

'Mmm, well you know how to calve a cow, I grant you that. Do you have a name, Miss McLaren?'

'Of course . . .'

He grinned at her. 'Would you mind sharing it?'

'My name is Kimberly. Kim, to my friends.'

'Very well, Miss Kimberly McLaren. You are my nearest neighbour so I hope I shall be allowed to graduate to Kim before long. Meanwhile, I shall wait until your father gets home from hospital and feels well enough to have a discussion about the tenancy and what is best for our mutual interests. Perhaps you would ask him to telephone me when he feels up to it?'

CHAPTER THREE

Kim didn't mention her meeting with their new landlord, either to Nessie, or to her father when she visited him at the hospital later that day. Mr Daniel Nichol could wait. She would not allow him, or anyone else, to upset her beloved parent now she was here to take care of him.

Ten days later Ross McLaren was allowed home, but only with strict instructions not to try walking on uneven ground and not to be on his crutches too often or for too long.

'My daughters will be needing more hay for their ponies soon, so I may call in and surprise you to check you are following my instructions,' Mr Sanders said with a smile and a twinkle in his eye.

Kim wondered fleetingly whether it was her father or Nessie he was hoping to surprise. Mr Sanders was a widower with two young daughters and Nessie seemed so very at ease in his company.

* * *

Nessie was cooking the dinner in the farmhouse kitchen when the phone rang. She answered it automatically but tensed when she heard Daniel Nichol on the other end. She assumed he would be wanting to come to discuss the tenancy with Ross, so she was surprised when he explained he was phoning to speak to Miss Kimberly McLaren.

'I understand she has recently visited New Zealand and I hear there is a meeting in town with a speaker who is expected to be both entertaining and interesting,' Daniel said. 'I thought she might like to hear him. Will you tell her I can pick her up at seven o'clock?'

'I . . . er . . . I think Kim is working in the garden.' This was awkward, Nessie thought. 'Can you hang on a minute please while I give her a call?' She knew Kim was in the farm office across the hall. She put her hand firmly over the receiver while she repeated the invitation.

Kim's eyebrows shot up in disbelief. An invitation from their new laird was a surprise. 'B-but I'm the speaker!'

'I know . . .' Nessie chuckled. 'Obviously he doesn't know that though.'

'Don't tell him! Say . . . say I'm busy. Er . . . no . . . Tell him I have an engagement this evening. Well, it's true.'

Nessie obeyed but she couldn't suppress a smile. It was rare to see Kim getting flustered.

'You could have accepted a lift with him,' she teased when she'd replaced the receiver.

'I wouldn't do that! However obliging or charming he pretends to be, he'll never convince me he has any right to claim vacant possession for Rowandene.'

'I'm afraid Ross will have to discuss it all with him soon,' Nessie said with a troubled expression. 'We can't put him off much longer. Maybe we should be pleasant to him at least.'

'I can't go with him anyway,' Kim said defensively. 'The committee have arranged to take me to dinner at the hotel beforehand as a thank you for stepping in at such short notice.'

'Mr Nichol will get a shock when Dr McLaren turns out to be his next-door neighbour *and* a female.'

'He probably just wanted company because he's a stranger to this area. I heard on the grapevine he had been working in Africa before he came here. I don't know if it's true.'

'I think it is. I heard he was in Africa when his family's lawyers bought the estate. It was Jock Kerr, the builder, who told me. He had been asked to check the gutters and the state of the house. Anyway, it was kind of him to offer you a lift.'

'If he was kind, he wouldn't be trying to take over Rowandene with vacant possession when Dad is a legitimate tenant. I'm sure it was that letter that upset him. It probably made him so preoccupied he wasn't looking where he was going outside in the dark.'

'Oh, Kim, dear, we don't know that. Ross doesn't seem to remember what happened.'

'Well, anyway, Dan-the-man will just be looking for company until he gets to know everybody.'

Nessie didn't argue. Kim had never considered herself an attractive woman, despite her being intelligent and capable.

***

Kim was the only woman of the eight people sitting at the dining table at the hotel, but she knew most of them by sight, some better than others. Three of the younger members on the committee of the County Farmers' Club had been involved in the Young Farmers' clubs when she was an active member herself. Harry Bell was sitting next to her and they enjoyed reminiscing about their days as Young Farmers. He had belonged to a different club, although they were both in the same district so had often competed against each other at local shows. Kim had attended many meetings and markets with her father, and they all asked after him and sent their good wishes for his recovery. They were laughing at a joke someone had told when Kim glanced up and saw members of the audience hurrying along the adjoining corridor towards the function room.

'It looks as though some of them got caught in that thunderstorm. I heard the thunder rumbling overhead while we were eating dessert.'

They were only feet away from the windows of the dining room and, of all the people in the crowd, Kim's eyes locked with the astonished gaze of Daniel Nichol. He paused briefly, lips parting in surprise. His eyes widened and Kim knew her reaction to him had been exactly the same. She clamped her mouth shut. Daniel was not alone. The young man beside him looked vaguely familiar, but for the moment she couldn't place him.

'That man was having a good look at you,' Harry said. 'Not that I blame him.' He grinned. 'You're even more attractive now than you were when you were a teenager, and you were a pretty young thing then.'

'Flattery will not earn you any favours,' Kim responded, her smile a little strained.

'Do you know him, the tall, dark fellow? He made sure he didn't miss anything.'

'He's our new landlord since Sir Martin Newall died. His name is Daniel Nichol. I believe he has recently moved into Wedderburn Hall.'

'Ah, so that's the man. Hasn't he been doing a stint of charity work in Africa as a vet? I heard some relative, his uncle or godfather, or something, purchased the estate on his behalf while he was away.'

'I don't know anything about that.'

'I'm forgetting you're not long back from the other side of the world yourself. You will have a bit of catching up to do—' He broke off as the chairman called them to order and said it was time to take their places.

Kim's heart sank as she followed the chairman and vice-chairman onto the platform. Only four rows from the front, and right in the middle, sat Daniel Nichol and his young companion. It was impossible to miss him, she thought crossly. He was eyeing her intently and she thought there was a hint of a sardonic smile around his mouth. Why couldn't he have hidden himself at the back or at the side somewhere so that she didn't need to see him?

The chairman proceeded to introduce her, saying all the usual flattering things.

'We are fortunate Dr McLaren has agreed to step in at such short notice after Mr Peacock was rushed into hospital with appendicitis. Dr McLaren is not long home from New Zealand. She cut short her trip because her father was ill, so she has not had time to sort out her collection of photographs or plan the talks she will be doing for the Young Farmers' clubs during the winter. However, I have heard Kim speak several times during debates in her days in Young Farmers and it is not surprising that she was selected by the joint Scottish and New Zealand universities for the tour, so I know we shall have an interesting evening, and if we're lucky maybe Kim will agree to come back at a later date and show us her photographs. Before I sit back and listen I would just like to say we all send Ross our best wishes for a full and speedy recovery and hope to see him at our next meeting.'

There was spontaneous applause and Kim felt proud of her father's popularity, but she noticed Daniel Nichol raise his dark eyebrows in surprise.

'Now I shall hand you over to Dr McLaren,' the chairman concluded, and sat down.

There was more clapping as Kim got to her feet. She was glad she had taken pains with her appearance and she knew she looked smart in her kilt and jacket and new black court shoes, all so different to her everyday trousers, sweaters and wellingtons. It helped her confidence.

The kilt had been expensive but her father had insisted on buying the very best in the modern McLaren tartan, ahead of her lecture tour of New Zealand. It was mainly blocks of greens and blues with a stripe of yellow and a stripe of red running through it. She had chosen a black jacket which fitted her slim figure to perfection, but it also matched the bright colours of the Stewart tartan kilt which she had from her days as a member of the Scottish Country Dancing team. Her mother had been a Carmichael, which was a branch of the Stewart clan, and Kim would have been happy to make do with that for her trip abroad, but she had to admit the made-to-measure kilt was superior.

The talk went well and there was genuine laughter once or twice when Kim recounted a couple of humorous anecdotes, one of which had been her own terror at the prospect of sky diving — something she had never expected to attempt but which she felt would have disappointed her hosts if she had refused. It had been a busy time and she had visited a lot of farms, so there were plenty of interesting things to talk about without the need for notes. In fact Kim forgot about individual members of the audience once she got started, and her own enthusiasm was infectious. She was modest about her achievements, so was unaware that it was her natural ease and ability as a public speaker, plus her sense of humour, that had singled her out as a worthy ambassador for the New Zealand tour in the first place.

After the meeting closed, the vice-chairman delayed her for a short time, enquiring about her father and if he was well enough for a visit. The two had known each other a long time and had often done deals together. Then he asked if she would care for a drink at the bar. She thanked him but refused. It had been a long day and she would be glad to get home to bed. As she passed the bar lounge, she noticed most of the audience had congregated there.

Outside she shivered a little after the warmth of the hotel. The sky still looked stormy as darkness descended, but at least the rain had stopped.

As often happens with thunderstorms, heavy rain started again when she had driven only a few miles along the road. She had just turned off the main road onto a narrow cross-country road when she met the milk tanker coming rather fast round a corner, so she was forced to drive through a long, deep puddle as close to the edge of the road as she could get.

She felt her car judder as she hit a hidden pothole beneath the water, but at least she had avoided a brush with the tanker. She had only gone another mile or so when her car began to lurch to the side. Her heart sank. She guessed it was a puncture in a back tyre. The rain had eased to a drizzle, but she would still get wet. She reached for her old anorak and pulled it on top of her jacket, but it would do little to protect her kilt.

She switched on the safety torch, which her father had always insisted she keep in the car. She sat it on the roof, its red light flashing. She was fairly well drawn into the grass verge and she had put the hazard lights on, but it was a narrow road if anyone came on her too fast. Still, there was nothing else for it but to change the tyre or walk the last four miles home.

She lifted the boot lid and took out the jack and lever and the tool for slackening the nuts. She prayed they were not too tight. She couldn't remember the last time she'd had a puncture. She frowned as she prodded the emergency wheel. It didn't seem all that hard considering it had never been used. There was a pair of old waterproof trousers which had belonged to her father beside it. They were none too clean and she doubted if she could get all the material of her kilt tucked into them. It would be mighty chilly to remove her kilt with so little underwear underneath the waterproofs, but it was the best alternative. She sat in the passenger seat with the door open and unbuckled her kilt. She was about to slip it off when the headlights of another vehicle swept round the corner. Fortunately, it was not going too fast and drew to a halt behind her. Before the engine had stopped, the passenger door was flung open and a young man bounded out.

'Hi, Kimby, I thought I recognised your Ford Estate. Are you in trouble? Ah, yes, I can see you are. That really is a flat tyre.'

Kim stood up, grasping the top of her kilt to prevent it slipping down. Kimby! Only one person had ever called her that. She peered at the smart young man in the lights from the Land Rover.

'Billy? Billy Nairn? Goodness, you were a boy the last time I saw you. When did you grow so tall?' She had known Billy since they were both children because he had come down from the north to stay with his aunt and uncle every school holiday. She had always been more than a head taller than him, but now he was a good six inches taller than she was. 'I thought I recognised you at the meeting, but I've never seen you in a suit before, looking so smart and handsome. I didn't know you were visiting your aunt and uncle at Wedderburn Lodge.'

'I'm not visiting, I am living with them — at least temporarily.' He grinned happily. 'After such flattery, if you'll lend me those old waterproofs I'll pull them over my trousers to protect my one good suit, then I'll change the tyre for you.'

Daniel Nichol came up behind him. Taking in the situation with a sweep of his eyes — from the kilt she was gripping tightly at her waist, to the waterproofs grasped in her other hand — he grinned. As his eyes met hers, she could see the amused glint. Kim felt flustered all of a sudden. 'I was preparing to change the wheel myself and I didn't want to ruin my kilt,' she said defensively.

'This evening continues to be as interesting and entertaining as I had been promised,' he said, with that grin widening yet further. 'Though my friend here failed to tell me he was on such familiar terms with our neighbour.'

Kim was hastily buckling her kilt, but she looked up at Billy, her eyes questioning. 'You said you were living down here, Billy?'

'Yes. Mr Nichol is giving me a trial as his land agent. Uncle William retired when Sir Martin Newall died, but he has agreed to continue supervising until he and Mr Nichol are convinced I am capable of taking over. I have been at college in Gloucestershire for four years, and of course you have been away yourself. We have a lot of catching up to do now I'm back. Are you home to stay now?'

'I'm afraid that rather depends on you and your employer, and whether you put us out of Rowandene.' She knew her tone was waspish.

Billy had slackened all the nuts and was in the process of lifting off the wheel, but he jerked upright, glancing from one to the other of them with a horrified expression.

'I'm afraid I have not had the pleasure of meeting Mr McLaren yet,' Daniel said drily, 'but I suspect we have a few matters to sort out. I am presently looking into the conditions of the sale and the lawyers who handled it on behalf of the charity who are getting a very generous donation from Sir Martin Newall.' There was a grimness in his tone now.

'B-but the sale has g-gone through?' Billy stammered in alarm. 'You are the new owner, aren't you? Uncle William is not selling me a pup, getting me here under false pretences, is he? I mean, there really is a job for me as your land agent, if I prove myself able enough?'

Daniel Nichol moved to Billy's side and patted his shoulder, almost in a paternal gesture.

'Yes, Billy, I am the owner now, and there is a job for you, so please be assured on that score. Your uncle is very keen to have you take over his old job, though I suspect he will continue working far longer than any of us expect, especially your aunt. However,' he sighed heavily, 'the estate was bought on my behalf. Evidently, Uncle Fergus considered it too good a chance to miss. He intends to make his own home down here, too, once I have settled in myself.'

In the dim lights Kim glimpsed a wry expression on his face. She guessed he had not been consulted on several aspects of the purchase. There seemed to be too many complications relating to the sale and purchase of the estate for either herself or Billy to understand what the future might hold. Perhaps the sooner her father had a talk with Daniel Nichol, the better.

'This spare wheel doesna seem as hard as it should,' Billy said, drawing their attention back to the job in hand. Daniel went to test it.

'It does seem a bit soft,' he agreed with a frown. 'I have a foot pump. Put it on, Billy, and I will blow it up if I can. It's not far to go so it should see you home, Dr McLaren, and—'

'Oh, for goodness' sake, drop the formality,' Kim said irritably. 'My name is Kimberly, or Kim if you like.'

'Kim for friends. Yes, that I do like,' Daniel said with a glimmer of a smile. 'We will drive behind you to make sure you get home safely, but don't drive too fast.'

'Oh, I'm sure there's no need for you to—'

'Of course there is,' Billy said with a grin. 'We've earned a cup of coffee, I reckon. Does Nessie still bake those nutty biscuits she always used to give us?'

'Very well.' Kim grinned back at him. 'I will submit to your wishes, Billy Boy.' She had, in fact, baked a batch of the nutty biscuits herself that morning. They were her father's favourite too.

When they arrived back at Rowandene, Ross and Nessie were both drinking their bedtime cocoa, but they stood up in surprise at the sound of male voices. Kim led them into the room.

'This is Mr Nichol, the new owner of Wedderburn Estate, Dad.' She turned to draw Daniel forward. 'My father, Ross McLaren. I think you've met my aunt, Nessie McLaren.' She waited while Daniel greeted them and shook hands, then she ushered Billy forward. 'You both know this handsome fellow.'

'Well, hello, young Billy!' Nessie greeted him. 'Where has that skinny young scamp gone? I can't believe you've grown into such a tall young man.' She indicated both men should take a seat.

'I heard you had done well at college, Billy. Agriculture, wasn't it?' Ross asked. 'The last time I was speaking to your uncle he spoke of how proud he was of you. You'll be looking for a job now?'

'The course was more estate and land management, really,' Billy said. 'You taught me everything I know about actual farming,' he admitted. 'I've learned quite a lot about trees and forestry management plus a few other subjects.'

'Billy is going to take over his uncle's place at Wedderburn,' Daniel said, 'with his initial supervision.'

'I thought he had retired from his work when Sir Martin died?'

'I don't think he will ever retire,' Daniel Nichol said with a smile at Billy. 'He asked me to take Billy on trial, with himself as his supervisor. So we're giving it a go.'

'You'll be living with your Aunt Annie then, Billy?'

'I am for the present, but Mr Nichol has promised to modernise one of the cottages for me once he's done up a wing of the Hall for his own uncle.'

'I'll make you both a hot drink,' Nessie said, beginning to rise. Kim pressed her down.

'I'll make it. You finish yours while it's hot. I had a puncture and they stopped to change my tyre so I owe them a cup of coffee, or tea. What will it be?'

'Hot chocolate for me, please,' Billy said with a grin, 'if you still make it as good as you used to?'

'Oh, Kim is still as good a cook as she always was, Billy.' Nessie chuckled. 'And she baked a batch of your favourite biscuits this morning. She must have had a sixth sense you'd be calling in.'

'What would you prefer, Mr Nichol?' Kim asked.

'I thought we'd dispensed with the formalities, Kim. You know it's Daniel, though lots of people call me Dan — or worse sometimes.' He grinned. 'I'll have the same as Billy, please. He seems to know what is recommended.'

A little while later Kim returned from the kitchen carrying a tray with three mugs of hot chocolate and a plate of biscuits. They were all chatting amicably and she breathed a sigh of relief.

'Dad, Mr Nichol has been wanting a proper meeting with you to discuss the tenancy situation, but I thought we should wait until you were completely recovered.'

'Och, lassie, there's nothing wrong with my brain, or my tongue, and I'm hoping there'll be nothing wrong with my leg either before long.' He turned to Daniel. 'It will suit me to get our affairs straightened out, Mr Nichol, whenever you're free. Am I likely to need my solicitor here at the same time?'

'Your solicitor? I hope not, Mr McLaren! I believe there have been enough misunderstandings involving lawyers already. If you are free tomorrow afternoon at two o'clock, it would suit me well. I would like to have things sorted out between us as soon as possible. You've probably heard that Mr Craig is retiring from Burnhead?'

'No, I hadn't. Is that voluntarily or under pressure?'

'No pressure from me, I assure you,' Daniel said coolly, with a glance at Kim. 'Though he may be under some pressure from his wife. I understand she wants to buy a bungalow in the village. That will be one of Billy's first tasks, to help me interview prospective tenants for Burnhead.'

'So it's not true then, that you were intending to take all the land into your own hands?' Ross McLaren asked tensely.

'Definitely not. I'm a vet and enjoy my work. My experience of farming is sketchy. I think between us, Billy and I will have plenty on our hands improving Home Farm and the woodland at Wedderburn. William Nairn tells me some of the woods are in need of attention, but he said Sir Martin seemed to lose interest latterly.'

'He was an old man and made no secret of the fact he wanted to live his last years in peace without officials telling him what he must do.'

'Aye, Uncle William said he couldn't be bothered with the form-filling connected to felling some of the trees and the clearing and replanting of the two top plantations,' Billy said. 'Even I can see it's time some are felled before they blow down.'

'My great-uncle may have made a generous gesture in buying the estate on my behalf,' Daniel remarked with a wry smile, 'but I'm beginning to wonder what he's let me in for.

It was his way of getting me back in the country. According to his solicitor, he didn't like the idea of me working with the wild animals, but it was an experience I wouldn't have missed for the world.'

'Aye, young folks like to broaden their horizons these days,' Ross sighed, thankful he had Kim safely home again.

'Well, Billy, I think we've kept these good people long enough. Thank you for our drinks and delicious biscuits.' Daniel looked at Kim as he rose to his feet.

'Thank you for changing my wheel and seeing me safely home,' Kim said. 'I'll get the spare checked tomorrow when I get the tyre mended.'

After they had seen their guests out, Nessie muttered, 'I have a confession to make. I had a puncture at the supermarket the day after Ross's accident. I discovered the spare wheel wasn't very good but forgot to ask the garage to check it.'

'Dear Nessie, it got me home all right.'

CHAPTER FOUR

After lunch the following day, Kim was surprised to be asked by her father to collect a box of calcium from the vet's at Lockerbie.

She frowned. She wanted to be around when Daniel Nichol met her dad.

She was not interested in seeing him again, she told herself irritably. She just wanted to make sure he didn't upset her father. She also wanted to make him understand how much of his own capital her father had spent over the years, maintaining the fences and ditches and repairing and painting doors and windows, not to mention modernising the buildings and putting in the milking parlour, as well as the cubicle shed to house the cows in winter.

'I was sure we had a stock of calcium,' she said, 'and we've not had any cows with milk fever since I came home.'

'A good stock never goes wrong at this time of year,' Ross said. 'Anyway, Joe said he ordered some tubes for a cow with mastitis, so they'll be ready to collect too. He needs them for the afternoon milking.'

'Very well,' Kim said, stifling a sigh. 'I'll go as soon as I've cleared away the dishes and tidied the kitchen. I think Nessie is visiting two of her clients at home today.'

'Yes, she is. By the way, Kim, Mr Sanders, the surgeon, said he was needing some more hay. He sometimes comes for it himself, but he was exceptionally good to me when I was in hospital, so if you could take the pick-up truck and drop some off for him on your way home I'm sure he would appreciate it. He's a very busy man. He has a daily woman to care for the house and be there for the wee girls coming home from school, but it's not the same as having a wife.'

'All right,' Kim agreed, but as soon as she was alone in the kitchen she frowned again. She had a feeling her father didn't want her present when Daniel Nichol came. Did he expect a disagreement? He had never shut her out before, and she'd often accompanied him to discuss the farm and any changes with Sir Martin Newall, even when she was quite young. The old man had always been pleased to see her and would have sweets or a bar of chocolate hidden away in his big desk in the library — even when she was a teenager.

***

Kim had to wait quite a while for the receptionist at the vet's to get the required medicines. Apparently they weren't ready for collection, just as she'd suspected. There were usually two girls on, but Edith explained the other girl had had to go home sick.

'We're having a bad day all round. One of the vets has had an accident with a stallion he was attending. He's been taken to hospital with a broken leg and wrist, as well as some internal bruising.'

'Oh dear, I am sorry to hear that,' Kim commiserated.

'Yes, Mr Turner says he's likely to be off work for quite a while so is going to see if he can persuade one of the retired vets to come in part time.'

'I see. Thank you,' she added, as the chatty woman handed over the tubes and the box of calcium. 'I'll take these and let you get on.'

Kim wasn't sure why she felt so on edge, but it was most likely because she wasn't at home to hear what Daniel Nichol had to say about the tenancy. By the time she'd dropped off the straw for Mr Sanders' ponies, their new landlord would be long gone, unless he and her father had had a disagreement and were still wrangling. Her father was a man with strong principles, not someone to be pushed around or treated unfairly.

A car drew up in front of her as she approached the doctor's house. She knew the girls wouldn't be home from school and nursery yet and the doctor would still be at the hospital. She wasn't sure where the stables were for unloading the two bales of hay, so she'd intended asking the housekeeper. It was a surprise when she saw Mr Sanders himself climbing out of the vehicle. She thought he looked weary as he stood up, rubbed his eyes, and then stretched his long limbs. As he straightened, he caught sight of the truck and Kim thought his face brightened as he strode eagerly towards her. His smile faded as he came close and recognised her.

'Oh, hello,' he said. His tone was flat and he seemed disappointed. Kim wondered who he had been expecting.

'I brought hay for the ponies, but I'm not sure where to put it,' she said.

'I thought it was Nessie when I saw the Rowandene jeep.'

'Nessie is seeing some of her clients today, and my father thought you'd be needing this,' Kim said. 'I was just about to ask the housekeeper where the stables are.'

'Mrs Bain doesn't come during the day today. She'll be here about five to look after the girls while I do my evening rounds at the hospital. I was just in theatre so I like to see my patients in the evening. We do need hay, though, so I'm grateful to you for bringing it, Miss McLaren.'

'Do call me Kim. Everyone else does.' Kim smiled. 'Nessie and I are very grateful to you for the care and attention you gave my father.'

'How is your father? Do tell him I'll pop by to settle up for the hay soon.'

'My father is doing very well, thanks to your skill, but Nessie and I have a struggle to make him take things slowly. Please call any time, but there's no charge. It's good that your daughters enjoy riding their ponies.'

'Oh it is, and Nessie has helped Jenny's confidence tremendously. She was quite nervous, and Evie, the younger one, is too confident by half! Nessie is so good with them both and she seems to know exactly how to handle them.'

'Nessie taught me to ride when I was young. She loves riding herself. Do you ride at all, Mr Sanders?'

'I do when I get the time. I still have my late wife's pony here, as well as my own. Maybe I could ask Nessie to come riding with us one of these days so we can exercise both the horses at once.'

'I'm sure Nessie would enjoy that, and she has no excuses now that I'm back home,' Kim said with a mischievous smile as she made her farewell.

It was clear the good doctor was very taken with Nessie, Kim mused, as she headed back home. She was approaching the farm road into Rowandene when she saw Daniel Nichol's car come out and turn in the other direction towards Wedderburn Hall.

She was undeniably disappointed that she'd missed him, but also anxious because he'd been with her father so long. Had they disagreed over the terms of the tenancy? She prayed her father hadn't been upset and his recovery damaged.

Kim went straight to the kitchen, expecting her father to be taking his tea. They always had tea and scones before milking time and it was a custom neither of them wanted to break. She'd set out the tea things and covered them with a clean cloth. She was surprised to see both cups had been used and the scones, gingerbread and biscuits all eaten. Her father was leaning back in his Windsor chair at one end of the big kitchen table. His eyes were closed and his feet were resting on a low stool. He looked weary, she thought, but then his eyes opened.

'Hello, lassie. Ye're back then. I was just summoning up the energy to move into the sitting room for a wee rest. I missed my nap after dinner with Daniel coming.'

'Daniel, is it?' Kim repeated in surprise. 'Are you on first-name terms then? Was he so easy to deal with?'

'We-ell, yes. He asked me to call him Daniel from the start. Once we'd agreed on a reasonable increase in the rent, we had quite a good discussion on several topics. In fact, Kim, I rather enjoyed his company.'

'I expect that's because you've not been to the market or anywhere else to have a crack with your usual cronies.'

'That's true, but Daniel was telling me a bit about his work in Africa. He really does enjoy being a vet, and I believe buying the Wedderburn Estate was entirely his great-uncle's idea. Apparently, his parents were killed when a ferry capsized when Daniel was just a boy. His great-uncle became his guardian and mentor and Daniel says he owes him a huge debt. His uncle never married, so Daniel is the only family he has. He's modernising the west wing of the hall for his uncle to live in, and the old man will be moving down here as soon as the sale of his own house has gone through.'

'So are we to understand that the vacant possession of the farms was a misunderstanding, then?' Kim said.

'Yes. His uncle left the negotiations entirely in the hands of his solicitor and the lawyers acting for the charity getting the proceeds. The old man has never even been down to this part of the country, even less viewed his purchase. Daniel is hoping young Billy and his Uncle William will be able to manage the estate before long so that he can go back to being a vet, even if it is only part time.'

'Our veterinary practice is looking for a part-time vet right now.' Kim told her father about the accident to one of the partners.

'That would probably be ideal for Daniel.'

'So what about the farms? What did he say about a joint tenancy for Rowandene, and is he going to get a new tenant for Burnhead now that Mr Craig is definitely retiring? It will need quite a bit of money to modernise the buildings if a new tenant wants to keep dairy cows.'

'Er . . . we-ell . . . He says he's not interested in farming any of the land himself. He realises Burnhead would need a lot of capital to bring it up to the standard of Rowandene.' Kim opened her mouth to speak, but her father held up his hand. 'Let me finish, lassie. Yes, he does know that we've modernised and improved the buildings here and maintained everything ourselves in recent years, so he says if I want it, and so long as I feel well enough to take it on as it stands, I can rent the land on Burnhead at the same rate as we've agreed here.' Kim noticed her father's eyes shining with their old enthusiasm and sent a silent prayer of thanks to Daniel Nichol. 'I thought I might keep a small flock of breeding sheep again,' her dad said enthusiastically. 'Jim Craig kept the fields fenced with sheep netting for his own flock. We could use the farmhouse for an extra stockman or shepherd since there are no cottages on Burnhead and we have no empty cottages here.'

'It sounds as though you've had a productive afternoon. I see you've both had tea in the kitchen. I would have set it on a tray in the office if I'd thought he would be staying.'

'Oh, he said it was more homely in the kitchen. He enjoyed it and he praised your gingerbread and scones.'

'Good. So are we to be joint tenants for Burnhead as well as Rowandene then?' Kim asked cheerfully.

'A-ah, er . . .' Ross looked uncomfortable.

'Father . . . ?'

'We-ell, the truth is, lassie, Daniel wouldn't agree to you being a joint tenant for Rowandene. I told him you've been a partner in the business since you were twenty-one, and that the stock and everything will be yours someday.'

'Then why? Is it because I'm a woman? Doesn't he think I'm capable?' she asked indignantly, her colour high, her eyes sparking green fire.

'I'm sure he doesn't think that. In a way I can understand his point of view. He did say he would review things after four years, if your circumstances are still the same.'

'What circumstances?'

'He seems to think that you are so well qualified, you might decide that farming is not challenging enough for you and you might go off and join that professor and his research, or do more travelling and lecturing.'

'I promised I would be home to stay,' Kim said, with a note of reproach. 'There's no fear of me leaving you again.'

'Mmm . . . maybe, but Daniel considers you're a very attractive woman, as well as being intelligent and with the world at your feet. He says if you were to marry, your husband would probably consider himself a joint tenant too.'

'That's rubbish!'

Ross held up his hand wearily. 'Dinna fly into a temper, lassie. In a way he could be right. That professor hinted he'd like to make you more than just a research partner. Both Nessie and I could see what he meant. He is single, isn't he?'

'That doesn't mean I want to marry him . . .'

'Maybe not, but the other night after you gave your talk to the Farmers' Club, some of them stayed for a drink at the bar. Daniel said they were all full of admiration for you, but two of them had obviously enjoyed a few drinks before the meeting began and they were drinking again. Their tongues were rather loose and neither Daniel nor Billy liked the way they were arguing about which of them would persuade you to be his wife and get his feet under the table at Rowandene.'

'I have no intention of getting married, but what difference should that make? Lots of women carry on a business while their husbands do their own jobs. Just what century is he living in? It's because I'm a woman, isn't it!' she finished furiously.

'I think I'll go through to the room now and have a wee nap,' Ross said with a sigh. 'Will you phone and tell Daniel about the vet's needing someone? It might help him settle down if he gets some familiar work that he enjoys.'

'No, I won't phone him! If he can't make me a joint tenant, why should I help him get a job.' Kim knew she sounded childish, but she was furious with Daniel Nichol for thinking he could decide her future. As it happened, someone else told Daniel about the job, and he jumped at the chance. Not that Kim knew that.

***

Kim saw Daniel in the village several times — when she called for their daily paper, or when they got the weekly farming papers which her father always looked forward to reading — but she made a point of avoiding being in the small shop at the same time as him if she could.

On one occasion she felt obliged to voice a polite 'good morning' and passed on, even though she knew he would have stopped to speak to her. The second time it happened, Kim's briskness was so evident, Mr Brooks the newsagent raised his eyebrows in surprise.

'Wee Kim must have a lot on her mind this morning,' he mumbled, as much to himself as to Daniel. He had known Kim since she was a child at school, and evidently still regarded her as a youngster instead of the capable young woman she had become.

It was about a fortnight later when Kim and Joe Baird decided they were going to need the help of a vet.

***

'I didn't tell my father I was coming out to check on Queenie,' Kim told Joe as he came back up to the farm to check on the cow. It was early evening and he'd technically finished for the day but had shared Kim's worries about the animal. It was Queenie's second calf and she was one of the best young cows in the herd. 'Mr Sanders warned Father that he hadn't to take any chances of getting his bad leg bumped by one of the animals, but I know he would insist on coming to help if he thought I needed it.'

'Aye, I understand, but I reckon we're going to have trouble,' Joe said anxiously. 'She hadna opened up enough for me to feel her after I finished milking so I went for my supper. There'll be trouble, I feels it in ma water.' Kim nodded. She was used to Joe's peculiar sayings, but he had a true stockman's instinct and she was uneasy herself.

'I can just get my hand in,' she told him. 'I'm certain the calf is coming backwards, but I think there is either something wrong or it's a monster of a calf. We shall have to give her more time and see if she opens up.'

'I'll go home and have a snooze in front o' the fire, but I'll come back about midnight,' Joe offered. 'I reckon it's going to need the two of us.'

'I have a feeling it may need a caesarean unless she opens up and I can manoeuvre that other leg into position. I don't want Father to know, though, so if I'm not already here at the calving shed, don't ring the bell. Come round to the sitting room window and tap on the glass in case I've dozed off, though I don't think I'll relax enough for that.'

With that plan in place, Kim made their bedtime drink earlier than usual and was relieved when her father seemed pleased to get to bed. She was already back out at the shed when Joe appeared, looking weary and rubbing sleep from his eyes.

'Joe, the calf is definitely coming backwards and I can feel a front foot as well. It seems to be tucked underneath. It would be best if we get the vet. Will you phone from your house so my dad doesn't hear? You needn't come back up. You have to be up again in a few hours to start the milking at five. I can sleep in a bit longer in the morning. Tell whoever is on call that I think it needs a caesarean, and hopefully they'll send an experienced vet and not one of the two trainees. I'll get everything ready.'

'Are ye sure, Miss Kim?' Joe asked anxiously.

'I am, Joe, so go get your sleep. I'll walk down as far as the dairy with you now and collect the stainless-steel buckets we keep for emergencies. I'll have the hot water, soap and a clean towel ready. We can only hope they aren't out on another call.'

'If they are, I'll come right back up, lassie.'

'It would be good if we had one of those phones you can carry about with you, like they have in America, without any wires,' Kim said. 'I have heard they are becoming more popular, but they are too big to fit in a pocket. We would need a bag to carry one around.'

'It wouldna be very convenient having a bag slung around your neck,' Joe muttered. 'I'll go and phone right away.'

Kim had everything as prepared as she could. She was considering going back into the house to wait when she heard a car coming and saw the glow of headlights. Goodness me, he hasn't had time to drive from Lockerbie, she thought. He must have had a call somewhere nearby.

It was a shock to see Daniel Nichol's tall figure come striding towards her, already clad in his waterproof trousers and smock. He paused to hose his wellingtons before entering the shed, even though they already looked spotless, but she was glad to know he took possible infections seriously. Rowandene had been one of the few farms to escape the last foot and mouth outbreak and her father was sure it was due to his stringent hygiene precautions. Daniel's mouth tightened when he saw her.

'Evening. So what's the trouble? Mr Turner's on call but thought I was nearer and it might be a caesarean?' His voice was brisk and cold. What Mr Turner, the senior partner in the practice, had actually said was, 'Kim McLaren thinks one of their young cows will need a caesarean. I can almost guarantee if Kim says that, she'll be right. She is as good a stockman as her father. Do what you consider necessary, but dinna cast aside her opinion just because she's a female.'

Daniel didn't inform his temporary new boss that he had already seen Kim McLaren in action and would not disparage her ability whatever her gender. Not to say he liked her recent attitude towards him. He was not used to women — indeed anyone, although he'd be kidding himself if he didn't admit to seeing her very much as a woman — avoiding him or treating him with indifference.

'Are . . . are you working for the practice?' Kim stammered as she led him towards the cow. She really hadn't expected to see Daniel Nichol.

'I'm helping out as long as they need me. Mr Turner is expecting a call from the north end of the practice, and he thought since I was so near, it would be better if I attended Rowandene. Do you have a problem with that?'

'Of course not, so long as you can do whatever is needed without killing the animal.'

He washed his hands and arms and moved into the pen, speaking quietly to the nervous animal. Kim followed him in and stood next to Queenie, stroking her soothingly, while holding her steady against one wall while Daniel tried to feel inside. He frowned.

'She is very tight. How long have you given her before you called us?'

'Long enough to open up if she is going to,' Kim said abruptly. 'This is her second calf and she has been working on, pressing, then getting up and down since midday.'

'And it's now after midnight. Your hands are smaller than mine. Did you feel her? What did you think?'

She told him what she suspected.

'Right. It seems we are going to need a caesarean. Will your father be happy with that?'

'He doesn't know. She is from one of our best cow families so he would not want us to kill her by dragging the calf out. We do sometimes have difficulty getting them in calf again after an operation, but anything is better than tearing her to bits.'

'I agree. Are you squeamish? Do you want to get Joe?'

Kim's mouth firmed and her eyes sparked ominously. 'I've seen operations in other places and assisted with two here, the first when I was fifteen. You can be sure I shall not faint,' she said coldly. He nodded and proceeded to inject Queenie.

The calf was still alive when he lifted it out, but it was a big bull calf and, true enough, one of the front feet was curled well forward under the its belly.

'You were right. No wonder she couldn't make any progress. That front foot will probably take a few days before it straightens. It would have torn her terribly trying any other way.'

Kim could tell Daniel was satisfied with his night's work, as she was herself, especially as they had a live calf. He worked methodically and neatly too.

'It's not the first time you've done that, is it?' Kim reflected out loud.

'No. I would not have risked coming here if I hadn't done a few operations before. Mr Turner wouldn't have suggested I come, either. He considers your father one of his most valued customers.'

He wondered if Kim had any qualms about spending time alone in the middle of the night with a man she knew little about. He glanced at her as he washed and dried his hands and stripped off his waterproofs. He wondered what she would say if he gave in to the temptation to pull her into his arms and kiss her as he'd wanted to do since the first time he'd seen her. He suspected she'd slap him.

She looked preoccupied and pensive. In actual fact she was contemplating whether she should ask Daniel Nichol in for a hot drink before he went home. Her father would be disgusted with her if she didn't. All the vets came in for tea after completing a job such as this one, even during the day, unless they had other clients waiting for them. Kim was fair-minded and she admitted Daniel had done an excellent job and he hadn't doubted her diagnosis.

At last she said, 'Would you like a hot drink before you leave?'

'I would be very glad of one, especially if it means the frost is thawing a little?' One eyebrow quirked up humorously and a faint smile curved his mouth. Kim scowled at him.

'Come in when you're ready then,' she said coolly, 'but don't knock or ring the bell. I don't want to disturb my father. Would you prefer milky cocoa or tea?'

'I don't want to be any trouble, but milky cocoa sounds wonderful right now.'

Kim had the milk heating and set out a plate of biscuits and two large mugs. She brought two plates and the butter as well in case Daniel fancied toast. Now that she was back indoors with a good night's work behind her she herself felt rather peckish, so she put two slices of bread in the toaster.

Daniel let his car freewheel silently towards the farmhouse and pulled up at the side. Kim had not heard a thing and she jumped when she realised he was standing close behind her. He put a firm hand on her shoulder.

'Steady on. You said to come in quietly, but I didn't mean to frighten you.'

'I'm not frightened! I just didn't hear you enter. I'm making toast for me. Do you fancy some?'

'Now you mention it, I could eat a horse.'

'I didn't offer you a horse, but I can cook bacon and eggs if you're so hungry. It will soon be dawn anyway.'

'Toast and hot chocolate will be lovely, finished off with one of your homemade biscuits. No wonder the vets all like to come here.'

'My granny was known for her hospitality. Father and Nessie have always kept it up.'

Daniel ate with relish. Kim had heated more milk than needed, so she topped up their mugs with more hot chocolate.

'That was absolutely delicious, and very much appreciated,' Daniel said, stretching his arms above his head and stifling a yawn. 'Does this mean you might speak to me the next time we meet in the village?'

Kim had been feeling replete and sleepily relaxed. She stood up quickly and began to clear away their mugs and plates. Daniel wished he could withdraw his question. He could see at once it had been a mistake, and yet he wanted to know what he'd done to make her avoid him or treat him so coldly.

'I can't put things right when I don't know what I have done wrong,' he said.

'You don't know what you've done wrong?' Kim's green eyes flashed angrily. 'You refused to take me on as a joint tenant with my father. Worse than that, you seem to have convinced him it was the best thing for both of us. You're a chauvinist, that's what you are!'

'Ah, now I begin to see. I am definitely not a chauvinist. I thought I was helping you to keep your options open and resume your chosen career as soon as your father has completely recovered from his accident.'

'Resume my chosen career?' Kim stared at him as though he was crazy.

'Yes. I owe my uncle a greater debt than I can ever repay, but I wish to God he hadn't felt the need to buy an estate to bring me home. If Uncle Fergus had only told me he was not keeping so well, that he was lonely and wanted me to return, I would have done so immediately. There was always a job for me in my old veterinary practice in Aberdeenshire if the worst came to the worst.'

'So you don't really want to be laird of the manor? But what has that to do with not allowing me to be a joint tenant?'

'I thought I was giving you an excuse to continue your work in research. I heard some professor had been down here to take you back.'

That was Willie Nairn giving him the gossip, Kim thought in exasperation.

'I thought you might want to make use of all the studying and hard work you must have done.'

'All I have ever wanted to do is farm and breed dairy cattle like my father.'

'But what about all the years of studying?'

Kim looked up and saw his look of genuine bewilderment.

'My father promised my mother that he would see I had the best education I was capable of, and the option to have a career and independence, like Nessie, if that's what I wanted.

I went to university to please my father and I worked hard to make him proud of me. I specialised in genetics and breeding because that's what interests me. He encouraged me, but I do not want to spend my life doing research projects in a laboratory.'

'I see . . . Your father thinks the professor is very keen to have you back, and as, er . . . more than his research partner?'

Kim flushed slightly and rolled her eyes. 'You and my father seem to have discussed my future too thoroughly for my liking. Neither of you can know what I want, or what is best for me. I certainly have no desire to be married to the professor — or anyone else for that matter.'

'Maybe not right now, but you may realise you're missing your professor more than you expected. It's an aspect I needed to consider when discussing the tenancy agreement. I have no intention of having an unsuitable tenant foisted upon me.'

'Are you suggesting—'

He held up a hand. 'There's no need to get angry with me again. I did not mean you personally. I meant whoever you marry.

'As your father's only child, you would provide a way into farming. I decided it would be wiser to see where we all are in four years' time. I would never consider tenants like those two drunk fellows at the meeting who argued about which of them would marry you.'

'You don't credit me with much judgement if you think I would want such men as husbands either! Guess what? I actually have a say in who I marry!'

'Actually, I believe you are a good judge of character, but we can all be misled if our emotions become involved. You are a very attractive woman for any man . . . but especially one wanting to farm, even without you being a joint tenant here at Rowandene. Several of the members regarded the two loud mouths with contempt for their drunken state, but they agreed you would make an excellent wife for the man who is lucky enough to marry you.'

'That's a pathetic excuse for not making me a joint tenant with my father! I have made it plain enough I have no intention of marrying anyone.'

'I have not known you long enough to know your intentions. I know you're intelligent, capable and you treat both your father and Miss McLaren with consideration and kindness. In other words, you are flesh and blood like the rest of us . . . I believe you have all the passions and desires that tempt many people into marriage, even when the candidate is unsuitable.'

'You don't know what you're talking about!' Kim declared.

'You're not telling me your professor, or one of your fellow students, has never awakened the latent passion I see in your flashing green eyes? I have noticed the auburn streaks in your chestnut hair, too, when the sun shines — and now, in the lamplight.'

Kim stood up swiftly without answering. She gathered the mugs and plates and carried them to the sink. She didn't realise Daniel had moved as quickly and was right behind her when she swung round.

'You didn't answer,' he said softly. His hands settled gently on her shoulders. Kim's eyes flew to his face. She opened her mouth to protest, but his lips brushed hers gently. His eyes asked for permission, begged for it — and her eyes undoubtedly gave it. He lifted one hand and his fingers fluttered down her cheek, caressing her. He murmured against her mouth, 'I have wanted to do this since the first day I saw you calving that heifer and stubbornly refusing my help.'

Kim's insides quivered with feelings she had never before experienced and a yearning she couldn't comprehend.

He slipped one arm behind her, drawing her nearer, holding her close against the length of him. He kissed her again, more passionately this time, as Kim pulled him closer. She felt the hardness of him against her stomach and she knew he felt the same desire he was awakening in her. She summoned all her willpower to draw her lips away and break the kiss.

Daniel was breathing hard. 'I apologise. That was totally unprofessional and inappropriate,' he muttered.

'We are both tired,' Kim mumbled. 'I shouldn't have invited you in tonight.'

He began walking towards the door but turned to look at her.

'I am glad you did,' he said softly. 'Goodnight, Kim.'

CHAPTER FIVE

The following day, when Kim heard Daniel's car, she knew he'd come to check on the cow. She had already been to see for herself and the wound was as neat and clean as could be. The animal was chewing her cud contentedly. Kim had not slept well for thinking about Daniel Nichol, the things he'd said and the emotions he'd awakened in her, stirring a depth of desire she hadn't known she possessed. She had been kissed lots of times but had never felt so aware. No one had ever come close to making her lose control until last night. She couldn't face Daniel again — not yet. She scurried upstairs to the bathroom, leaving her father to answer the door and accompany Daniel to the calving shed.

Over the next few days, Kim found various excuses for not collecting the newspapers from the village shop in case she ran into Daniel. She didn't know how she could face him. She could not forget the way he had made her feel. Inwardly, she scolded herself for being a coward.

Eventually, of course, she had no excuse and she cycled to the village for the papers. Billy and his uncle, William Nairn, were just coming out of the shop as she parked her bicycle. She breathed a sigh of relief. She knew they'd have collected the papers for Wedderburn Hall as well as their own, just as Daniel collected theirs if he was at the shop.

'Ach, lassie, 'tis good to see ye,' Mr Nairn greeted her cheerily. 'If we had known ye were short of transport—' he nodded at her bicycle — 'we could have brought your papers.'

'Oh, I have plenty of transport, but it's a lovely day and I fancied a cycle ride.' She didn't confess that if she had seen the Wedderburn car parked outside, she had planned to hide until it had gone. 'It's not often you collect the papers, is it, Billy?'

'No, it's usually Daniel or Uncle William who comes for them, but now old Mr Nichol has moved in, he likes his papers early. Daniel was called out to help Mr Turner. The boss is reputed to be the best vet with horses but is having difficulty foaling a Clydesdale mare. He must think Daniel can help.'

'I see.' She grinned teasingly. 'So it took two of you to come for the papers.'

'We-ell, I met Uncle as I was setting out. He came with me because he has a list of shopping to get for Aunt Annie and she said he was chuntering about shopping being a woman's job. I'm keeping the peace.'

'So it is a woman's job when there's things on the list that ordinary folk have never heard of,' William muttered. 'It's that woman who is staying at the Hall who wants them.'

'I'm surprised at that. I heard old Mr Nichol had brought his housekeeper with him, but Mrs Nairn told me she's a pleasant, comfortable wee woman who cooks good plain food.'

'Aye, so she is, but that's Mrs Dolly Dunn ye're talking about. Her sister-in-law has taken ill so she's headed back to Aberdeen for ten days. She stocked up the old man's freezer with the things he enjoys. It seems he can manage the microwave all right, and make toast for himself. That's more than I can do, so my Annie said she would keep an eye on him and make sure he was having proper meals.

'But she didna bargain for this Roon-Kurcher woman turning up out o' the blue and demanding all sorts o' fancy stuff. This lot is for her.' He stared derisively at the box of foodstuffs he was holding. 'They don't keep half the things she wants in our wee village, but if she thinks I'm going into Dumfries for her, she can think again! And Billy, you just tell her you have work to do for Mr Daniel and ye havena time to be running errands for the likes o' her. She can drive herself there in her posh sports car.' He lowered his voice confidentially. 'She's got her eye on Mr Daniel, so she has.'

'Now, Uncle, we don't know that. After all, she seems to know old Mr Nichol as well.'

'You invite us to Rowandene for a cup o' coffee, lassie, and we'll tell ye a story that'll make your hair curl.' William's eyes danced wickedly.

'Uncle!' Billy protested. 'You shouldn't gossip. Anyway, Kim's hair is curly enough already, and Aunt Annie will be needing this stuff for *'er madam's lunch, don't you know.*' He feigned a posh accent but he couldn't suppress a grin.

'Aye, well, she can wait or eat something out o' the freezer as she's supposed to do. Come on, Kim, lassie, we'll put your bicycle in the Land Rover while you get your papers.'

Kim raised her eyebrows in a silent question as she looked at Billy. He shrugged and nodded.

'I suppose I always enjoy a cup o' coffee and one o' your biscuits,' he said resignedly.

They entered the kitchen by the back door to find Nessie making a cup of coffee for herself.

'Ross is working in the office so I've just taken him a cup,' she said. 'I will put more milk on to heat. I remember you always liked yours milky, Billy.'

'I do, thanks.' He gave her a grateful smile. 'Are you still as busy with your clients?'

Kim guessed he hoped to detain her, but when she glanced at his uncle, she knew Nessie's presence would not deter him from saying whatever it was he wanted to tell them. He still had that wicked glint in his eyes and she doubted if anything would stop him. She remembered how he used to love telling stories to her and Billy when they were young, and how he made them shiver if it was a ghost story. He had always added his own embellishments.

'Have ye heard about the fancy dame who is staying up at the Hall?' he asked Nessie.

'No. I heard old Mr Nichol's housekeeper was away. Is the new woman her replacement?'

William Nairn made a rude noise. 'This madam wouldn't know when the kettle was boiling to make a cup o' tea. No, no, she is a real fancy piece is Miss Roon-Kurcher. She arrived two evenings ago in a swanky blue sports car. She had driven down frae Aberdeen, I think. She's trying to treat Annie like her unpaid servant. If she carries on, I shall have to have a word with Daniel.'

'Uncle William, you can't do that!' Billy exclaimed, his eyes wide.

'I can, and I will, if she stays much longer.' He turned to look at Kim. 'The evening she arrived, Annie made up Dolly's bed with clean bedding, but Madam said she was not staying in the servants' end. She insisted she wanted to stay "in the main residence", *don't you know!* Daniel is only using the few downstairs rooms Sir Martin used. He said he owed it to his uncle to make him a comfortable home first, so he has modernised the west wing. Madam expected my wife to open up the other rooms in the main house. Annie told her the upper floors had not been used for years and Daniel only uses the bedroom downstairs. D'ye ken what she said to that?' He stared from Nessie to Kim, his sandy eyebrows twitching like hairy caterpillars. Kim wanted to laugh, but when she caught Billy's glance, she saw he had his tongue pressed high in his cheek. He rolled his eyes and gave a faint shake of his head. She knew that look of old. He had something to hide from his uncle and aunt.

'I suppose she asked where the nearest hotel is,' Nessie suggested.

'Indeed she did not! She said Daniel's bed would do perfectly and she would share it with him. The brazen hussy!'

Kim met Billy's glance and guessed he had shared his own bed with a lady friend or two while he was away. Clearly, he didn't consider this woman's suggestion as outrageous as his uncle and aunt did.

'My Annie was having none o' that.' William shook his head and his eyes gleamed triumphantly. 'She explained about the arrival of Madam Stella and her needing a bed. Daniel told Aunt Annie to take her to his uncle and she could use the housekeeper's bedroom.'

'Her name is Estelle, Uncle,' Billy reminded him.

'I never heard o' anybody called that,' William said stubbornly. 'Old Mr Nichol calls her Stella and that's a queer enough name. Well, lassie—' he stood up and smiled at Kim — 'that was a grand cup o' coffee but we'd better get these groceries home now.' Nessie accompanied him out to the Land Rover but Billy hung back.

'You'll have to excuse Aunt Annie and Uncle William being so old-fashioned, Kim. They have never moved with the times like we have.'

Kim nodded but made no comment. Billy would probably consider her old-fashioned, too, if he knew how she felt about one-night stands. She had a feeling of disappointment that Miss Roon-Kurcher knew Daniel well enough to share his bed and to be so frank about it.

* * *

Estelle had stayed two nights at Wedderburn Hall, consigned to the housekeeper's room, and she determined to do something about it. She was also restricted to the old man's west-wing apartment. Old Mr Nichol had always made her welcome when they were neighbours up in Aberdeenshire, but then she had only visited during the day. He seemed uncomfortable having her staying under his roof.

'When does Daniel come in to see you?' she asked plaintively. 'This is the third day I have been here and I have seen no sign of him.'

'He is working. He had no difficulty getting himself a job as a vet down here. One of the partners in the local practice has been hurt. He jumped at the chance to get back to working with animals,' Fergus said with a sigh. 'I fear I made a mistake buying this estate for him, hoping it would help him to settle down.'

'At least it brought him back from Africa,' Estelle said. 'There's plenty for him to do modernising the rest of Wedderburn Hall. I would love to stay here and help him with it.'

'He doesn't seem interested in the house. A week ago another of the young vets broke his leg playing football, so Mr Turner, the main partner in the practice, has offered Daniel a permanent post, with a view to becoming partner after a six-month trial for both of them. He has got the farms signed up for a four-year tenancy, and Mr Nairn and his nephew, Billy, are managing the woodland and the rest of the estate. There is nothing to stop him working as a vet. It is what he has always wanted to do. He tried to tell your father that, but he didn't want to listen.'

'He could at least come to see if you're all right,' Estelle said sullenly.

'Mrs Nairn will have told him I have company while you're here. He knows I'm fine.'

I'm not! Estelle wanted to shout. She scowled in silence for a while.

'I'm going for a drive to explore the local town,' she said sourly. 'Do you want to come?'

'A drive in that flying machine of yours, and no roof to keep the wind out.' He shuddered. 'No, no, lassie. I'll 'bide by the fire until you return.'

Daniel had been visiting one of the farms when he saw Estelle speeding by in her blue sports car. She wore sunglasses and a silk scarf tied round her long blonde hair.

He had got on well with the morning's calls and knew the remaining three weren't urgent, so he turned towards Wedderburn Hall. He felt a little guilty that he hadn't seen Uncle Fergus during the last two days, but he was still smouldering with anger at him encouraging Estelle Roon-Kurcher to visit.

Daniel had believed they would be far enough away from Aberdeen to prevent her visiting. Instead, she had come to stay. Not only that, but she'd hinted to Mrs Nairn that he would welcome her sharing his bed. He had lived in a rural area all his life and knew how quickly gossip spread, and grew.

Daniel parked his car near his uncle's back door and jumped out.

'Hello, Uncle Fergus. I have a few minutes to spare between visits so thought I'd call in.' His voice was cheery because he *had* managed to evade Estelle.

'Ah . . . hello, Danny. Stella only left a few minutes ago. She will be sorry to have missed you.'

'Why did you invite her to stay? Were you feeling lonely?'

'I didn't invite her to visit. As a matter of fact, I was surprised when she turned up without warning. I wondered if you'd arranged for her to visit while Dolly Dunn is away.'

'Certainly not!'

'Good. The Nairns see that I'm well looked after and I enjoy a chat with William Nairn most mornings — at least I did until Stella arrived. He hasn't called since she came. Sometimes he takes me with him and Billy in the jeep and he explains what needs doing to improve the woodlands. He knows all the folks around about. Sometimes we call at one of the cottages and they always make us a cup of tea and a scone. I am not lonely now. The folks are very friendly.'

'Yes, I am finding they're very hospitable. What brings Stella here if you didn't invite her?'

'I don't know. I've not heard from her father since we moved away. He wasn't very happy about me spending money to buy this place. I thought Stella must have come to see you. She is disappointed she can't stay in the main house, but Mrs Nairn explained that most of it has not been lived in for years.'

'Well, you must tell me if you do ever feel lonely, Uncle Fergus. I could take you out with me sometimes, if you're content to wait in the car while I'm doing routine work. Whatever you do, don't encourage Stella to visit again. You must tell her she has to leave when you hear Mrs Dunn is due back.'

'I thought you and Stella got on well together. She always said you did. Will you be taking her out for a meal one evening?'

'Not if I can help it, Uncle.' He sighed heavily. 'Why do you think I escaped to South Africa? It felt as though Stella had already moved in with us before I went away. She called on you every day. I thought you encouraged her.'

'If I did it was for your sake. The way she talked, I thought you were more than friends.'

'Definitely not! And now you know we're not, promise you'll persuade her to leave soon — or I shall be running away to Africa again.'

'Oh no! Ye wouldn't do that, would you, Daniel?'

'Of course not. But remember, when I want a wife, I shall choose my own. And if I can't have the one I want, I shall stay a bachelor like you.' He grinned. 'You've always seemed happy enough.'

'Ah, Danny . . .' Only his mother had called him Danny. The old man sighed heavily, then looked up and met his eyes. 'If you meet the woman you want to spend your life with, seize your opportunity and don't waste time.' He paused before saying, 'Your mother was the only woman I ever loved or wanted for a wife.'

Daniel gaped in surprise. He'd had no idea.

His uncle nodded and went on. 'I was ten years older than she was so I hesitated to tell her how I felt. Then I introduced her to your father . . . He was nearer her age, young and fit and full of life. The grief I felt when they were killed was terrible, but they gave me you. I've always felt you were like my own son because she was your mother and your father was my cousin, and the closest friend I ever had.' It was the longest speech Daniel had heard from his great-uncle.

'I'm sorry, so sorry,' Daniel said quietly, crossing the floor to stand beside his uncle's chair and press his shoulder. 'I never knew. I never guessed . . .'

'How could ye, laddie?' He reached up and patted Daniel's hand. 'But now you know why I missed you so much when you went away to Africa. Promise me you'll not go away like that again, at least not while I'm alive.'

'I give you my word I shall not leave you again, Uncle Fergus. I believe we shall both be here for the rest of our lives.' His thoughts flew unbidden to Kim McLaren.

'So you really like it here then?' Fergus asked eagerly, his eyes bright with hope.

'I do. I like the countryside, the people are friendly and hospitable, and Mr Turner wants me on board full-time as a vet, with a view to becoming a partner. It's the life I enjoy, Uncle. It's what I trained for and what brings me satisfaction. Don't get me wrong, I'm grateful to you for buying the estate. I'm beginning to enjoy going round and planning improvements with Billy and William Nairn. I have decided to join the two farms together under one tenant, and I'm sure Ross McLaren will make an excellent job.'

'What about this house? It is too big for the way most people live these days, unless you want to be part of the gentry, and I don't think you're cut out for that.'

'You're right there.' Daniel grinned. 'Now that I've made this part of the house comfortable for you, I'm quite content with the rooms the last owner used. The facilities are modern and the few rooms in use are warm and comfortable. If I get a wife, we shall decide together what we need to do.'

***

When Estelle returned and learned that Daniel had spent some time with his uncle she was furious.

'Why didn't he let us know? I would not have gone out on my own if I had known he was coming to see me. When is he coming back?' she asked eagerly. 'I thought we could dine at one of the hotels in Dumfries. One of the shop assistants told me there is a good hotel a bit further away on the banks of the River Nith. Maybe he will be back this afternoon?'

Fergus recalled his conversation with Daniel and chewed his lower lip, feeling uncomfortable. He had known that Edward Roon-Kurcher was pushing Daniel too hard to do his bidding, instead of allowing him to choose his own life, but he hadn't realised that Estelle's constant visits to their old home had been another reason for Daniel escaping to Africa. Estelle was a beautiful young woman, even if she was an indulged only child. It was clear to him now, though, that she was not Daniel's choice for a wife.

'I don't know when he will drop in again. They are short-staffed with one of the young vets being unable to drive or go out on calls.'

'Oh, for goodness' sake! Surely he should be satisfied with the estate you bought for him? I would enjoy being lady of the manor and Daniel would make a good laird. I shall make the Hall the envy of the county. I didn't get to see much of it with Mrs Nairn being here — I thought she was unnecessarily vigilant — but I can see from outside that some of the front rooms on the second floor have beautiful big windows. It will make such a difference when I redecorate and install heating and more bathrooms. I could furnish each of the public rooms in a different style.'

Fergus's eyes widened. He observed Estelle more carefully as she described her dreams. This was a different side to the young woman he'd thought he knew.

'I don't think Daniel aspires to being a laird in that respect, my dear. He loves his work as a vet.'

'That's ridiculous. If he has a house as beautiful as I visualise making Wedderburn Hall, he will not want to go attending to filthy animals.'

Fergus considered his next words carefully. Maybe they were not strictly true, but it was a fact that neither he nor Daniel would spend money as extravagantly as Estelle envisaged.

'Being a vet is Daniel's life, Stella. I believe he tried to convince your father of that. It is all he ever wanted to do, even as a boy. It gives him all the satisfaction he desires, but . . .' He held his hand up when she pouted and began to protest. 'But apart from satisfaction in his work, Daniel used his own capital to make a comfortable home here for me and Mrs Dunn.' He waved his arm around his sitting room.

'Yes, but—'

'I spent my money buying Wedderburn Hall because I was anxious to bring Daniel home again. Maybe I did pay more than I should have done for a small estate but we were misled.' This, at least, was true, he comforted himself, although he felt George, his own solicitor, should have looked into things more carefully. But they were both getting old. He watched Estelle closely as he continued. 'That doesn't worry, Daniel. He is happy with one of the tenants. The other plans to retire, and when he vacates his farm, all the land will be run as one larger farm.'

'So he will have more money from the rent then . . .'

'We-ell, yes, but it is only one farm, not a whole estate, nor anything like as big as the original estate used to be when the Hall was built. In the past, Home Farm mainly supplied the occupants of the Hall when there was a vast workforce. It may have the potential to be more profitable now, but I understand it would need improvements first. I believe Billy Nairn is going to consult Dr McLaren when he can get round to it. It may improve the financial situation a little in due course, but now that Daniel is working full-time as a vet again, he will want to gather his own capital to buy into a partnership in the veterinary practice. He and Mr Turner, the senior vet, have already discussed it.'

'He must be mad!' Estelle stamped her foot. 'Surely an estate should bring in plenty of money without him working at all. I can't believe he's happy to live in a pokey corner of what could be a beautiful mansion like a bloody . . . like a . . . a squatter!'

'He seems comfortable enough for now. It would require an army of staff to maintain Wedderburn Hall if all the rooms were opened up. It would be a waste of money, especially when improvements need to be made to parts of the estate first. Have you been for a walk around yet?'

'No. I'm not interested in a smelly old farm. My father has always said you are the richest man he knows, and Daniel . . .' She broke off, seeing the fleeting expression of regret, or was it disenchantment, which crossed the old man's face.

'And your father thought Daniel would inherit my wealth?' he finished dryly. 'Well, he has. He has inherited this estate. It may turn out to be a white elephant, of course. I doubt if Daniel will mind that, though, so long as he has his own work. The Nairns are keen to bring the woodland back to the way it used to be in Mr Nairn's younger days, and Danny is satisfied with that, so I'm not sorry I bought it. It brought Daniel home and that's all that mattered to me. You would do better to marry a wealthy stockbroker, my dear, if you want to live in a mansion.'

He sighed heavily. He understood the situation now. Back in Aberdeenshire he'd believed Estelle would help Daniel settle down. Instead, he'd been driven away. True, the boy had returned once he realised how badly he'd been missed. Fergus's health had suffered, but it was not so bad since the local doctor had prescribed him the magic pills to reduce the awful chest pains. Angina, he called it, and told Fergus never to go anywhere without his pills. Fergus knew he was a fortunate old man and from now on resolved never to interfere in Daniel's private life again.

* * *

Kim had had plenty of time to come to terms with *that* kiss. She had made up her mind to be polite, if a little distant, in future, especially when she'd heard about Miss Roon-Kurcher coming to stay. Clearly, a kiss meant nothing to Daniel if he was used to sharing his bed with lady friends. She realised Billy saw nothing wrong in the idea of sharing a bed either, and he seemed to assume Kim felt the same. She knew many of her fellow students had had sex at one time or another, but few of them had gone on to have long-term relationships, and one or two had paid a high price.

Kim decided there must be something wrong with her as she had never been tempted — until now. It was not something she was ever going to discuss with Billy, however close they had been in their youth. Let him think whatever he liked.

* * *

Before Kim left for university, her father had always prided himself on the records he kept, and Joe Baird had been conscientious about filling in the large calving chart, marking the date cows calved and any treatments needed, the date they'd been put with the bull again or artificially inseminated, whether they'd settled in calf again or required further service. Joe and her father also carried a wealth of information in their heads about individual animals, but as the herd had expanded, Ross McLaren had decided to pay the vet to come once a month to do a routine pregnancy diagnosis. It was usually one of the younger vets who did such visits, so Kim had no qualms about taking Joe's place and helping her father by taking note of the results. She kept the record book, marking whether an animal was in calf. If not, did it need any treatment? It could make a serious difference to cash flow if a bull proved to be less fertile than he should be, especially if he appeared to be working well with a bunch of heifers, only to find out three months later that few, if any of them, were in calf.

Kim was on her own, checking the animal pens that would guide them to one end to be held for examination by the vet, when the car drew up.

It was Daniel. Of course it was. She knew he was now working full-time but had expected him to attend more unpredictable calls. She willed her heart to slow its silly racing as she walked forward to meet him.

'We're all ready and waiting,' she said. 'My father will have heard the car so will be out in a moment.'

'And good morning to you, Kimberly,' Daniel replied with a smile, raising one dark brow quizzically. Kim was relieved to see her father coming towards them, greeting Daniel with his usual cheery smile.

When they'd finished, Kim said she would take the cows back to the field where the rest of the herd were grazing, but her father quickly intervened.

'No, no, lassie. You go in and get the coffee on. I'll tell young Jimmy to see the cows into the field.' He turned to Daniel. 'You'll be ready for a cup of coffee, Daniel? It is Mrs Scott's day for working here so she's been baking scones this morning.'

'Well, I wouldn't say no, if you're having one,' Daniel replied with a grin.

'We are. Take him in, Kim. I'll be back in a minute.'

'I promise to behave like a gentleman this morning,' Daniel said in a low voice close to Kim's ear as they walked towards the house.

'You will not have any option. I have heard how you play fast and loose, sharing your bed with your lady friends. I have no intention of being one of them.' Kim cursed herself silently. She should *not* have said that. Daniel was bound to guess one of the Nairns had been gossiping and she'd no desire to cause trouble.

'What's that supposed to mean?' The smile had died from Daniel's face at her cool tone. He stepped in front of her so that she had no option but to look at him. He frowned.

Kim would have walked around him into the house, but he caught her arm.

'You have no reason to say that, Kim. I admit I shouldn't have allowed myself to get carried away the last time we were alone, but I don't make a habit of behaving badly.'

'I suppose that's a matter of opinion, but I didn't think *gentlemen* shared their bed so readily whenever lady friends visited.' She couldn't resist emphasising the "gentlemen". Daniel was not amused. She saw his brain working out what she meant, then his eyes widened and he looked furious.

'For God's sake, don't tell me you heard about Miss Roon-Kurcher suggesting she could share my bed at the Hall! I'll ring Billy Nairn's neck. Has he nothing to do but spread gossip?'

'Billy never mentioned it,' Kim said, and stepped by him to open the door, leaving Daniel no opportunity to ask how she had heard.

Mrs Scott was collecting her dusters to clean the bedrooms and Kim was very glad of her presence. She deliberately detained her so that Daniel could not persist with their conversation. She asked Mrs Scott about her son Jimmy, who had done general work at Rowandene since leaving school. She knew how proud she was of him.

Mrs Scott still cleaned two days a week, having originally helped out full-time after Kim's mother died. She was a widow now and glad to continue earning a small wage, as well as enjoying the company.

Hearing about her from Ross, Daniel had asked her to clean and cook two mornings a week for him too, so he also made an effort to converse.

It was a relief when her father joined them for coffee and the conversation became general, but Daniel was annoyed that Kim had heard of Stella's outrageous suggestion to share his bed. He made a point of avoiding being at the Hall except to sleep, but it was a relief when he heard Dolly would soon be back and Stella would have to leave.

CHAPTER SIX

Estelle knew she had to do something and quickly when she heard Mrs Dunn would be returning soon, now that her sister-in-law was out of hospital. It was clear no one was going to encourage her to stay by opening up rooms in the main part of the Hall. She had barely seen Daniel, had missed him again earlier, and that infuriated her. She was confident she could persuade him to let her modernise the place if she could get him on his own long enough to use her feminine wiles. She would persuade him to give up his filthy work as a vet, too, once they married.

She mulled over what his uncle had said about Home Farm having potential for improvement. She had not the faintest idea what might be involved, or that even small repairs and developments took both money and time before they showed any financial return. But she made up her mind to impress Daniel and show him how efficient she could be.

She knew a Dr McLaren lived at Rowandene Farm because she had overheard the Nairns discussing the farmer, Mr Ross McLaren. She assumed Dr McLaren must be his son, so she lost no time in telephoning. The person who answered was a Mrs Scott, who said she was only the cleaner at Rowandene but she could leave a note for Dr McLaren if that would do.

'Yes. Please tell Dr McLaren that the estate manager wishes to have a consultation about improvements to Home Farm at two o'clock this afternoon.' Mrs Scott scribbled the message on the notepad and left it on the kitchen table so that Kim would see it when she and her father came in for lunch.

Estelle made sure she had her gold-plated pen and leather-bound notebook in her handbag ready to meet Dr McLaren after lunch. She would make a note of all the improvements the doctor recommended and put them into neat order for Daniel. She was determined she would convince him that she would be an asset when she was his wife. She would help him make the estate more profitable, even if she did intend spending the extra income on making Wedderburn Hall the envy of the district and the perfect setting for the laird and his lady.

* * *

Kim was surprised when she saw the note Mrs Scott had left.

'It's not like Billy to be so formal. He's called me Kim all his life and he knows Mrs Scott as well as we do. In any case, I can't think why he wants to see me, Dad. You've already promised to sow the grass seed for Mr Lenox if he decides to reseed the field that borders ours, haven't you?'

'Seems strange,' Ross agreed. 'I didn't think Billy was taking on anything to do with the management of Home Farm so long as it was ticking over and providing them with their eggs, milk, cream and butter, plus a pig to kill now and then.'

'And a few of Mrs Lenox's capons to roast,' Kim added with a laugh.

'Not to mention a couple of lambs and a side of beef for the freezer,' Ross agreed with a chuckle. 'All Sir Martin Newall ever wanted was for him and his housekeeper and the Nairns to be well supplied with good fresh produce. I suppose new brooms usually sweep cleaner, even if it doesn't last long. Home Farm could certainly be a lot more productive.'

'It would need more labour than just Bert and his wife, though,' Kim declared. 'It would need some money spent on improvements too, especially if they had a new manager who wanted things brought up to date.'

'It would that.' Ross frowned. 'Bert and his wife are well into their sixties, but I understood Daniel Nichol intended to leave things as they are until Bert decides to retire.'

'I can't imagine Home Farm without the Lenoxes,' Kim mused.

'No, they have been at Home Farm since I was a lad.' Ross nodded. 'Things were different then though. There were four men working it. Of course Sir Martin was younger and he took an interest in things. I remember he was one of the first in the district to convert the byre to a tandem milking parlour. It was an innovation at the time. It's long out of date now, of course, but the Lenoxes only keep about six dairy cows. They still have a bit of everything else, though, as most farms did when I was young — pigs, poultry, sheep . . .'

'Oh well, I will meet Billy and see what he has in mind. I don't suppose I'll be long and will be back in plenty of time to help Joe with the milking.'

'All right, lassie, if you're sure. I'm going down to Burnhead. The Craigs move out tomorrow.'

'Are you still considering taking on Mr Craig's nephew to work for us?' Kim asked.

'Aye, I think so. It's his wife's nephew, actually. He's going to be at Burnhead all of today, helping the Craigs sort out their stuff and tidy up. I'll have a talk with him on his own. He's twenty-four and seems keen on sheep and tractor work, but has no experience of milking. I know he keeps two working collies of his own. I must admit I'm quite looking forward to having some breeding sheep again.'

'I don't know much about lambing ewes,' Kim said. 'We've not had any since I was about ten.'

'No. I got rid of the sheep and streamlined the work as much as I could when your mother died,' Ross said with a sigh. Then he changed the subject abruptly. 'The young man's name is Eric McMurray, but the Craigs call him Mac. His mother seems keen to come and keep house for him, at least until he decides to take a wife. The Craigs have quite a lot of furniture they'd like to leave for him. They're moving to a modern bungalow and have no room for it all . . . Did I tell you I saw Nessie out riding with Mr Sanders the last time I was down at Burnhead?'

'No, you never told me that!'

'It slipped my mind.'

'I knew Nessie was teaching the little girls to ride, but . . .'

'Mmm, but they were on their own. Jim Craig said he's seen them a few times riding along the lane at the bottom of Burnhead fields then back to the village across the doctor's small paddock.' Ross grinned. 'He thinks they would make a grand couple. Maybe he's right. I'd like to see Nessie happily settled, and she would make a fine mother to the two wee girls.'

'Ye-es, she would. I don't remember Nessie having any serious relationships since I got old enough to notice such things,' Kim mused.

'She went out with various young men while at university, and an odd one since, but she never seemed to want to get serious. Perhaps this one's different . . .'

Kim pulled on her wellingtons, knowing the yard at Home Farm was always muddy, and after the heavy rain last night it would be worse than usual. She wondered if Billy intended walking over the fields, or what else he had in mind as he wanted to speak to her instead of her father.

Bert Lenox always kept the fences in good repair, but he didn't apply much fertiliser to the grassland and there had been no grain crops grown at Home Farm for a long time. Bert still preferred turnips for the cows' winter feed, although most farmers were changing to silage now that milking parlours were replacing byres and the cows were in cubicles instead of being chained by their necks. In addition to his other work, Bert always grew an acre of potatoes for the Hall and their own use, and often he grew some carrots, cabbages and beetroot too. This had apparently become a habit during the war when food was scarce, but now he was on his own he had to harvest everything himself so he was certainly not a lazy man. She hoped Daniel Nichol was not expecting him to do more, or intending to push him to retire before he was ready.

Kim drove along the farm track, which was a short cut between Rowandene and the Wedderburn Hall land, but a short branch off it brought her straight into the yard at Home Farm and saved time driving round by the road, which was the way Billy would come. There was no sign of the truck he used for his work on the estate, but Mr Lenox appeared at the door of one of the sheds.

'Ah, hello, it's you, Kim. I heard an engine. I hoped it was one of the vets. I've one of my cows having trouble calving. There's something wrong, but I canna get her to stand still while I tie her up to let me feel her. Could you come and steady her against the wall for me, lassie?'

'Of course I will.' Kim followed him into the shed.

'The poor beast is in a state. She knows something's wrong. She's not usually as flighty and panicked as this,' Bert said anxiously. Kim knew this was true. Mr Lenox was a canny man and all his animals were quiet. He treated them as he might have done his children if he had had any.

Between them they got the cow tied up by the neck.

'I think if you stand where she can see you, Mr Lenox, it may help to keep her calmer. She knows you and is used to you stroking her. I'll feel her. Is this the bucket of water?'

'Aye, it is. I'm sorry it's not very warm,' he said apologetically. 'We heat all the water from the boiler in the house and I forgot to stoke it up after I used the water in the dairy this morning.'

Kim stripped off her anorak and her pullover and laid them on a bale of clean straw. Her thin cotton blouse had short sleeves so that was no problem. Almost at once she could feel that one of the calf's front feet was turned backwards while the other was coming straight.

'Mr Lenox, I need to push the head and foot back a bit so that I can free the twisted foot and get it coming straight. She may jump a bit, but I'll be as gentle as I can.'

'Do you want me to come to that end instead, lassie?'

'No, I think you're doing a better job at keeping the poor animal calm than I could. Anyway, my hands are smaller than yours.' Kim worked patiently and managed to straighten the foot and bring it forward a little.

'The calf is coming straight now, Mr Lenox. Maybe we could give her a wee while to settle and gather her energy ready to press. If we're lucky, she may calve by herself. Has she worked on a long time?'

'Aye, I'm afraid she has. I thought the vet would have been here by now. The poor beast is exhausted.'

'Do you have a calving jack if she needs a pull?'

'No, but if ye look behind you, young Kim, ye'll see two ropes and a smooth bar of wood on the straw. They're what I use if a calf needs a pull.'

'All right.'

'I heard a car. Maybe that's the vet.' They waited but nobody appeared. Bert patted the cow and talked soothingly, as he would to a child, then he went to the door to look out.

'Are you the vet?' he called. He came back into the shed, muttering in disgust.

'If she's a vet I'll eat my hat, or I would if I had one. She'll not be any use here. Dressed in high heels she is, and a fancy sort o' dress. Ye'd think she was on her way to a wedding.'

'Maybe she's one of the new young vets they've taken on.'

***

Estelle had driven along the public road, but when she opened the gate into the farmyard, she stared in dismay. She could not drive her dear little sports car into all that mud. She waited, but nobody came. She could hear the murmur of voices in a shed. Exasperated, she climbed out and picked her way gingerly, clinging as close to the buildings as she could, searching for any dry patch she could find. Twice she almost lost her footing in the mud. Her shoes were ruined. She was furious. She stepped into the shed and stopped, eyes wide, mouth agog.

'Oh my God! What are you doing?'

Kim frowned at the hysterical voice. It was evident the calf was going to need a pull. She was gripping the ropes, now slippery with the slimy excretions.

'Will you pass me that bar, please?' she asked politely.

The woman gaped at her. 'I'm not coming anywhere near you.'

Kim muttered in frustration but kept hold of the ropes while she bent and half-turned, trying to reach for the bar herself. As she turned back to attach the ropes to the bar, the cow groaned and pressed hard, sending a gush of fluid cascading down Kim's blouse. If she hadn't turned away for the bar she would have seen and jumped back in time. She swore under her breath. The woman shrieked at the sight of the blood-streaked fluid. 'You've killed it! I'm going to faint.'

'Dinna faint here, woman,' Bert Lenox growled. 'Ye'll never make a vet!'

'Better still, get back to your bloody car,' another voice hissed angrily.

'Daniel!' Estelle protested. None of them had noticed him enter the shed. 'Have you no consideration for me?' she asked pathetically.

Kim was too busy easing the calf's head out and wiping away mucus to help it breathe, to pay much attention to the petulant whine. She prayed the cow would not go down with the hind end of the calf still in her. Then she felt a body close behind her, two arms reached around, and a hand gripped the bar on either side of hers.

'We'll give her a moment or two then pull,' Daniel's deep voice said quietly. 'I would have been here sooner but I was at the north end of the parish.'

'I'll move out of the way and let you—'

'Stay where you are. You can shield me. No good two of us getting in a mess.' She could hear amusement in his low tone. 'Pull now,' he urged, as the cow began to press again before Kim could reply.

She was too aware of his long, hard body pressed firmly against the length of her back to do anything but obey. Seconds later the calf slithered out and the cow sank down onto the straw, panting.

'A fine bull calf you have, Bert,' Daniel called cheerfully before he turned to look at Kim. His mouth quivered as he suppressed a smile. 'You make a great shield.'

She felt such a mess and knew she must look one, but when she glanced down she was worse than a damp, sticky mess. Her blouse was almost transparent and clinging to her due to the amniotic fluid.

'Oh my goodness!' she gasped. She turned to Bert. 'W-would Mrs Lenox mind if I used your bathroom to c-clean myself up a bit?'

'She'll be pleased to see ye, lassie. Ye've done a grand job. I reckon the calf would have been dead, aye, and maybe the cow tae, if ye hadna come when you did. Did ye want to see me for anything in particular?'

'Not really. I was supposed to meet Billy Nairn here. I'm not sure what he wanted, but he's late.' She moved towards the straw.

'Don't come near me, you filthy creature!' the woman yelped. 'You're not decent . . .'

'You are sitting on my anorak and pullover. I need them,' Kim said coldly. The woman jumped to her feet and Kim grabbed her clothes.

'What are you doing here, Estelle? This isn't your usual kind of place,' Daniel asked.

'I had an appointment with Dr McLaren, but he's late,' came the sulky reply.

Daniel threw back his head and laughed aloud.

Kim didn't wait to hear more. She hurried into the farm-house and Mrs Lenox's motherly ministrations.

'That is Dr McLaren you saw calving the cow,' Daniel chortled. 'Why do you want to see her, and why here of all places?'

'That was Dr McLaren? That woman in those filthy clothes? How could a person like that possibly advise me on how to make a dirty dump such as this into an efficient and more profitable farm?'

Daniel felt Bert stiffen beside him, and saw his eyes widen then narrow warily at Estelle's words.

'There appears to be a misunderstanding,' Daniel said with a frown. 'I understood Kim was expecting to meet Billy Nairn. Did you get her here under false pretences?' He knew of old that Estelle could be sly when she wanted her own way, but what could she want here, and with Kim? 'Was it you who arranged to meet her instead of Billy?'

'So what if I did! Your uncle said you're short of money. He said this place could make more profit if it was more efficient, so I decided to do something about it . . .'

'I beg your pardon?' Daniel snapped, his eyes narrowing. Estelle realised he was only just managing to control his anger. 'You . . . *you* decided? You know damn all about farming! Come to that, I doubt you could run a house efficiently, much less tell Billy Nairn, or me, how to farm efficiently. I think you had better leave now.'

'But I wanted to prove to—'

'I will open that gate. You'll need to drive into the yard to turn your car round.' His mouth was tight with anger, both at Estelle and at his uncle.

'Drive my little car through all this mud?'

'There's nowhere else to turn. Unless you want to reverse all the way back to the road junction? You never were very good at reversing, as I recall.'

He strode across and opened the gate while Estelle tiptoed slowly round the edge of the buildings again, looking surly.

'You could have helped me!' she accused when she reached the gate. 'My shoes are covered in mud. They will make a mess in my car.'

'What did you expect me to do about it?'

'You could have carried me.'

'Lord, you're not fit for country life, even if your father is an auctioneer and spends his life mixing with farmers and animals.' He closed the gate after her departing car.

'Will ye take a cup o' tea with us, Mr Nichol?' Bert asked.

'I would really appreciate one. Thanks, Bert,' Daniel said gratefully, then, 'Hey, wait a minute, why the Mr Nichol? I thought I was Daniel to you by now?'

'Maybe, but it sounds as though we have serious matters to discuss when your lady friend thinks I'm not efficient and you're needing more money.'

Daniel halted. He turned to face the older man. 'Let me make two things clear, Bert. That interfering woman is *not* my lady friend. Secondly, she had no reason to be here. If she tried to interfere with what you do, she would not be a friend of anybody in this area. As for money, if I had a fortune I would never let Miss Roon-Kurcher get her hands on it. She would want to make Wedderburn Hall like Buckingham Palace. As things are, I earn a good salary now I am working full-time as a vet again. I am doing a job I enjoy. I have no complaints about money. If I ever do, I shall let you know myself. Meanwhile, if you are happy with your work and your life, then so am I.'

'Aye, Mary an' me have been at Home Farm most of our lives. We're happy here.'

'I'm pleased to hear that. Although when I look around I think there are one or two things I should have done to make your life a bit easier.' He noticed Kim had kicked off her wellingtons at the back door. 'We ought to lay some concrete in this yard for a start. It would make your wife's life a bit easier, as well as your own. The mud must trail into the house in weather like this.'

"Tis the rain last night made it so bad,' Bert said apologetically. 'But Mary doesna grumble.'

* * *

Kim knew Mrs Lenox well. She had often visited Home Farm with her father when she was quite young. Billy had tagged along, too, whenever it was school holidays and he was staying with his aunt and uncle. Mary Lenox always had a selection box of chocolates for them at Christmas, chocolate eggs at Easter, and homemade tablet or treacle toffee around Halloween. Kim ran straight up the stairs to the bathroom, glad to peel off her sticky wet blouse. Even her bra was wet and her face and hair were splattered. The water was only lukewarm, but she stripped to her waist and washed herself thoroughly. She pulled on her woollen pullover. It would have to do until she got back home, and at least she felt clean and decent again. She could smell newly baked scones and knew Mrs Lenox would be making a hot cup of tea for her. She hoped that hysterical woman was not still here.

The kitchen at Home Farm was a sunny room with plenty of space for a large table and chairs. The Aga had a boiler beside it and took up most of one wall, but you had to go through the small scullery to get to it. The kitchen sink, washing machine and kitchen units were in the scullery and Mrs Lenox did most of her washing and food preparation there. Kim went in, intending to go straight through to the main kitchen, but she had reckoned without Bert leaving drips of water on the scullery floor after washing his own hands. Kim, in her stocking soles, slid helplessly forward. Daniel had just dried his hands and managed to catch her before she fell to the floor. Her pullover was short and too bulky to tuck into her jeans. Inevitably, it rumpled up as Daniel's hands gripped her. He spread his fingers automatically to support her, and his eyes widened as his thumbs brushed the gentle swell of her naked breasts.

Kim gasped.

'Lord, you do tempt a man, Kim,' he whispered.

Kim straightened up and took a step back.

'Everything I had on was damp. This is all I have,' she muttered, unable to look him in the eye. His touch seemed to waken all sorts of feelings she had never known before.

'I'm not complaining,' he said softly. 'Not at all.'

'Come through here for a cup of tea when you're finished, Mr Nichol,' Mary Lenox called cheerfully. He and Kim jumped, then moved as one through to the main kitchen, taking care not to slip on the trail of water drops.

While his wife poured tea and passed around the plates of scones and cake, Bert said, 'I hear ye're going to give a talk to the Young Farmers' Club next week, about your work in Africa. Young Billy Nairn says you have some pictures that you can show on a screen. I wouldn't have minded seeing them myself.' He chuckled. 'My days as a young farmer are long past. Are you going, young Kim?'

'It should be interesting. We could probably pay a visitor's fee.'

'I imagine they would welcome you for free, having given them a talk on New Zealand,' Daniel said.

'The club invites all guest speakers, coaches and anyone who has helped, or hosted the club on farm visits, to their dinner and dance in the autumn,' Kim told him. 'It's always a good meal and they usually have a decent band too.'

'You and Billy can come to the talk as my helpers, if you like.'

'I think Billy is a paid-up member since he came to live here permanently. He's a couple of years younger than I am anyway so will have a few years yet as a member.'

'I see. As for you, Bert, why don't you come to the Farmers' Club next month? I'm giving a talk and slide show to them too.'

'Oh my father will enjoy that,' Kim said eagerly. 'It's time he started going to the meetings again, now his leg is stronger. His car is an automatic so he has no problem driving. I'll tell him and I'm sure he'll give you a lift if you want to go, Bert.'

'Aye, I would like that.' Bert beamed.

Kim's earlier embarrassment with Daniel was forgotten in the friendly atmosphere of the Home Farm kitchen, but it returned when they stepped outside and were alone together.

'It's strange that Billy never turned up, and didn't phone to say he'd been held up. I hope he's not had an accident in the woods or anything.'

'It wasn't Billy who asked you to come,' Daniel informed her.

'It was. Mrs Scott left a note to say he wanted some sort of consultation at Home Farm.

'Did it say it was from Billy?'

'Er, no . . .' Kim frowned, trying to remember the wording. 'Not exactly. It sounded very formal for Billy. It said the estate manager wanted to see Dr McLaren. I thought it was strange. I wondered if Mrs Scott had made a mistake, and why would Billy ask for me to have a consultation with him. My father has already had a discussion with Bert about reseeding the field next to ours. There's no suitable drill for grass seeds here at Home Farm so my father offered to sow it.'

'There was a misunderstanding,' Daniel said grimly. 'The message was from Miss Roon-Kurcher. She had some notion of picking the brains of the famous Dr McLaren and turning Home Farm into a gold mine. Apparently, Uncle Fergus told her the estate doesn't bring in much money and Home Farm could be a lot more profitable.'

'So that was your lady friend! The hysterical woman who was here?'

'No, dammit, she is not my lady friend,' Daniel retorted irritably. 'She is simply someone I've known for most of my life. Her father and my uncle were neighbours. Anyway, she'll be returning to Aberdeen soon. Mrs Dunn is due back and there are only two bedrooms in my uncle's wing.'

'But there must be about twenty spare bedrooms in the main Hall,' Kim replied, deliberately looking wide-eyed and innocent.

'Don't you start provoking me. I don't know what Uncle Fergus has been saying. I shall ask him when I see him. He has a jolly good pension himself, so I know he's not short of money. As for me, I can't understand why Estelle decided to interfere.'

'I don't think your la— your friend and I would have got on very well. She didn't even have a pair of boots to walk round a farm.'

Daniel attempted to move the conversation away from Miss Roon-Kurcher.

'As a matter of interest, what would you have suggested as improvements to Home Farm, supposing it had been Billy asking you?'

'I'm sure Billy would never go behind the Lenoxes' back. I imagine he would have discussed things with you or your uncle first anyway.'

'I know you're right — Billy is straight and I trust him. But . . . for the record, tell me two things you would do to improve Home Farm, assuming Bert is content to stay a few years longer.'

'Put in a separate hot-water system for the dairy and milking parlour, and concrete this muddy yard,' Kim said promptly, before dodging under his arm and darting to her vehicle. He didn't allow her to escape so easily. He reached her jeep as she scrambled inside and he prevented her from closing the door on him.

'I've already told Bert we will concrete the yard after seeing what it's like today. What do you mean about the water system?'

'All the hot water for the house and the dairy, even for the young calves, has to be heated from the boiler in the house, even in summer. It must get dreadfully hot in the kitchen keeping the boiler stoked most of the day. Bert had forgotten to stoke it up after he used all the hot water in the dairy this morning, so the water in the bathroom was lukewarm.'

'Ah, I see. So you had to have a cool wash down.' His lips twitched and she saw a glint in his dark eyes, but he was still holding the car door so she couldn't shut him out. 'You smelled delightfully clean and fresh — from Mrs Lenox's coal-tar soap presumably? Your skin felt like silk . . .'

Kim glared at him and yanked the door out of his grasp then started the engine. She heard him chuckle and saw him salute as he stepped hastily back from her wheels.

Kim could almost feel the touch of his hands on her bare skin as she drove home, and she both smiled and trembled at the memory.

* * *

A few days later Billy phoned to offer Kim a lift to Daniel's talk. She accepted gratefully. She'd remembered it was on but knew she'd not have gone on her own. As it happened, it was Daniel driving when the car drew up. Billy was in the back, keeping a rolled screen in place and balancing two circular frames already loaded with slides ready for the show.

It was a good evening. Daniel was an excellent speaker and he included both humour and anguish, as on the occasion a baby elephant died. Kim felt his emotion and regret at being unable to save the young animal. Equally, he was able to laugh at himself when he showed pictures of his introduction to the different way of life, the hot climate and some of the primitive conditions.

Afterwards she helped Billy carry things back to the car, but this time he put them in the boot.

'The show's over now. Daniel didn't want the slides falling out on the way here. He had them all arranged in the order of his talk. It was good, wasn't it?'

'Yes, I thoroughly enjoyed it. It's an interesting subject, but Daniel is a superb presenter too.'

'I'm pleased you think so, Dr McLaren,' Daniel said quietly, coming up behind her.

'I'm getting a lift back with Jackie Anderson,' Billy informed Daniel. 'We're going for a drink and a catch-up with some of the lads.'

'I expect your aunt knows you'll be late?'

'I didn't know myself. We only arranged it ten minutes ago, but I'll not be that late anyway. We all have work tomorrow and Jackie won't be drinking as he's driving.'

'So long as your folks won't worry and blame me. I'll probably see you tomorrow sometime. Jump in, Kim, unless you intend walking home?'

Kim didn't reply but got into the car, silently cursing Billy for not telling her he wasn't coming home with them. She wasn't sure she could trust herself if Daniel turned on his charm. She was finding his flirtatious teasing increasingly difficult to resist.

The pictures of Africa had shown two attractive women who seemed on very friendly terms with Daniel, and she wondered if they'd also shared his bed. He might say Miss Roon-Kurcher was not his particular lady friend any longer, but maybe she'd not been aware of that when she arrived unexpectedly and expected to share his bed again . . .

'You're deep in thought. Penny for them?'

'They're not worth that.' She gave herself a mental shake. 'I'm on call tonight from ten. I would have swapped duties if I'd known Billy would be leaving us to drive home alone.'

Kim shot him a sharp glance. She saw his mouth twitching and knew he was suppressing a smile.

'It would not have been worth your while,' she said drily.

'You sure about that, Kimby?'

'Of course I'm sure.'

'Oh dear. I must be losing my touch. I thought you'd have enjoyed a little kiss and cuddle in the shadow of that stretch of woodland on the way home.'

'Then you thought wrong,' she retorted, more firmly than she actually felt. They were approaching the woodland that bordered the road and were travelling fairly fast, but almost as though Daniel read her thoughts, he slowed the car and glanced at her with his dark brows raised in question.

'Sure?' he asked.

'Certain,' she said, but she wished her heart wouldn't beat so fast at the mere mention of a kiss and cuddle with him. She breathed a sigh of relief when he put his foot down again and they sped towards Rowandene, but when he pulled into the farm he stopped the car well away from the door. He turned towards her.

'What have I done wrong?' he asked softly.

'N-nothing. Y-you're just imagining things.'

'I don't think so. I would like to take you out for an evening on our own, to a good film, or better still, for a meal and the theatre in Edinburgh perhaps. I really would like us to get to know each other better.' He was not teasing now. If she didn't know better, and if she hadn't seen how smart and well-groomed Miss Roon-Kurcher was, she might have thought he was pleading with her.

'I think Miss Roon-Kurcher might have something to say about that.'

'Miss Roon-Kurcher has nothing to do with me and my life. Anyway, she cleared off back to Aberdeen the day after the fiasco at Home Farm.' He couldn't hide a gleeful smile. 'Her car got splattered in mud, even some on the inside after she skidded. So, what about an evening out together?'

'I-I'll think about it.' She reached for the door handle, but he'd slipped his arm along the back of her seat, and with his other hand he gently but firmly turned her face towards him. She knew he was going to kiss her, and she was incapable of resisting. She even wondered if she'd met him halfway.

When she got into the house she planned on heading straight to her room so she could analyse the evening and the response Daniel Nichol awakened in her. As she passed the door into the kitchen, she heard her father and Nessie talking and then their laughter. She smiled and would have passed on by, but her father called out.

'Nessie has a surprise for us, Kim, and something to show you.'

She opened the door and went in. 'What is the surprise? Something nice, I hope?'

'A lovely surprise.' Her father chuckled. 'Show her, Nessie.'

Blushing slightly, Nessie held out her hand to show a beautiful engagement ring: a ruby with a diamond on either side. She looked younger and almost shy, but her eyes shone with happiness.

'Oh, Nessie! You're engaged! To Mr Sanders? That's wonderful news, and ruby is your birthstone, isn't it?'

Nessie nodded happily, and Kim hurried round the table and hugged her warmly. 'I am so happy for you. Have you fixed a date for the wedding? This is so exciting. I had no idea things were this serious. Tell me everything . . .'

'There's not much to tell yet,' Nessie said. 'Ross has invited Mel — Mr Sanders! — and the girls for lunch on Sunday so we can all discuss things. So far we've only told Jenny and Evie, but Mel is telling Mrs Bain in the morning. We didn't want her hearing from someone else and we want to assure her we shall need her to carry on working as she does now. She is a widow and I don't think she has much of a pension from her husband. She has already guessed there might be changes, but I told her I intend to carry on my own business whatever happens. We can't decide whether to build a small office for me adjoining Mel's house or whether we should move. My tenants are moving south at the end of next month so Fairvale will be vacant. It could be an option. Whatever we decide it will take time to get plans passed to make alterations, so I'm hoping Ross and you won't mind if I carry on using my present office plus its wee cloakroom with the toilet and hand basin. I thought we could lock the door so the rest of my rooms can revert to the house as they were before Ross made me an apartment of my own — not that I often stay in it,' she chuckled, 'except to sleep of course.'

'Oh, Nessie.' Kim hugged her again. 'Don't worry about any of that. We shall miss you terribly, of course, but at least we can come and visit if you're in the village.'

'Mmm, but nothing will be ready in time if Mel has his way. He would like us to get married in September.'

'Things will fall into place, lassie,' Ross said happily, 'and Mr Sanders is right. Once you've both made up your minds, there's no point in wasting time.'

'Dad's right,' Kim said, 'and we'll help in any way we can if you do decide to move houses, won't we, Dad?'

'Aye, we will.'

'Fairvale is at the opposite end of Ryankirk to Mel's house, but the school is in the middle of the village and so is Mrs Bain's house, so the distance is about the same. If I'm honest I would prefer to move to Fairvale. It's the older end of the village and the houses are all built of stone and generally larger, although they're not so modern inside. My parents were happy there, and so was I.'

'Aye, lassie, but then you moved back here again to help me look after Kim when Miriam died. You've had a lot of upheavals in your life. It's time you found some peace and joy. You deserve all the happiness life can give you.'

'Oh, Ross, you have always been good to me. You've always been a wonderful big brother.'

'Mr Sanders is a fine man. He hasn't had an easy life himself, losing his wife with cancer when the children were so young.'

'His name is Melvin, but all his friends call him Mel. I'm sure he would like to count you as a friend, Ross. Evie can't remember her mother at all, but she was only a year old, and Jenny was barely three, when she died. They . . . they seem so happy with our news. Jenny says when we marry they will have a mother of their own, just like the other children in their class.'

'And so they will, Nessie. You were wonderful to me when my mother died, and you have a truly kind heart,' Kim said.

'Does Fairvale have more rooms than Mel's house?' Ross asked.

'Yes it has, and it would be a fresh start for all of us,' Nessie said. 'It has two paddocks as well, so there'd be more room for the ponies. Mel seems in favour, but he's not seen inside the house yet. He is enthusiastic about building proper stables for horses and an extension for my office, but I think the small room at the back would probably do for me.'

'It sounds ideal,' Kim said.

'The house will need redecorating, of course. And we would need to make a doorway to the side, and maybe add a small porch or shelter of some kind, so my clients can come straight to the office and bypass the drive to the house, a bit like you have made for me here, Ross. Maybe you will show Mel, and explain how you did things here, when they come on Sunday?'

'I'm sure there'll be no problem, lassie.'

CHAPTER SEVEN

Ever since Kim learned to cook, she and Nessie had worked well together in the kitchen so they had no problem deciding what they'd each make for Sunday's dinner.

'If Mel and the children arrive early you'll want to spend time with them and maybe show the children the calves and chickens, so it would be better if I do the main course,' Kim suggested, 'especially if we're having roast beef and Yorkshire puddings. They need to be made at the right time.'

'That's true, and you always make a better job of them than I do,' Nessie said. 'You're a born cook, Kim — just like your Granny McLaren. My mother always said you would take after her because you were so practical, even when you were tiny.'

'But you taught me all the cooking I know, Nessie,' Kim reminded her.

'In the beginning, maybe, but you were eager and quick to learn. I can make most things myself, but I think Mrs Scott taught you quite a lot too. You enjoyed spending time with her when you were younger and I was working. Anyway, I shall be grateful if you'll do the main course. How about a good pan of chicken and rice soup for starters. That's Jenny's favourite and I can make it in advance.'

'What shall we have for dessert?'

'The girls love anything with jelly,' Nessie said promptly, 'but Ross's favourite has always been trifle and I know Mel likes that too. I'll make a trifle and set an extra jelly. The girls can choose jelly and ice cream if they don't like trifle.'

'They will probably try both.' Kim chuckled. 'I know I would have at their age. I might have both even now.'

'I don't know how you keep so slim, Kim. I envy you.' Nessie sighed.

'But you're not fat!'

'Maybe not fat exactly, but well rounded,' Nessie said wryly. She blushed a little. 'Mel says he doesn't want me any other way.'

'Oh, Nessie, I'm sure you'll be very happy together. I'm looking forward to getting to know Mel as more than the good consultant surgeon who helped my father. Presumably we're allowed to call him Mel as you do, are we?'

'Of course. I never thought I could be this happy,' Nessie admitted in a low voice, 'but, oh, Kim, I'm so nervous about— well, about some aspects of getting married. I-I mean nobody expects a woman of thirty-six to still be a virgin. I was never tempted to sleep around after a casual night out — not like people seem to be doing now, at least according to Billy.'

'Surely you don't believe everyone has sex after a night out, Nessie?'

'I don't know. People say casual attitudes started in the nineteen sixties. We're well into the seventies now and relationships seem to be getting even more casual.' Nessie's tone was vaguely troubled.

'I admit I was a bit shocked at first to find a lot of students experimenting when they got to university and away from home and parents,' Kim said. 'Some of the girls I knew regretted it later. I think some people feel under pressure to be the same as their friends.'

'I got the impression Billy gained plenty of experience while he was away from his folks,' Nessie said. 'He seemed to think you had too, the way he was gesticulating. He saw nothing unusual in Miss Roon-Kurcher sharing Daniel's bed either.'

'I think Billy has gained more experience than we would have expected, knowing what a shy boy he used to be. I neither admitted nor denied his assumptions about me. I have never been tempted to do things for the sake of experimenting or keeping up with other people. I share your values, Nessie, even if we are both old-fashioned. From what you say, I think Mel will respect your principles.'

'Ye-es, he is very understanding about . . . about things. It's just that he's so experienced himself.' Nessie blushed. She couldn't bring herself to tell Kim that he'd said he was looking forward to teaching her to enjoy loving and being loved. She knew she would feel tense and unsure until she and Mel had consummated their marriage, and it was one reason she didn't want to wait long before their wedding.

News of Nessie's engagement brought an air of anticipation to Rowandene. There had been just the three of them for so long and Kim looked forward to having the children to visit, along with Mel. Their small family was doubling up and she knew her father was delighted at the developments. Nessie was his only sister and he loved her dearly. They had always been close, but he felt she'd made big sacrifices for them. He had a genuine liking for Mel, as well as great respect for him as a surgeon. If he brought happiness and security to Nessie's life, then Ross McLaren would be happy for them all.

* * *

Unfortunately, Sunday morning at Rowandene didn't begin well.

As soon as Kim went into the shed where the recently calved cows were kept she saw that one of the older cows was unsteady and swaying on her feet. She was a high yielder and had delivered her fourth calf two days earlier. Since her father's accident, Kim had taken over gathering up any animals needing special treatment before they went into the milking parlour, but Kim knew instinctively it would be a mistake to try to move Rowan Violet. Almost certainly she would collapse in the middle of the yard, or it would be even worse if she went down in the milking parlour and couldn't get up. Kim got the others out of the shed and closed the door. As soon as she'd driven them to the gathering area ready for Joe's attention, she went to find her father to tell him Violet had milk fever. She collected a bucket of hot water from the dairy and put in the bottles of calcium to warm up to blood temperature. Her father joined her and brought the flutter valve and sterilised needle with him. Together they got the cow securely into one corner and Kim steadied her while her father inserted the needle into the vein in her neck and patiently allowed the liquid to drip into the cow's blood stream. They both knew that if the liquid went into the vein too quickly it could cause heart failure, and the death of the cow.

Ross fixed a second bottle of calcium to the drip. 'She's not in a good way. It's a good job you saw her and didn't let Joe risk taking her into the milking parlour.'

After breakfast Kim still felt uneasy about the cow. She went back to the shed to have another check.

'She's lying down, but I don't see much improvement in her yet,' she told Ross.

'I'll keep an eye on her, lassie. Don't you worry about the animals when you're busy doing the cooking. Nessie is really happy that we're making Mel and his wee girls welcome here for Sunday dinner.'

'It's the least we can do, and we're both happy for them. Besides, I enjoy cooking the roast and all the things to go with it.'

Mel Sanders and his daughters arrived earlier than expected. He greeted Nessie with a kiss, and Kim grinned at her flustered manner and pink cheeks. She was usually so calm and took everything in her stride.

'I know we're too early, but these two rascals are so excited they couldn't wait to get here. They haven't given me any peace since they got out of bed.'

'Auntie Nessie said she'd let us see the animals,' Jenny said, and moved to Nessie's side to hold her hand. Evie moved to her other side, looking up with wide, trusting eyes as she slipped her small hand into Nessie's free one.

'Did you remember to bring your wellingtons?' Nessie asked after kissing each of them on the cheek.

'We did!' they chorused. 'They're in the boot of Daddy's car.'

Ross came to the door. He had heard the car and hoped it was the vet who he'd had to call as the cow was not improving. He greeted Mel and the girls warmly and put his own wellingtons back on, ready to join the party visiting the calves and chickens and the big bull with a ring in his nose, and anything else there was to see. The girls were full of questions, but their father seemed interested, too, as he walked beside Ross, remarking on things that were unfamiliar to him. He noted that Ross now had only a very slight limp and seemed free of pain, at least most of the time.

Kim returned to the kitchen and began whisking up the Yorkshire pudding batter ready for when the roast came out to rest. She heard the car draw up at the back door and guessed it was the vet but was surprised to see which one.

'We didn't expect you, Daniel. You're on call today?'

'No, but he's out on another call and I told Angus — Mr Turner — that with Rowandene so close, I'm quite happy to come here anytime if I'm at home and free. He says you've a cow with milk fever and she's not responded to the calcium?'

'That's right.' Kim peeled off the white apron she always wore for cooking, and Daniel admired the sight of her slim green skirt and matching silk shirt. 'I'll show you where she is and see if I can find my father.'

'I can look for him if you're busy.'

'I'm cooking today. Father will want to see you anyway.' They walked side by side. 'He's with Nessie, showing Mr Sanders and his wee girls round the farm. Did you hear he and Nessie are engaged?'

'No. I hadn't heard that. It's a wonder if Billy and his uncle have missed that bit of news. Are you pleased about it?'

'Oh yes, I'm very pleased, and so is Father. Nessie deserves some happiness and they seem well suited. Here we are.' She went to open the heavy sliding door of the shed, but Daniel moved quickly.

'I'll do that. You're too smart for such work today.' They both stepped inside and Kim gasped when she saw the cow lying flat out and looking much worse than she had earlier. She knew that when cows lie flat like that they can soon fill with air and the pressure on their heart could cause them to die quite quickly. Daniel looked at her.

'Mr Turner said she'd already had calcium, but are you sure it was into the vein?'

Kim stiffened and gave him an outraged stare.

Daniel knew by the way she tightened her lips and rolled her eyes heavenward that he'd committed a blunder. He held his hand up in a placating gesture. 'Sorry . . . sorry.'

'I'll give my father a shout.' Kim turned silently on her heel. It didn't take her long because Ross had been half listening for the sound of the vet's car while he was showing Mel Sanders around the farm buildings.

'He's in there.' Kim nodded towards the shed. 'It's Daniel Nichol. I'll get back to the kitchen.'

A little while later Kim heard the laughter of the children, and Nessie and Mel returning with them. Nessie helped them take off their wellington boots and supervised hand washing in the small downstairs cloakroom.

'Dinner is ready when you are,' Kim said, going into the hall to greet them. 'My father said we're not to wait for him.'

'They won't be long,' Nessie said. 'I saw Daniel going back to his car. He has given the cow some phosphorus and was going to get a vitamin injection for her as a booster. Ross invited him to join us.'

'Did he? For lunch?'

'That's all right, isn't it? There's plenty of food. I'll lay an extra place. We'll go straight through to the dining room and get seated, unless there's anything I can do?'

'No, everything is ready. I'll put the Yorkshire puddings in to cook while we're eating our soup.'

'All right. We don't want them to waste, do we, girls?' Nessie asked.

'Oh no. I love Yorkshire pudding!' Jenny said with relish.

'I like it too,' Evie echoed in a small voice. 'We don't have it much at home, do we, Daddy?'

'I'm afraid we don't, at least not when I'm cooking,' Mel said wryly. 'Mrs Bain is a good cook, but she has a day off on Sundays unless I'm on call.'

'Mrs Bain always makes Yorkshires for us when she comes on Sundays, even if we're having chicken or stew,' Jenny said with satisfaction. 'She makes them in little bun tins if we're not having roast meat.'

'Nessie makes good roasts and Yorkshire puddings,' Kim told the girls.

'Will you make some for us when you are our mummy?' Evie asked eagerly.

'Of course I will, my dears,' Nessie said, flushing a little as she glanced at Mel. Kim saw him give her a wink.

'I'll go and bring the soup through.' Kim had heard her father come into the hall through the side door and she expected Daniel would be with him, so she was surprised when she heard a brief knock on the back door and Daniel came into the kitchen, still in his shirt sleeves but with his jacket slung over his shoulder.

'Oh! I thought you were with my father . . .'

'He said to come through this way and you'd find me a pair of his slippers to wear. I usually have my shoes in the car, but I put my wellingtons on and came straight here this morning.'

'I suppose we should be honoured that you give us special service,' Kim said brusquely.

'I see you've got the bristles up again, Miss Hedgehog,' Daniel mocked, but his eyes sparkled with humour. 'Will it help if I apologise again for doubting your word, however briefly?'

'It was my father who gave the cow the calcium into the vein and he has been doing it for years.'

'Yes, so I gathered, but you'd be surprised how many of the farmers cannot manage that, or even under the skin.'

'I'll find the slippers,' Kim said. 'You can wash your hands at the sink in the back kitchen if you like, or go through to the cloakroom. We're eating in the dining room today.'

'Thanks, the back kitchen will do fine for me.'

'All right, but I'll find you some slippers first. I'll carry the soup in and start dishing it out, so come on through as soon as you're ready.'

'Mmm . . . it smells delicious.'

'It is delicious.' She paused, and he glimpsed the smile tugging at her lips. 'Nessie made it.'

'I see, but I thought you were cooking?'

'Yes, I am. We often do it between us. I'm doing the meat course so you had better hurry.'

'Yes, Miss . . .' Daniel made a quick exit in case she threw the dishcloth at him, but Kim heard him chuckling and wondered why she let him bring out the worst in her.

She saw at once that Nessie had seated Daniel next to her and she frowned, but it made sense. Her father was seated at the other end of the table with a child on either side of him. They were not at all shy and seemed to have taken to him. Mel was seated next to Jenny, with Nessie across from him, next to Evie, ready to help her cut up her meat if needed.

It was a lovely meal, with conversation flowing easily between the three men, and Kim realised her father was enjoying having some male companionship for once. He seemed to get on well with both Mel and Daniel.

When the meal was over, Ross pushed back his chair.

'I like to have a seat for a while after such a good meal. You're all welcome to join me unless you have other things to do?' He looked questioningly from Nessie to Mel.

'Nessie promised to show me the office you made for her with the separate entrance to keep it self-contained and professional.'

'It was easily done, as you will see. Just a wee bit of adaptation,' Ross nodded. 'I see the rain is coming on, though—' he looked at the children — 'so if you two want to come and join me in front of the fire, I'll tell you a story.' His eyes twinkled and Jenny and Evie immediately pushed back their chairs and each took one of his hands.

'He is good with children,' Mel said, watching them go. 'They don't remember either of their grandfathers.'

'Ross was always good with youngsters, even when he was a very young man himself. I remember he was so patient with me and he was a young man of seventeen when I was born,' Nessie said. 'He never resented me. He ought to have been blessed with half a dozen like Kim.'

'I should think one Kim is enough for any man to manage.' Daniel chuckled.

'I shall go and clear away the rest of the dishes since you're going to hurl insults,' Kim said, pretending to be hurt.

'You've done enough, Kim,' Nessie said. 'I'll tidy the rest. Don't protest. I noticed you had already washed all the pans and the roasting tin and put them away. You've already stacked most of the plates in the dishwasher.'

'You have a dishwasher?' Mel asked in surprise.

'Yes, Ross bought it some time ago to make life easier for Mrs Scott,' Nessie said.

'My father wondered whether you had one, Mel?' Kim asked. 'He was thinking of buying you one for a wedding present.'

'Was he? That would be a very generous gift, wouldn't it, Nessie? I reckon we should both be grateful for such a useful machine.'

'We would indeed,' Nessie agreed.

'You do know it was a man who first invented a machine for washing dishes, don't you?' Kim asked with wide-eyed innocence.

'A man?' Daniel queried.

'Yes. It was about 1850, though, and of course it was made of wood, and wasn't a great success. I've forgotten the name of the woman who invented one a bit later. You still had to turn it by hand, but it was better organised inside, I think.'

'Well, I will prove I'm perfectly able to wash whatever dishes are left,' Mel said. 'With Nessie's help, of course.' He grinned and sent Daniel and Kim a look which they interpreted as a message for them to stay out of the kitchen.

'All right,' Kim agreed. 'I had promised to play bat and ball with Jenny and Evie on the lawn, but I don't think the rain looks like stopping. Nessie, what do you say if I go up and investigate the attic. I'm sure the dolls' house is still up there. Do you think they'd like to play with it if I bring it down?'

'I'm sure the girls would love it. You had a farmyard too. I expect it must be up there somewhere. It will all be very dusty, though, Kim.'

'One thing will be enough,' Mel said with a laugh, 'or I shall never get them home again.'

'If you do go up, Kim, for goodness' sake be careful. It's such a narrow, twisted stair to carry things up or down.' Nessie looked at Daniel, brows raised. He gave a hint of a smile and a slight nod.

'I would like to have a quick check on the cow,' he said. 'Will you come with me, Kim? Then I'll help get what you need down the attic stairs.'

'Yes, that would be much safer,' Nessie said, nodding in satisfaction. 'Thank you, Daniel. I assume you're not on call?'

'No, not today. Kim, we shall need our coats and wellingtons.'

'It is plain we're not wanted in there,' Kim said with a grin as they went out together.

'My feelings exactly. Not that I blame Mel for wanting Nessie to himself.' He chuckled. 'She is a lovely person and you can see the girls adore her already. I think they'll make a happy family.'

'I do hope so,' Kim said with feeling. 'I can't think of anyone who deserves happiness more, and Nessie is so understanding and kind, as I should know.'

Daniel grasped her hand in his strong, warm one and they ran together through the rain to the shed, arriving breathless. 'I think you have to experience such a loss to really appreciate the effect it has, especially when you're too young to understand why your world has turned upside down. Maybe Mel has considered that aspect when he sees how gentle and kind Nessie is with his children, but it's obvious he's in love with her.'

'For once, I agree with you,' Kim said seriously.

'I'm glad we agree on something. Ah, look, Kim!' He moved closer to the pen where the cow was now standing up. He grinned with relief and satisfaction.

'She's chewing her cud. And she's steady on her feet now. She must be feeling better, whatever magic you used,' Kim said.

'No magic. Instinct, experience and modern medicines. She has drunk most of the water your father set beside her too. Thank goodness she's going to recover. I hate to lose an animal, and your father says she is one of his best.'

'She's one of the highest yielders. I suppose that, and her age, is partly the reason for the trouble.'

'There's no job more satisfying than saving a good animal. I've never regretted insisting I wanted to be a vet.'

'Did your uncle want you to do something else then?'

'No, not Uncle Fergus. He said it was my life so I had to make my own choice. It was Estelle's father who wanted to train me as an auctioneer. I refused to consider it. I admit I was probably a bit bloody minded at that stage in my life. I resented someone who wasn't even family trying to tell me what I should do with my future. I really longed for my parents then. Estelle and her parents never understood. Her father told me more than once that Uncle Fergus had spoiled me and given me too much of my own way.'

'It sounds as though he liked his own way too.'

'Too right he did. When I realised he and my uncle thought Estelle and I would eventually marry I began to feel trapped. Her father also expected I'd become a partner in his auctioneering firm.'

'So you've no regrets?'

'No, none at all. Uncle Fergus couldn't have been kinder, or more generous, but from time to time he had to go away on his own business and he was the only real link I had with my parents. I often felt lonely then, so I ought to have realised Uncle Fergus might be lonely, too, when I went off to Africa. I know how lucky I was. He had no need to take me in at all. Although they were fairly close in age, and good friends, he was my father's uncle. As a bachelor, and only my great-uncle, he would have been justified in sending me to a children's home.'

'Oh no! That would have been a dreadful thing to do,' Kim said with a shudder. 'At least I had my father and the home I'd always had, as well as Nessie a lot of the time, and Granny and Grandfather were still alive at first. We have always been close, the three of us.'

'I feel closer to Uncle Fergus since he came to stay down here than I did as a boy. Recently, he told me he'd always loved me like his own son because my mother was the only woman he had ever loved or wanted to marry. He never told her. He said he felt he was too old for her because he was twenty-nine and she was only nineteen. He introduced her to my father and he must have been dismayed when the two of them immediately fell in love. They married young. I could never have guessed all that, but I am glad he told me. I don't suppose I would have understood at the time, but I do now.'

'I know what you mean. It never occurred to me that my father might want to marry again when I was young, but when I see how happy Mel and Nessie are together, I think he must have felt lonely sometimes. Maybe he did long for a companion, but I was too young to know.'

'There's a lot of things we can never understand, or know, about another person, I suppose.' He sighed, then smiled at her. 'Now we had better rescue your father from his storytelling with that dolls' house.'

CHAPTER EIGHT

Daniel had been right about Mel seizing an opportunity to have Nessie to himself for a while.

It didn't take Mel long to see how Ross had made a separate entrance to the office and disguised it using a hedge so that it looked entirely separate from the main house.

'We could certainly do something similar at Fairvale from what I've seen of the outside. I know you would prefer us to make our home there rather than at my present house, dear Nessie, and I don't mind where we live so long as I have you beside me. We could go on Wednesday afternoon and have a proper look around when the tenants have moved out. Then we can decide what changes would suit all of us.'

'You don't think it will cost too much?' Nessie asked dubiously.

'You don't need to worry about that. I earn plenty to keep all of us comfortably. You don't need to continue working at all unless you want to, but you seem to enjoy your work so I assumed you'd want to keep it on, especially now you've built up your own list of clients.'

'I do enjoy it, but I promise not to take on too many clients.'

'We shall also have one of the houses to sell. I suggest we invest the money from that to give us a nest egg in case it's needed for a rainy day. Now, let's forget about the mundane things until tomorrow.' He took her hand. 'Show me your sitting room.'

'It's just through here.' He followed her in and looked around the cosy, pleasant room. 'I really like this painting.' He stood for a moment looking up at the woodland scene above the fireplace.

'Ross bought that for me for my twenty-first birthday. He let me choose which one I wanted. These two over here are by the same artist. They belonged to my mother. Kim has a similar one in her bedroom.'

'They're very true to life.'

'Yes, that's what I like about the artist's work. These doors lead to the small cloakroom and a tiny kitchen.' She opened the door to show him. 'And this was the back stairs when there were live-in maids. It leads to a large room above. It needed to be big because there were three maids in the days when my grandparents lived here. It's my bedroom now. Ross partitioned off one section to make me a small bathroom of my own, but there's also a door onto the main landing so I can use either staircase. We all come and go quite freely, but Ross couldn't do enough to make sure I retained my independence and had a place to entertain my own friends in private whenever I wanted. Kim has long since outgrown the need for me, but we've all been happy together so I stayed. The rent from Fairvale allowed me to build up some savings too.'

'I can understand Ross being grateful for your help, even though you were still quite young yourself. It's a worry to me sometimes, making sure Jenny and Evie are well cared for, but Mrs Bain is very reliable.' He looked around. 'Where does that door lead?'

'Back into the main house.' Mel had noticed a key in the lock and he looked at Nessie, holding her gaze, his eyes alight with love and laughter. He turned the key and gave her a boyish grin.

'Does this mean we can snatch half an hour or so to ourselves, my love?' She smiled back at him, her cheeks slightly pink now, the way he enjoyed seeing her. He still couldn't believe he had found a woman as sweet and innocent as Nessie, at his age, and especially in his circumstances. He moved to her side, his gaze soft with love and desire. Nessie's blush deepened as he drew her close and kissed her longingly. He continued kissing her as he manoeuvred them to the settee, drawing her down with him and pulling her onto his lap. Nessie knew Mel was longing to make love to her, but he had told her he wanted their first time to be in their own bed where they couldn't be disturbed. Her heart beat faster at the mere thought of it and she returned his kisses with more passion than she ever had before.

Encouraged by this more relaxed Nessie, and knowing the girls would not find them in here, he half lay across the settee, pulling her with him. He undid the button of her skirt and eased her blouse free. Nessie's breathing came faster as his fingers released the hooks on her bra and his hand cupped her breasts, first one and then the other, stroking her nipples until they rose to his caresses. She responded to his kisses with a passion to match his own. He had never doubted that he could teach Nessie what it was like to love, and be truly loved, but her response was already more than he had dared to hope. He opened the buttons of her blouse so that his lips could follow where his fingers had led.

'Oh, Mel . . .' Nessie breathed softly.

'You like that, my love?' he asked tenderly.

'Y-ye-es, oh yes . . .'

Mel's mouth found hers in a passionate kiss while his free hand lifted her skirt and allowed his fingers to explore slowly and gently. He heard Nessie's indrawn breath and his kiss deepened as his fingers probed. Nessie, his innocent Nessie, was already moist with longing. He found it hard to stop now, but he knew he must. This was not the time or place to make her completely his.

'We must arrange a date for our wedding,' he breathed, his mouth soft and caressing against her cheek.

'Y-yes, soon . . .'

'I believe you want me almost as much as I want you, my own sweet Nessie.'

'I never knew I could feel like this, Mel,' she whispered, and he cradled her head against his chest and rearranged her clothes.

'I suppose we should see what the girls are doing?' He sighed, reluctant to let her go.

'Yes, I suppose so . . .' Nessie agreed, though she made no move out of his embrace.

'Can we fix a date for our wedding?' Mel murmured, his chin resting on her soft hair.

'I think we must.' Nessie blushed as she raised her head to look into his eyes. 'I don't want to wait now — now that I know . . .'

'My darling, Nessie. There is so much more . . . I long to make you completely mine. Can we forget about houses and alterations and simply fix a date?'

'When can you take time off from the hospital?'

'I must give a bit of warning, but how about the last Saturday of the school holidays. I would like us to go away on our own for a couple of weeks and the girls will go back to school on the Monday. It would be easier for Mrs Bain to look after them.'

'I'm sure Kim will lend a hand too. Maybe take them riding a couple of evenings and bring them here at the weekend? When are the school holidays?'

'They start next weekend and the girls return to school the first week in September, so our wedding would be the first Saturday in September if you agree?'

'Mmm, that's only seven weeks away.' Nessie gave him an impish glance. 'But I can't wait.'

'I can see I'm going to have a more ardent wife than I ever dreamed.' Mel grinned.

***

The stairs up to the attic were narrow and twisted, but there was a huge floor space. A lot of things had been covered with old blankets, and Kim was pleasantly surprised when she uncovered the dolls' house to find it reasonably clean. Daniel had followed her all the way into the attic instead of waiting at the bend of the stairs for her to pass the little wooden house down to him, as she had expected. He moved silently behind her and as she straightened, he wrapped his arms round her, holding her close.

'I have thoroughly enjoyed my day with you all,' he whispered against the soft skin of her neck. 'I'm beginning to feel it was worth coming back from Africa now.' He began to describe some of the things he had not mentioned in his talk, such as the foods he'd had to try, and he made her laugh when he described how he felt trying a drink that looked like blood and tasted foul but was passed from person to person. He had a way of making things both interesting and humorous.

'I'm beginning to feel we're getting to know each other at last,' he murmured softly. Kim's breath was coming faster than she would have liked at the feel of his tall, hard body pressed against her and his strong arms holding her securely beneath her breasts. Slowly, he turned her around until she was looking into his face. 'Don't you agree?'

'Y-yes, I think so.' Kim's spirited character could not leave it at that, though. Her eyes danced with glee. 'It doesn't mean I shall not be bristly sometimes . . .'

'Ah, I know a good cure for that.' Before she realised his meaning, he bent his head and claimed her mouth, taking her by surprise. He made the most of his opportunity, deepening the kiss, exploring and awakening a satisfying passion in return. Kim's arms seemed to have a will of their own when they crept around his neck. He sighed with pleasure and pressed her closer against him, one hand stroking her back. He was reluctant to break their embrace, especially when her hand moved to his shirt, opening some of the buttons so her fingers could explore the slight fuzz on his chest before they came to rest on his heart and felt its increased beating. He looked into her eyes and held her gaze. His own hand gently stroked her breast, feeling her nipple harden in swift response. He would have liked to feel her warm flesh, as she was exploring his, but he knew instinctively that he must take one step at a time to earn Kim's trust. For a moment he held her gaze and saw the latent desire in her eyes. He lowered his head and kissed her with increasing passion. But eventually he sighed and released her reluctantly.

'I suppose we'd better find these toys. Your father will be exhausted with storytelling by now.'

'Mmm,' Kim sighed, then smiled up at him. 'I expect he'll be wondering where we are, unless Nessie and Mel have joined him.'

'I doubt they will have done that.' He chuckled softly. 'I heard Mel saying he hoped they could snatch a little time to themselves inspecting Nessie's apartment.'

'I don't suppose they do get much time on their own,' Kim reflected. 'The children will never be far away. We'd better get these toys downstairs then.'

'I'll carry the dolls' house. It's not so heavy.'

'If you're sure you can manage the stairs?'

He nodded.

'Then I'll bring this wee crib with teddy and a rather scruffy doll. I'm not sure what the girls will make of them.'

'You must have been a loveable child, playing with your dolls,' Daniel mused, trying to imagine the slender, efficient, sometimes prickly young woman as a little girl. He heard her sigh. 'Do they bring back happy memories, Kim?'

'Mostly, I suppose they do. Father made the dolls' house, that's why it's so substantial. He made this little crib with its rockers, too. I was only seven or eight then. It was before Mother died.'

'Ah, I see,' Daniel said softly.

'As I got older I spent a lot of time outside as my father's shadow. Nessie had her own work and Mrs Scott couldn't be here all the time, especially in the school holidays. My interest moved from dolls to cows and sheep and hens, and I got a pony of my own. I loved that. I'm hoping to get a pony again now I'm home for good.'

'Really? I wouldn't mind having a decent horse again myself. Maybe we could ride together sometimes?'

'Mmm, maybe we could. Somewhere up here in the attic there's a farmyard. My father made sheds and pens and fences similar to the ones we have here now. I think he was planning the changes he wanted to make to Rowandene. We had lots of animals and some small tractors and trailers. I loved it. I was always farming in my own way.'

'It sounds as though you loved the farmyard as much as this wee house.'

'I loved them both, but the house will be enough for Jenny and Evie today. They might spend some time with us if Mel and Nessie go away on a honeymoon. They can enjoy the other toys then. As far as I know, they've not set a date for their wedding yet.'

They made their way back down the stairs and Kim paused on opening the door into the sitting room, putting a finger to her lips. Her eyes sparkled. Her father was sound asleep in his big, comfortable chair and the two little girls were lying on the hearth rug, each with a cushion for a pillow, and both asleep. Kim stepped back and closed the door quietly.

'We can put these in the dining room until they waken,' she whispered. 'It will soon be time to go back out to work anyway. We'll go into the kitchen and I'll make some tea.' She blushed. 'That is, unless you're wanting to leave now?' Kim looked up, realising she didn't want Daniel to go just yet. She felt comfortable and at ease in his company today — and more than that . . .

'I'm in no hurry to leave. I would like to come and help you with your chores, if you'll have me?'

'I shall probably be feeding the calves and the other young stock. Dad will likely help Joe finish the milking and deal with any cows needing extra attention, like the one with the milk fever, or if any have mastitis. He trusts Joe, but he likes to deal with any ills himself.'

'I understand that. Angus Turner says your father is one of the best stockmen he knows, and he doesn't give credit lightly.'

* * *

Although Kim had opened the sitting room door quietly, the movement had wakened Ross. He stirred and stretched, then remembered his two young companions. Jenny opened her eyes and looked up at him. She gave him a beguiling smile.

'We don't have a grandfather of our own. Will you be our grandfather? Please?'

'Aye, I would like that, wee Jenny.' Their low voices wakened Evie. Moments later the pair of them were bouncing on Ross's knee and giving him hugs.

'My goodness me! What are you two up to?' Mel said, pausing in the doorway as he and Nessie were about to enter.

'We've got a grandfather of our own now,' Jenny informed him.

'Have you?' He looked anxiously at Ross. 'Have they been a nuisance?'

'Not at all. We all had a nice wee nap in front of the fire,' Ross said with a grin.

'Granddad McLaren told us a lovely story and we fell asleep,' Evie said, obviously enjoying using this new title.

Daniel and Kim came into the hall.

'We've made some tea in the kitchen if anyone is interested,' Kim announced with a smile.

'I am,' Evie said eagerly.

'Can we have orange juice?' Jenny asked as they all followed Kim through to the kitchen. 'I do like it here,' she added, looking around the big kitchen. 'What a giant cooker! Where does that door go?'

'That will take you out into the yard,' Ross told them, 'but I see it's still raining so you'll have to come back another day to explore properly.'

'Where does that other door go?' Evie asked.

'It goes into the pantry where we store lots of food,' Kim said with a smile.

'We store our food in the 'fridg-rater,' Jenny said.

'And in the cupboards up high,' Evie added, 'where we can't reach.'

'I think it's time I took these two home,' Mel said reluctantly. 'I don't know how I'll get them to sleep tonight. They were too excited to sleep last night and then they were up at the crack of dawn this morning wanting to get here.'

'You don't need to take them home so early,' Kim said. 'Dad and I have some jobs to do, but Nessie will be here. There's plenty to eat for supper — that's what we call our evening meal — if you don't mind helping yourselves to cold meat and salad and pickles. There's a chocolate cake too,' she added with a smile at the girls.

'Oh, Daddy, can we stay? Please?' the girls chorused.

'We don't want to outstay our welcome,' Mel said uncertainly. He looked at Nessie.

'There's no fear of that, laddie,' Ross said. 'They're fine wee bairns. I have enjoyed having company today. Besides, Kim bought a big pork pie from Mr Jones, the butcher. He makes them himself.'

So it was unanimously decided they would all stay for supper, including Daniel. At Nessie's suggestion, Mel agreed he should make a quick trip home to collect the children's pyjamas and dressing gowns so that she could bathe them and get them into their night clothes ready to pop into bed as soon as they got home.

'We left the toys in the dining room,' Kim said in an aside to Nessie.

'Oh, that's good. First I might make a batch of scones for supper, and show the pair of them how to make a scone man or a wee cuddy. You used to enjoy that.'

'That's true,' Kim said with a smile. 'I liked making the man best. You can put more raisins on for buttons, as well as eyes and a mouth. A donkey only has two eyes and a nose.'

* * *

In spite of the rain, Daniel seemed to enjoy finding his way around the various buildings and looking at all the animals. He helped Kim fill up the tank where the calves sucked their milk from a line of teats, and he was patient with the two very young calves, letting them suck his fingers and making sure they got sufficient colostrum from a bucket each.

'We seem to have finished quicker tonight,' Kim said. 'That must be because you helped me fill up the hay and carry the cake and the milk.'

'I'm glad to have been some use and helped to earn my lunch. I'm not so sure I ought to impose on you all and stay to supper, though.'

'When my father says you are all welcome to stay, he means it,' Kim reassured him. 'I believe he has enjoyed having company, including the children's.'

'Yes.' Daniel grinned. 'I liked the way they adopted him as their new granddaddy. But it's not your father's approval I'm unsure about, so much as yours?'

'Mine? It's my father's house. He's the boss.'

'But you're the cook. Are you sure I shall not be one too many?'

'Of course not! It won't be a formal meal. You'll have to help yourself to what's on the table. We don't stand on ceremony as your Miss Roon-Kurcher and her family probably do.'

'Do I hear the prickles rising?' Daniel teased. 'Remember, I've found a cure . . .' Kim gave him a wary look, but as she went to pass him on her way out of the calf house, he reached out and drew her to him.

'This may be my last chance for a goodnight kiss, and I also need your approval, as much as your father's.' He put a finger under Kim's chin and raised her mouth to his in a lingering kiss which brought the colour to Kim's cheeks.

'You're very welcome to j-join us for supper, Mr Nichol,' Kim said primly, but her eyes were alight with laughter as she ducked under Daniel's arms and made for the house.

* * *

When the evening meal was over, Mel stood up and pulled Nessie to her feet, keeping his arm around her.

'We have an announcement to make. We have fixed a date for our wedding and we hope it will suit all of you.'

'You've fixed a date?' Kim chuckled. 'When? Next week?'

'I wish it was so soon, my dear Kim,' Mel said. Nessie blushed at his ardent look. 'It is the last Saturday of the school holidays and Nessie and I hope to go away on our own for two weeks. The girls will be at school during the day by then. Will that suit everyone?'

'Of course it will,' Ross declared. 'We shall make it suit, whatever else comes up.'

'You will be my bridesmaid, won't you, Kim? Jenny and Evie will be flower girls and carry posies, and we shall have to choose two pretty new dresses,' she added, smiling at them. They both pushed back their chairs and ran to hug Nessie, putting their chubby arms around her neck and kissing her.

'Will you be our new mummy when we have all been to church?' Jenny asked.

'I shall, if you want me to be your mummy?'

'Oh we do, you know we do,' they chorused.

'So who is your best man, Mel?' Ross asked. 'Or have you not asked him yet? I don't suppose you have had much chance.'

'We-ell, as a matter of fact, as soon as Nessie agreed to marry me, I couldn't keep it to myself. I mentioned it to a close friend and colleague. I knew I could rely on him to be discreet and not spread gossip around the hospital, especially since we hadn't set a date yet. Unfortunately, he's only gone and got a new job down south. He leaves in a fortnight's time. He won't be able to make it back so soon.'

'Ah, that's a pity,' Ross said.

'You could ask Daniel now you know him, and you seem to get on well,' Nessie said, smiling widely across the table at both Daniel and Kim. 'He will not be gossiping to all your nurses because he doesn't know them. You are both doctors after all, except that Daniel's patients are animals.' She turned to Kim. 'I didn't want the people at the hospital to know, you see, not until it's all over. Mel understands I don't want a big wedding with the long white dress and trimmings. I am far too old for that sort of fuss.'

'Of course you're not too old!' Kim declared. 'You're only thirty-six.'

'Exactly what I told her,' Mel said, 'but so long as she agrees to be my wife, I don't mind if she turns up in her underwear.' He grinned. 'What about it, Daniel? I know we've only just met, but I'd be greatly obliged if you would agree. If I ask one of my other colleagues, I'm sure to offend some of them. Besides, I'm not sure any of them could resist spreading the news around. They would have accepted Bob because they know we have been friends since university and he's always the soul of discretion.'

Daniel glanced at Kim and his eyes danced with amusement. He had seen the way her eyes widened at Nessie's suggestion. He knew she was to be the main bridesmaid.

'I would be delighted to be your best man, Mel, so long as I don't need to organise a stag party? I don't know many people around here yet. The ones I do know are mostly farmers.'

'There will be nothing like that,' Mel said.

'We don't have very many relations between us,' Nessie said, 'so it'll be a quiet wedding. I would like a smart dress and matching hat. Would you be happy with the same, Kim?'

'Of course I would.' Kim smiled at Nessie's anxious look. 'I think we should take ourselves on a shopping spree to

Edinburgh. If we hurry up, you could ask Mrs McIver if she'll make ankle-length dresses for Jenny and Evie.' She turned to the little girls who were fidgeting with excitement. 'Maybe we could borrow her pattern books and then you could choose the dresses you like best. Nessie will help you choose a pretty colour that you both like. And you'll need new shoes. I shall need new ones too.'

'Can we have silver shoes?' Evie asked.

Kim glanced questioningly at Nessie, who shrugged and rolled her eyes. 'We shall have to see what they have in the shop. I want some pretty white shoes for myself,' Nessie told them. 'You might like some the same, then you could wear them to Sunday school and show your friends.'

'I would like that,' Jenny said in excitement.

'Me too,' Evie echoed.

All too soon it was time to go home, although the girls vehemently declared they were not tired or ready to sleep. Nessie and Mel smiled tenderly at each other, knowing they would sleep the moment they climbed into bed. Before they stepped outside, Evie turned back and ran to Ross. She put her chubby arms around his legs, looking up at him with an imploring smile.

'Please can we come back again, Granddad? Soon?'

'Of course ye can, lassie. I've enjoyed seeing both of you.' He smiled warmly at them. Satisfied, they scrambled into the car and waved goodbye. Mel gave Nessie a lingering kiss.

'I wish I didn't have to leave you behind,' he whispered.

'The weeks will not be long in passing, and I shall see you at the house on Wednesday.'

'I'll be there as soon after one as I can manage.'

'It's time I was leaving too.' Daniel sighed. 'I have truly enjoyed my day with you and your family, Ross, and the food was delicious. You have two splendid cooks.'

'Aye, they're not so bad, are they?' Kim and Nessie smiled and raised their eyebrows.

'I would have liked to repay your hospitality, but steak and chips is about my limit. And I would like Uncle Fergus to meet you all, but he only eats softer foods these days.'

'Och, you don't need to worry about feeding us, laddie. I can come and visit your uncle anytime you say is convenient. I used to visit Sir Martin Newall often when he grew too frail to get around much. He liked a chat and to hear the news of the district. To tell the truth, I thought I was doing him a favour by visiting him every week, but I've missed our discussions more than I expected. He had a good memory, for all he was frail.'

'I'm afraid Uncle Fergus's memory has deteriorated more than I realised.' Daniel frowned. 'I find it a bit worrying, but Mrs Dunn has known him all her life. It doesn't seem to trouble her. She looks after him well and anticipates his needs. If you're willing to visit him occasionally, I know he would be pleased — and you too, Kim. I don't think he approved of my decision not to include you in the tenancy just yet.' He gave her a wry smile.

Daniel shook Ross's hand in farewell. Then his eyes moved to Kim and he held her gaze as he leaned closer. He thought there was a flash of something like panic in her green eyes when she thought he was going to kiss her as he had earlier, so he contented himself with a light kiss on her cheek. Even so, Kim saw her father's eyes widen in surprise and his bushy eyebrows rise.

'So you and our young landlord have buried your differences then?' he asked when they'd closed the front door behind their guests.

'How do you mean?' Kim asked.

'I know how annoyed and frustrated you were with him over the tenancy business when he refused to include you. You have inherited my caustic tongue when it comes to letting people know you are displeased. I almost felt sorry for the poor fellow.'

'I don't think Daniel Nichol needs anyone's sympathy,' Kim retorted, 'and I still think he was wrong to deny me the right to be a joint tenant.'

'He did have his reasons, lassie. When I see all the letters your professor writes to you, I wonder if he may have been right and there's a possibility of you getting married to someone with no interest in farming.' As they entered the living room where Nessie was now watching television, he added, 'In fact, I noticed the professor's letters have become even more frequent recently.' He looked questioningly at Kim, then suddenly turned on his heel, muttering, 'I forgot to bring the Sunday papers in and I need to make a phone call.'

Nessie looked up, then reached forward to turn the television sound lower.

'Don't switch it down for me,' Kim said.

'I'm not. I take it that's your professor Ross is talking about? He is a bit worried since the letters started arriving every other day.'

'He is *not* my professor,' Kim stated emphatically. 'And why does everyone have to remark on my correspondence?'

'Oh, Kim dear! I didn't mean to upset you.'

'I know . . .' Kim sighed. 'I suppose there have been a lot of letters recently. Has Father said anything to you about them?'

'Not exactly, but I get the feeling he's a bit uneasy. He thinks the professor must be very keen to persuade you to marry him.'

'His name is Kelvin — Kelvin Bradley. He has asked me to marry him several times, but I don't love him. I have no desire to live in Edinburgh, either, even though he does have a lovely house and a large garden.' She looked Nessie in the eye. 'Do you think I am cynical, Nessie?'

'Cynical?' Nessie frowned. 'I have never considered you cynical, Kim. Why do you ask?'

'Well, Kelvin has asked me to marry him several times, but this recent spate of letters is more to do with picking my brains, at least that's how it feels. I am sorry if that sounds conceited, especially as he was my professor while I was first a student.'

'A very clever student, though, Kim. You would not have won those awards or been selected for the trip to New Zealand if you had not been outstanding.'

'That had nothing to do with the project we were working on. Sometimes I seemed to see things more clearly than Kelvin. Also, I refused to brush aside small details when things didn't quite turn out as expected, or rather when they made the result less exact. We did come very close to a real quarrel when I refused to add my name to one of the experiments. I knew the results were not as clearly proven as they needed to be for the project to carry on. Kelvin said they were only for the treatment of animals, not human beings. As though that should make any difference! I was furious at his attitude. This is between ourselves, Nessie.'

'Of course.' Nessie nodded.

'Kelvin is not writing me passionate love letters, so much as trying to persuade me to go back to Edinburgh, if only for a few months, to help him with his present project. But even if I wanted to do that, and if it was a success, Kelvin intends to claim the honours for himself this time.'

'Maybe that does sound cynical, Kim, but it also shows you can see the situation clearly. I have always thought you were a sound judge of character. Even when you were quite young, you summed people up and you either liked them or you didn't. There was never any half measure for you. I only met this Kelvin twice, but I had a feeling he was not the right one for you. From what you say, I am certain of it now.'

'Mmm, well, I've decided the only solution is for me to stop replying to his letters, because each one gets more persistent, even though I have made it plain I have no intention of doing what he wants.'

'You should tell Ross what you have told me. It might put his mind at rest. I know he's concerned about your future, Kim. And yes, do stop answering his letters. See if he stops pestering.'

'That's OK, so long as he doesn't take it into his head to come down and see me in person.'

'All the more reason to explain to Ross what the letters are about. If he understands the situation, he will not offer his usual friendly hospitality so readily as he would if he thinks the professor might be the man you are going to marry — even if the professor is not his choice.'

'Mmm, maybe you're right, but not just now. The programme coming on is the one Dad likes to watch every Sunday night. I'll give him a shout to remind him.'

Later, Kim wished she had followed Nessie's advice at the time.

CHAPTER NINE

The weeks before the wedding were passing swiftly and it was harvest time. Ross had bought a small second-hand combine harvester two years earlier, but he was the only person at Rowandene who could operate it — he determined to teach Mac, the new worker at Burnside. Mrs Scott's son, Jimmy, was a hard worker and always willing, but he simply didn't understand machinery beyond the tractor. Consequently, Kim had taken over baling the straw using the baler. She did not consider herself mechanically skilled, but she did pay close attention to instructions and whatever her father showed her. She managed reasonably well so long as there were no major breakdowns, and she'd always tried to be home from university during harvest time, but sometimes it dragged on into October in a bad season.

Fortunately, things seemed to be falling nicely into place, and Kim and Nessie spent a happy day together in Edinburgh buying outfits for the wedding. There was a dress in cream lace over a cream silk lining and it had a matching jacket which fitted Nessie as though it had been made for her. The boutique was quite expensive, but the quality was good and it also had a wide selection of accessories, including a hat which was almost a perfect match.

'Do you think I shall look very dull with everything in cream?' Nessie murmured anxiously.

'You never look dull with your fresh complexion and dark hair, Nessie. Besides, you will have your bouquet. Mel said he was getting you red roses with some kind of blue flowers. That will be a lovely splash of colour.'

'You suit the cream better than almost any of my regular clients, with your lovely fresh skin,' the boutique owner remarked, 'but I selected it because I fell in love with it myself. It is ideal for a wedding, but I do have a very smart lavender-coloured suit in a warmer material, if you prefer a colour?'

Kim's eyes lit up when she saw it. 'Try it on, Nessie. Just to see how it feels.' Nessie grinned and tried it on too.

'It also fits you extremely well without any alteration,' the proprietor agreed with satisfaction.

'It does,' Kim said. 'It will be perfect for a going away outfit with your black patent court shoes and handbag. We'll take them both.'

'Kim! I can't possibly do that . . .'

'I will buy the suit for you as an early birthday present.'

'It's far too expensive.'

'I could maybe give a little discount if you do decide to take both,' the owner murmured, but she was not a pushy woman and Kim liked that.

'I am determined we must take them both. It's time you treated yourself and I'm sure Mel will be pleased. He will be so proud of his new bride.' Eventually, Nessie was persuaded to take both outfits and also cream shoes and a matching handbag.

'It is just that we were never brought up to be extravagant.' Nessie sighed, knowing Kim was right, and she did want to make Mel proud. 'Now we must choose something lovely for you, Kim.'

The boutique owner brought several outfits to try when she realised Kim was to be bridesmaid. Kim really liked a silk dress with a fitted bodice and swirly calf-length skirt in shades of turquoise. It appeared to change from green to blue and various shades in between, depending how it caught the light.

'That fits you so well, Kim, and it emphasises your narrow waist. It will be perfect for the Annual Dinner Dance too.'

'Mmm . . . it is lovely, and I would like it for a dance, but not for a morning wedding. It is sleeveless, and see what a deep V it has at the back.' She twisted around before the triple mirrors to get a back view.

'There is a little velvet bolero with long, tapered sleeves in the same shade, if that would help,' the proprietor suggested. She beckoned one of her assistants to bring it. 'There is also a small velvet cap the same as the bolero. We could easily add a little decoration suitable for a wedding.'

Kim tried on the bolero. It was a beautifully snug fit.

'That would be perfect, Kim. You could wear the diamond brooch that belonged to your mother on the shoulder, and we could have lemon and white posies to contrast with the turquoise. I think Jenny and Evie should have white, though it would have been nice if we could have added something in the same colour as your outfit.'

'Are they wee flower girls?' the assistant asked.

'Yes, four and six,' Nessie said. 'We're having their dresses made locally.'

'My sister had flower girls in white, and Madam trimmed their dresses with a pink satin sash and two pink rosebuds each, to match my dress.' She looked at the boutique owner. 'We have velvet ribbon in a similar shade to the bolero,' she said diffidently.

'That is an excellent suggestion, Francine. Will you bring the box of ribbon please? I believe we have two widths in that colour, haven't we?'

In the end, Nessie decided on two lengths of the broader ribbon for sashes and a good length of the narrower ribbon to make either bows or covered buttons for the front of the bodices, and ribbons for the posies.

They decided to leave their parcels and collect them before they went to catch their train home. It would allow time for the velvet cap to be trimmed too. After enjoying an excellent lunch, which Kim insisted on paying for as her treat, they were both well satisfied with their day.

* * *

Ross had visited Fergus a couple of times since Daniel had spent the Sunday with them. The elderly gentleman seemed pleased to have company and to talk to someone who had known the district, especially Wedderburn Estate, all his life. Ross was happy to reminisce. In return he learned that Fergus had known Mrs Dunn — Dolly, as he called her — all her life.

'Her mother was a widow,' Fergus told him. 'She lived in a wee cottage nearby and worked as my housekeeper. She was a good woman with a kind heart, and honest as the day. Her name, and Dolly's then, of course, was Tarbett. Dolly's mother wasn't all too fit at the time Danny's parents were killed. Dolly intended getting married and coming back to live in the village, so I asked her if she would come and help her mother because Daniel was a lively laddie and very unsettled.'

The old man shook his head sadly as he recalled this dark period in all their lives. 'I am his only blood relative so naturally I wanted him to live with me. So you see, Danny has known Dolly most of his life too. Dolly married John Dunn, the brother of her best friend. He worked as a gardener and handyman for several of the big houses, but he and Dolly continued to rent her mother's cottage and she still kept house for me, and for Danny, too, when he was home from university. Dolly was glad of the work when her husband was killed cycling to work one frosty morning. It's good to have honest and loyal workers and know you can trust them.'

Ross nodded. 'Joe Baird, our herdsman, started work at Rowandene even before he left school. His grandfather and his uncle had worked for my father so we knew his family.'

'I heard you've had some hard knocks in life yourself, Ross. Danny told me your wife died, leaving you with a ten-year-old lassie to raise on your own. Did ye never think of marrying again?'

'No, I never met anyone I wanted to replace Miriam. I was fortunate because my parents were still alive, although they were not so fit, and they were living in the village. Nessie, my sister, was in her last year at university. When she got her degree, she started work with a firm of accountants. She was twenty-one and she had always spent her free time with us at Rowandene so she moved back to be company for Kim. There's just eleven years between them. My parents left Nessie their house, Fairvale, in Ryankirk Village. I advised her to keep it and rent it out to bring in a bit of extra income while she built up her own accountancy business. She has done well, but I don't know how Kim and I would have managed without her. She and Kim are still the best of friends.'

'Maybe you would bring your daughter with you when you come again? I would like to meet her. I believe she and Danny had a disagreement over the tenancy of Rowandene?'

'Aye, they did,' Ross said with a smile. 'I reckon they are both used to having things their way, but I do see Daniel's point of view.' He frowned and his eyes darkened. 'One of the professors she knew at university asked her to marry him. So far, she has refused, but he's persistent. He writes often — too often for my liking. I expect I'm prejudiced, but I couldn't take to him myself, at least not as a prospective son-in-law. Of course I shall make the best of it if Kim decides to marry him, so long as he makes her happy.'

'I see . . .' Fergus mused. 'At one time I thought Danny would marry our neighbour's daughter, Stella. They saw a lot of each other when they were younger. Her parents are still extremely keen on the match, but mainly because her father wants to train Danny as an auctioneer to take over the firm. I'm afraid I may have encouraged Stella before I knew Danny had no interest in marrying her or in being her father's whipping boy. After she got herself and her precious car covered in mud, I think she'd had enough, at least for now. She took herself back to Aberdeen, which is just as well because Daniel is his own man — as his father was. I have always liked to make my own decisions and go my own way too, although things might have been different if—' He broke off when Dolly Dunn put her head round the door to ask if she should bring in the tea tray.

'Yes please, Dolly,' Fergus said with a smile. 'Have you met Ross McLaren from Rowandene?'

'No, we haven't met, but I have heard a lot about you, Mr McLaren, from William and Annie Nairn. Young Billy swears you're the best farmer in the county.'

'He does, eh?' Ross grinned. 'He's not a bad lad himself, young Billy. We have known him since he was a wee laddie. He came to stay with the Nairns before he even started school. His mother was expecting twins and not in good health, and she already had two bairns. He stayed on while she was recovering from the birth of his twin brothers. I'm not sure she ever made a full recovery so he came to the Nairns every holiday after that. They were pleased he wanted to stay with them. I reckon they would have adopted him if they could. He's the nearest they have to being blessed with bairns of their own.'

A fortnight later, again on a Sunday afternoon, Ross announced he was going to see Fergus for an hour or so. He asked Kim if she would like to accompany him, as the elderly gentleman had asked to see her.

'We shall be back to working at the harvest tomorrow, lassie, if this weather holds, so you might as well relax when you get the chance. I see the wedding presents have started coming for Nessie, so the pair of you will have a busy time ahead.'

'We've plenty of baking done and more in the freezer if needed.' Kim grinned. 'I think Nessie is surprised that so many of her clients have already bought lovely gifts. They all seem so happy for her, and pleased to hear she's keeping on her business.'

'Aye, well, she has done her best to help them all. Some of them have reason to be grateful. Still, it is grand when people show their appreciation.'

'So far, the dishwasher you've ordered for them is the thing they both appreciate most.' Kim laughed. 'I'm surprised Mel didn't have one at his house already, but apparently it had never occurred to him.'

'I don't think men think about such things until they're prompted by their women folk. I don't suppose Mrs Bain felt she could ask for one, but she will probably be glad of it if she is keeping on her work cleaning the house and looking after the children when Nessie is working. So are you coming with me then, Kim?'

'All right. Give me five minutes to change into something respectable for a Sunday afternoon.'

'Perhaps a light summer dress. It's a warm day. A good harvest day.' He sighed. 'Your grandparents were always against working on the Sabbath, except for caring for the animals, of course.'

* * *

Fergus Nichol was a lot frailer-looking than Kim had expected, but his manners were impeccable. He was obviously well educated and from a good family. He greeted them both as though their visit gave him great pleasure, then he ushered them into his pleasant sitting room and made sure they had comfortable seats.

'It is a real pleasure to meet you at last, Dr McLaren,' he said to Kim. 'I have heard so much about you from Billy Nairn and his uncle.' His brown eyes twinkled. 'I've heard a bit from Danny, too.'

'D-Danny?'

'Daniel. I have always called him Danny, but I've known him since he was born. I hear people call him Daniel down here.'

'Y-yes. Well, we do, don't we, Dad?'

'Yes, but he is our landlord, as well as our nearest neighbour,' Ross said. 'I believe the other vets call him Daniel too.'

'Speaking of him being the landlord, Dr McLaren . . .'

'Oh, do call me Kim, please. Everyone else around here does.'

'Very well, my dear. Speaking of Danny then, I hear you and he had a disagreement over the tenancy?' His eyes seemed to dance with a mischievous glint. Although he was only Daniel's great-uncle, their dark eyes sparkled in the same way.

Kim raised her chin and eyed him warily. She didn't deny she'd disagreed with their landlord. 'He obviously doesn't think a woman would be as good a tenant as a man, but I aim to prove him wrong someday.'

'I don't think he ever said that, Kim,' Ross chided gently. 'His main objection was that you will likely marry within the next few years and your husband might not be a suitable joint tenant.'

'I have no plans to marry, and he could give me some credit for choosing a husband with similar interests to my own. Even if I fell in love with a man with different interests, lots of women manage farms themselves while their husbands continue their own profession.'

'I believe Daniel knows that, Kim,' Ross said patiently. 'But supposing that profession meant you both had to live in Edinburgh, or even abroad?'

'I wouldn't make such a choice . . .' Out of the corner of her eye she saw Fergus smiling in amusement.

'Now I see why Danny is so interested in your future plans, my dear. You certainly have plenty of spirit, and that is what Danny appreciates in a woman. It would never do for him to get a wife who gave him all his own way.'

Kim blinked in confusion. They were not discussing a wife for Daniel. Fortunately, at that moment, Mrs Dunn tapped on the door and brought in a tray of tea with scones and fruit cake. Kim got up to bring forward a small table so she could put the tray down, and Mrs Dunn smiled gratefully.

'Bring an extra cup for yourself, Dolly, and come and meet Kimberly McLaren in person after listening to young Billy singing her praises so often.'

'He does say both you and Miss McLaren are very good cooks,' Dolly Dunn said with a smile. 'He suggested I should ask you for the recipe for your nutty biscuits. He tells me they are his favourite.'

'Billy likes food in general.' Kim chuckled. 'But he does like something sweet. It is a wonder he never puts on weight.'

'He was always active as a laddie,' Ross said with a smile, 'and Daniel tells me he is still the same and often walks miles through the woodland, checking for disease or any blown trees.'

Dolly went to get a cup and saucer for herself and pulled up a chair beside Kim when she had poured tea for them all and passed around the plates of food. Kim learned that Annie Nairn had become a good friend to Mrs Dunn and they now went down to the village together to attend the monthly meeting of the Women's Rural Institute, or WRI. Quite often they went together to the church, too, when there was an evening service.

'So are you settled in down here?' Kim asked.

'Oh yes, and I love the comfortable wee home Danny has made for us. Plenty of space for both of us. We each have some privacy but it's not so big that I need help with the cleaning, not like I did at the big house when we all lived together in Aberdeenshire. The poor laddie has not done much for his own comforts yet, though. He says if it was adequate for Sir Martin Newall then it is good enough for him, and he has left the door between the two parts so that he and his uncle can visit each other any time.' She didn't add that Daniel had kept it locked while Miss Roon-Kurcher was staying. 'I expect if he gets a wife she will want to make changes.' The two men were talking together and Dolly Dunn lowered her voice. 'I believe

Stella has high ideas to change everything,' she murmured. 'She will spend every penny he has if she gets her way.'

* * *

Some days later Billy Nairn told Kim he heard she had met Mr Nichol and Mrs Dunn. He told her there was no love lost between Mrs Dunn and the Roon-Kurcher woman. Dolly reckoned Estelle's parents spoiled her from the day she was born and her father would buy her the moon if he could. Apparently, she had been nervous about moving so far away from her old home in Aberdeenshire but was glad now she had stayed with Mr Nichol and come to Wedderburn Hall.

'She hopes Daniel has escaped Mr Roon-Kurcher's clutches for good, and hopefully his daughter's too,' Billy said with a grin. 'I can't imagine our Mr Nichol letting anybody tell him what to do, even if that woman is a fancy-looking piece.'

CHAPTER TEN

It was a beautiful day for the wedding. Nessie and Mel believed they had kept their news very quiet, but Kim didn't think they had been successful considering all the people who had called at Rowandene with gifts. Mel and his children were well known in Ryankirk and Nessie had lived in the area all her life, and she had clients from a wide area too.

Daniel had arranged to meet Mel in the vestry after driving the bridesmaid and flower girls to the church. Then they would come into the church together direct from the vestry, while Nessie and Ross would follow in a wedding car.

Kim had known Daniel would arrive in good time. It was one of the things she appreciated about him — being reliable and prompt when he made arrangements. He and Mel had met several times since that first Sunday at Rowandene, and Daniel had agreed to be best man. The two of them discovered they had quite a few interests in common. Both enjoyed riding and exploring the countryside, and they both cared about the environment. Kim knew they'd exchanged several books, so she guessed they had similar tastes in reading. They often compared notes and ideas discussing the differences and similarities in treatments for humans and animals.

Jenny and Evie were quite familiar with Daniel now. He helped the two little girls into the back of the car and told them how pretty they looked. They grinned happily at him as he passed them each a posy of flowers. He held the door open for Kim and he leaned close as she bent to get into the car.

'You look beautiful,' he said softly. He smiled when she blushed. Kim never looked for compliments, even less expected them, unlike Stella, he thought, then wondered what had brought her to mind on such a day as this.

It was a surprise to them all when they arrived at the village church to find so many people waiting to greet them, waving and cheering. Daniel helped Kim out first and then the two little girls. When Evie saw so many people, her little hand reached for Kim's and she looked up anxiously.

'They have all come to see how pretty you look, Evie. You will know some of them from nursery school, I think.' Some of the children called to Jenny and waved and she waved back, grinning widely.

'Oh, there's Mrs Taylor, my teacher,' she said with a big smile. A motherly-looking woman stepped forward briefly.

'This is a happy day for you all. How lovely you look, Jenny, and you too, Evie.' She stepped to the side again to let them pass. Kim hesitated and looked at Daniel.

'If you can see the girls into the church yourself, I would like to move the car along a bit to let the wedding car stop right at the entrance.'

'All right.' Kim nodded at his suggestion. 'When you come back, take the path to the right before the church door and it will bring you to the vestry and a side door. Just go in. I'm sure Mel will be waiting.'

'Thanks, Kim. I hadn't considered how I would find the vestry until now. I didn't expect to see so many people,' he added.

'Neither did I. Nessie is in for a surprise. And Jenny is pleased to see all her friends.'

Nearer the church door, Mrs Bain was waiting.

'Bainey, Bainey,' Evie called eagerly. The older woman stepped forward, smiling warmly.

'How lovely you all look, Miss Kim,' she said, and Kim thought she saw a tear in her eye.

'You are coming into the church, aren't you, Mrs Bain?'

'Oh yes, but I wanted to see if the wee lassies needed anything first. My daughter is with me, but she's over there talking to her mother-in-law. They all enjoy a wedding, and Nessie is very popular in the village. It is kind of her to invite us to the reception.'

'Oh, Mrs Bain, you deserve an invitation more than anyone. I know how good you are with these wee rascals.'

Evie and Jenny looked up with wide smiles. 'Do you like our flowers, Bainey?' Jenny asked, and held them up so she could take a closer look and duly admire them.

'And see our new shiny white shoes,' Evie said, pointing her toe for inspection.

Later, Kim thought how smart the two men looked in their morning suits as she and the little girls walked slowly down the aisle behind Nessie and Ross. Daniel was just a fraction taller than Mel, but they were both lean and muscular, standing erect as they waited for the bride to join them.

* * *

After the service, there were lots of photographs taken outside before they made their way to the reception at one of the two local hotels. In spite of Nessie's desire for a quiet wedding, there were forty or fifty people at the luncheon. Ross had insisted on paying for it, telling Nessie she deserved it twenty times over. Kim had gone with her father to choose the menu, so she was pleased the chef had made a good job of everything. She had baked the two-tier wedding cake herself, but a young woman from the village had done the decorating and made a beautiful job. It was something she did as a hobby, but she was very professional. She had confided to Kim that she hoped to open a small bakery and do more cake decorating and some catering when her children started school. Everything went smoothly and it was a happy occasion all round.

When it was time to leave, Nessie and Mel had hoped to get away without fuss, but both Mrs Bain and Kim had provided the two children with confetti made from dried rose petals and they were determined to scatter it over their dad and Nessie. Then, of course, there were lots of hugs and kisses and promises to be good for Mrs Bain and Kim, who would be looking after them for the next two weeks.

'I'm sure they'll be fine,' Mrs Bain said quietly to Kim. 'They're good wee bairns. They rarely have a tantrum or a sulk and Nessie has left them a real surprise each.'

'Yes I know.' Kim grinned. 'She's been collecting small toys, novelties and treats for ages to give them a surprise. She made the snowmen herself to put everything in.'

'She didn't tell me that! I thought she must have paid quite a lot of money for them, and they're such a lovely idea. It will be a revelation when they take the hats off and so many wee surprises come tumbling out.'

They all waved as the happy couple drove away. Kim turned and almost bumped into Daniel standing close behind her.

'It has been a lovely wedding, hasn't it? I'm honoured to have been a part of it.'

'You both looked very handsome,' Kim said with a smile.

'I believe the children are going home with Mrs Bain. Your father and Uncle Fergus will come home with us, if that's all right?'

'Of course it's all right. It is your car. It is Father and I who should be grateful for the lift. How did your uncle get here? I could have sat in the back with the girls and made room for him to come with us if I had known.'

'Oh, he was happy to come with Billy and his aunt and uncle. Between them they seem to know everybody so they will have been introducing Uncle Fergus to lots of folks I expect. He has always enjoyed meeting people, but he is not so good at remembering them now.' Daniel frowned. 'In fact, his memory causes me some concern. We're lucky Dolly agreed to move with him and continue keeping house.' They walked together to the car, but when Kim went to climb in the back, Fergus ushered her into the front seat.

'Ross and I will take the opportunity for a bit of a chat ourselves now. It has been such a lovely day and I have met so many people.'

They were all in good spirits as Daniel drove up to Rowandene. At least they were until Ross suddenly leaned forward, grasping the back of Kim's seat.

'That yellow sports car, Kim! It looks like your professor's. Are you expecting him?' His tone was unusually sharp and tense.

'No, I am not. Certainly not today of all days!'

Daniel slowed the car, intending to reverse and turn ready to leave, but Ross jumped out without waiting for it to stop completely. They watched him stride to the man lounging against the sports car and smoking a cigar. Kim could see by her father's body language that he was not happy at Kelvin's appearance. She felt irritated herself. Instead of reversing, Daniel deliberately stopped the car facing the sports car and its driver. Busy watching her father, Kim barely noticed as he slipped his arm along the back of her seat.

'I get the impression your father is not too happy to have a visitor?'

'No, certainly not today. It will be time to start milking. Joe can't do everything on his own.' She turned to him with a troubled frown.

'It has been such a lovely day for everyone. Don't let anything spoil it,' Daniel murmured. Before Kim realised his intention, his arm tightened around her shoulders, drawing her close. He glanced at the man glaring at them, then bent his head and purposefully kissed Kim full on the mouth. It was not a brief kiss either. His lips moved to her ear. 'I wish it had been our wedding day,' he whispered.

They heard a soft chuckle. Kim gasped and glanced behind, remembering old Mr Nichol was in the back seat. His dark eyes were dancing with glee. Kim's eyes widened as she looked at Daniel. He gave her a warm smile.

'Everything will be fine if you follow your heart, Kim,' he whispered.

'I hope you're right. Dad doesn't look happy. I had better go and see what they're saying.'

* * *

Professor Kelvin Bradley was more than a little disgruntled by his cool reception at Rowandene. The first time he had visited, Ross McLaren had made him welcome and been generous in his hospitality, even though Kim had been away in New Zealand.

Today, Kim's parent didn't even invite him into the house. He seemed tense and on edge. Kelvin frowned. He was ready for a cup of tea and something to eat. Kim had told him it was to be a morning wedding, a quiet affair. He had expected they would be back home by one thirty at the latest, with the rest of their day free for him. He had been waiting an hour and a half already. He had tried the door, believing country folk never locked their houses, and he even searched for a key underneath the plant pots but found nothing. The door at Rowandene was often left unlocked or a key hidden for whoever needed it, but today, Ross had made sure everything was secure with so many lovely wedding gifts in the house.

The professor stared across at the car, willing Kim to hurry up and come to welcome him. He was dismayed when he saw the good-looking chap lean across and kiss her with some deliberation. He didn't like the way Kim smiled back at him either as she eventually climbed out of the car.

As soon as Kim joined them, she realised her father had no intention of offering his usual hospitality.

'You're looking very smart, Kim,' Kelvin greeted her. 'I've been waiting ages. I thought you said it was a morning wedding.'

'Yes, it was, but we had all the usual formalities people have at weddings. The photographs took quite a while, and everyone seemed happy to linger over the luncheon. In fact, it has been a really lovely day. Most of the village turned out to watch. The atmosphere was so relaxed and it was a superb meal, wasn't it, Father?'

'It was indeed. They did us proud. I'm ready to sleep now instead of getting changed and going out to work.'

'You're surely not expected to work today!' Kelvin exclaimed.

'Cows dinna milk themselves,' Ross said brusquely, 'and the young animals still need feed.'

'But surely you could have arranged for your man to do it?'

'Joe was at the wedding,' Kim told him with a chuckle. 'He and his wife have known Nessie all her life. In fact, Joe's wife and Nessie were at primary school together until Nessie moved on to the Academy. We couldn't have left them out.'

'You said it was to be a quiet wedding,' Kelvin snapped.

'Well, so it was in comparison to the usual country weddings,' Kim assured him. 'Anyway, I was not expecting you to be here at all, especially not today.'

'I thought you would be free after you had been a witness. I want to talk to you. I'm parched after hanging about so long.'

Kim bit her lip and looked at her father, raising her eyebrows.

'I suppose you'd better make the man a cup of tea,' Ross said, more tersely than Kim had ever heard him. 'You'll not have long for chattering though. The calves will be waiting for you . . .'

Kim and her father both knew that one of them could do the work if necessary, and Joe had returned as usual to bring the cows in from the field and get on with the main part of the milking.

'Perhaps I had better stay until tomorrow and we can talk then . . .' Kelvin began.

'There will be no time tomorrow. We promised to collect the children first thing,' Ross intervened. Silently, Kim wished she had explained to him earlier why Kelvin was writing so persistently. She realised he really was worried about her future and the possibility of her going back to live in Edinburgh. 'Kim promised to entertain the wee girls and do the cooking for them. Nessie and her husband are on honeymoon for a fortnight.'

Kim had already got things well organised for Sunday's meals, and Ross knew that, but she remained silent. She had been surprised, and secretly pleased, when Daniel had said he might come down for a while unless he got an emergency call out.

'Well, perhaps you'll hear what I have to ask you while you make some tea then?' Kelvin muttered, sounding surly. Kim realised he was not only used to getting his own way, he expected people to fall in with his plans and ideas without argument. Well, he would have to accept that her life as a student was over. She was her own person and she lived in the adult world and had her own responsibilities. She had explained all this several times already. She was more annoyed and impatient because it had been such a lovely, happy day and his arrival had spoiled it. She was going to have to be blunt, even to the point of offensive, to get through to the man, whom she had considered a genuine friend.

Kim hated being hurtful to people, but as she had feared, Kelvin was offended by her blunt refusal to fall in with his plans — ever. When he eventually took his leave, he made spiteful remarks about the man in the car 'being all over her with his kisses'.

Kim knew she would not hear from him again. She realised she felt relief rather than regret.

CHAPTER ELEVEN

Mrs Bain was grateful to Kim for taking the two little girls for the day. She had feared they would miss their father badly when they woke up and realised all the excitement of the wedding was over and that the start of the new school term loomed the following day.

Kim had prepared a roast chicken with gravy, stuffing balls, bread sauce and roast potatoes, green peas and baby carrots. She remembered the girls loved Yorkshire pudding for their Sunday lunch, whatever the meat, so she prepared the batter and left it in the fridge. She had already made a chocolate rabbit, and orange jelly and ice cream, but in case that was not filling enough for her father, and Daniel if he came, she prepared a cheese board and some fresh green grapes.

Ross offered to collect Evie and Jenny. They were delighted to see him, and Mrs Bain relaxed and smiled warmly when they tried to reach up to hug him. He lifted each one high in the air, making them giggle with joy.

'It will be all right if we don't bring them back until nearly bedtime, will it, Mrs Bain?' Ross asked. 'Kim wondered if it would help if she gave them their bath and got them into their pyjamas.'

'Oh, that would be a great help, if you're sure?' The two children were already scrambling into the back of the car, but she lowered her voice. 'They will not have time to worry about going back to school tomorrow. Shall I give you their night things now?'

'Yes please.'

'I'm going to my daughter's for Sunday lunch, as I usually do, but I shall be back here by four thirty, so if they are any trouble just bring them back early. It's very kind of Kimberly to have them all day.'

'We both enjoy their company and I don't think they'll be any bother. Enjoy your lunch. You will have a busy week ahead, I expect, but I think Kim promised she would take them riding two evenings, so maybe that will be something to look forward to.'

'It will indeed. They both love their ponies and it will take their minds off the absentees.'

***

Kim heard the car but was surprised when a brisk rat-tat-tat sounded on the back door, swiftly followed by Daniel striding in.

'I didn't expect to see you so early,' she greeted him in surprise.

'I see the yellow car has gone,' he said, smiling, his brown eyes bright. 'Or has he put it in one of the sheds undercover?' His smile faded.

'And good morning to you, too, Daniel Nichol. Does this mean you have no visits to do today?'

'Well, it is supposed to be my weekend off. Young Robin is on call and Mr Turner knows where I am if they really need me. You didn't answer my question. Is your professor still here?'

'No. He left barely an hour after we got home.'

'He's gone back to Edinburgh? He's not staying locally overnight?'

'I believe he has gone back to Edinburgh,' Kim said evenly. 'Does it matter?'

'Oh, yes. His presence would have ruined my day.'

'Ruined your day? How so?'

'He would have claimed your attention.'

'Of course he wouldn't. Dad has gone to collect Evie and Jenny. He really has taken them to heart, I think.' She smiled warmly.

'I don't blame him. They are lovely children. Even I can see that, and I'm not used to children. They're not spoiled or sulky.'

'No, they have such sweet natures and their big smiles make you feel like smiling too.'

'I have heard you were very like them yourself, Kim, when you were a small girl.'

'Oh, I suppose you have been listening to William and Annie Nairn. I saw a lot of them when Billy and I were young.'

'It is true they do have a great opinion of you, and they are proud of your success at university too. They think you've been a good influence on Billy. But it was Mr Turner who remembers you as "an adorable wee lassie" — his words.'

'Mr Turner? He is getting on now. I didn't think he would remember me as a child, or even notice I was around when he was here attending animals. My father has always said he is one of the best vets we have had. He keeps his mind on his job.'

Before Daniel could reply, they heard the two children chattering as they followed Ross into the kitchen.

'These two young ladies tell me they were up very early this morning so are ready for a drink of juice and some biscuits,' Ross said with a grin, seating the two children at the kitchen table. 'Good morning, Daniel. You're here bright and early. I expect you'll be ready for a cup of coffee with me, then you can help me entertain these two rascals for a while, looking round the calves and the chickens.'

'I think you might see two baby kittens, too, if you're lucky,' Kim told them. 'They are in the calf house where the baby calves stay. They are too young to leave their mummy, though, so you will only be able to see them with her.' She poured out glasses of orange juice and took over some chocolate finger biscuits, then she made coffee for herself and the two men and produced a plate of buttered fruit scones and some nutty biscuits.

'I thought I saw you making a rhubarb pie, Kim?' Ross prompted. It was one of his favourites.

'I have made one, but that is for tea this afternoon, if *everyone* behaves. If it stays as sunny as this, we might have a picnic in the garden.'

'Oh good-ee,' Jenny cooed.

'We love picnics on the grass,' Evie told her. 'Can we play with the dolly in the crib when we've been to see the animals? Can we take teddy and dolly to see the flowers?'

'Of course you can.' Kim nodded, smiling.

It was a lovely day all round. After lunch, Ross suggested the girls should accompany him into the sitting room and he would read them a story. Daniel offered to help Kim clear away the remains of the meal and wash up the dishes.

'You only offered because you know we have a dishwasher,' Kim teased.

'I expect there will be roasting tins and pans to wash. Remember, I am quite used to doing my own cooking and clearing up.'

'Even on a Sunday? I thought Mrs Dunn made Sunday lunch for both you and your uncle?'

'She usually does, if I'm not on call, but I told her I expected to be out today. I was hoping you would invite me, you see.'

'Even if I hadn't, I'm sure my father would have. He seems to enjoy your company.'

'It is mutual. He is a knowledgeable man and I could learn a lot from him about the countryside and the wildlife, aside from his animals. I'm glad your professor has departed, though. I got the impression your father wasn't overly pleased to see him.'

'My father was afraid I would marry him and go to live in Edinburgh,' Kim muttered irritably. 'You didn't help, either, stating your reasons for not including me in the joint tenancy. I came home every holiday and quite a lot of weekends when it was a busy time, especially harvest or when Joe had his holidays. I wouldn't have done that if I preferred city life.'

'You must admit the professor was persistent,' Daniel said. 'Your father said he wrote you letters every few days. You can't blame him for being concerned.'

'Maybe not. Anyway, that is the end of a pleasant friendship, and I am sorry about that.'

'Are you, Kim? Did you want the man, but not his way of life?'

'I didn't want him as a husband, but we had been good friends for a long time and I am sorry to lose a friend.'

'So you didn't love him?'

'Why are you being so persistent in analysing my feelings for Kelvin?' Kim asked irritably.

'Maybe I was jealous because you were such good friends.'

'But you have no reason to be jealous!'

'I don't think you realise what an attractive woman you are, Kim, as well as being intelligent and accomplished. I can't blame the professor for wanting to marry you. I have always thought I could never marry unless I fell deeply in love, as my father apparently did with my mother, but even when you are all prickly and indignant, furious too sometimes, I am still dangerously attracted to you. Haven't you realised that?'

Slowly Kim turned to face him as she finished drying her hands.

'Are you, truly?' She moved closer and lifted her face to his. Daniel needed no persuasion. Kim enjoyed his firm, cool lips on hers and the way he pressed her against him so that they were both consumed with a passion neither were prepared for. Kim had never experienced anything like this with any other man. It was only the sound of the sitting-room door opening that made them draw apart. Kim was glad it was only the children tiptoeing into the kitchen, and not her father.

'Grandpa Ross fell asleep after he finished our story,' Jenny said, 'so can we go play in the garden please?'

'Can I take teddy for a walk to see the flowers?' Evie asked.

Kim looked at Daniel and saw the laughter in his eyes, and yet there was a gentleness in his expression too. He leaned forward and whispered in her ear. 'Thank you. I regret we were interrupted, though.'

'Are you whispering secrets, Mr Nichol?' Jenny asked accusingly. 'Are you going to hide something for us to find?'

'You can call me Daniel, Jenny, now that I am a friend of your daddy and your new mummy.' He smiled warmly at the little girl. 'I hadn't thought of hiding anything, but that is a good idea. If you would like to play that game, I shall go and hide this bright yellow ball. You stay with Kim until I come back then you can both search all around the garden while Kim and I sit on the grass and watch you.'

Sometime later Ross came out to join them.

'It is a beautiful day,' he remarked. 'I hope it stays like this for the next few days until we finish the harvest.'

'I expect you are ready for a cup of tea after your nap, Dad?'

'Aye, that would be a good idea. Do you want me to make it as you're settled out here?'

'No, but you can keep an eye on the girls. I promised them a picnic, but I think it might be easier for you two men if I set it out on the little folding table.'

'I will come and carry it for you,' Daniel said promptly.

'Can we help?' Jenny asked. 'Please? I can carry things.'

'All right, come with me then.'

'Mmm, the sausage rolls smell delicious,' Daniel said, 'but I'm sure none of us should be ready to eat after the big dinner we all had.'

'I love sausage rolls,' Evie said eagerly.

'Yes, so Mrs Bain told me. Well, when Daniel has taken the table out, I will put the sausage rolls on a white napkin in this small wicker basket then they can't roll off. Jenny, I have a little tray of fairy sandwiches for you to carry.'

'I will come back for the tea pot and cups,' Daniel offered. Kim had made a plate of small iced buns with a cherry and coloured sprinkles on top, as well as her father's favourite rhubarb pie.

'I made everything tiny so that the girls can try a bit of whatever they fancy, but my father does enjoy a scone at tea time so I have split some and put the butter and jam on ready to eat, if you would like to take them and the rhubarb pie, Daniel?'

'I am very glad I came. I think Dolly was quite pleased she didn't need to make Sunday lunch for me. She is worried about her sister-in-law. She seems to have had a relapse. Dolly wondered if she might need to travel up to Aberdeen again to see her. They have been friends since they were at school, as well as Dolly marrying Freda's brother.'

'That's a shame. You must tell us if there is anything we can do if she does go to Aberdeen.'

'Mrs Nairn has already offered to cook for Uncle Fergus, and I usually make my own meals anyway, except on Sundays.'

'Grandpapa says are you two bringing the plates?' Jenny called from the doorway, jumping from one leg to the other in excitement. 'The wee cakes look lovely. I can't wait to start.'

'Take this extra rug out with you, Jenny, please,' Kim called. 'Then you and Evie can sit on it if you want.'

* * *

'You have made them a lovely picnic, lassie,' Ross said, smiling at Kim. 'The bairns have really tucked in.'

'Only the bairns?' Kim asked, her green eyes dancing with laughter as her father helped himself and Daniel to another piece of rhubarb pie.

'We have all enjoyed it,' Daniel assured her. 'I can't remember ever enjoying a picnic more.'

'I expect you did when you were a wee boy,' Kim said.

'Mmm, maybe.' Daniel frowned and turned to speak to Ross. 'Do you know a man named Cummings, Donald Cummings?' he asked.

'Cummings from Sunnyhill?' Ross asked.

'Yes, that's the man.'

'He breeds some good horses, and he was quite successful with two that he had trained for racing last year and the year before. I haven't heard of him doing much this year. We bought Kim's first hunter from him, but he bought it back for another client when he heard she was going to be away at university for a few years.'

'He's selling up.' He looked across at Kim. 'He has a lovely chestnut mare if you fancy having another horse. I really fancied buying one of the stallions for myself.'

'A stallion, eh? Do you fancy owning a horse like Red Rum?' Kim teased.

'Red Rum? He's a gelding, but he's the only horse to win the Grand National three times, isn't he? He has done well. But no, I've no desire to win races, even if I was small enough to make a jockey. I believe they allowed a woman jockey to compete this year for the first time?'

'They did.' Kim nodded.

Daniel smiled. 'A decent hunter would do me, but the stables at Wedderburn have been badly neglected. They're so big and the whole lot needs a new roof, not to mention repairs to the walls and windows, and all the doors need replacing.'

'Aye, it's years since they were used.' Ross nodded. 'Sir Martin Newall had a nasty fall when he was in his late forties. He was lucky not to end up paralysed, but he never rode again. The stables were as big as a house anyway. I suppose they were built in the days when everybody used carriages for transport. I'm surprised at Cummings selling up, though. He's only in his forties. Unless he's made his fortune, or maybe lost it. It is an expensive business, training horses.'

'Yes . . .' Daniel hesitated and chewed his lower lip, then looked Ross in the eye. 'It's not common knowledge yet, and he doesn't want people to know until he has sold off most of his breeding animals. He has cancer. The doctors have given him six months at most.'

'Ah . . . My word, I'm truly sorry to hear that,' Ross said with sincerity. 'Our stables are still useable, Daniel, and we're not far away, if you would like to buy yourself a horse and keep it here.'

'We were talking of converting them into a shed for very young calves with small individual pens,' Kim said, 'but we haven't done it yet.'

'No we haven't, and we still have quite a bit of tack,' Ross said. 'Now we know the circumstances, maybe we should go over there and look at the mare Daniel mentioned. Nessie has started riding again. She uses the horse that belonged to Mel's first wife. What do you think, Kim? You always enjoyed riding.'

'Well, I'm certainly home to stay now, and it would be nice to meet up with Nessie and the children sometimes.'

'I'm going over there tomorrow afternoon,' Daniel said. 'Why don't you both come with me? I'd be happy to pay the going rate for stabling, and I must say I have been longing for a good horse again. I sold mine when I went to Africa.'

So it was arranged that Daniel would pick up Ross and Kim and the three of them would go to Sunnyhill to see the horses the next afternoon.

CHAPTER TWELVE

As it happened, Daniel left home fairly early the following morning, knowing he had several routine calls to make before he collected Ross and Kim, plus there was often an emergency on a Monday if some of the animals weren't checked over the weekend. Fortunately, all went well and he collected Ross and Kim soon after lunch.

Donald Cummings seemed pleased to see them, but Ross was shocked and saddened at the younger man's gaunt appearance, sunken eyes and yellow skin. While the men were greeting each other and discussing the horses, his wife drew Kim aside.

'I remember when you brought your pony for Donald to sell because you were going away to university and knew you'd not have time to exercise her and groom her the way you had always done. You were very upset, but you hid it well.'

'I'm surprised you remember,' Kim said. 'But yes, I was very upset that day.'

'When they've finished looking at the horses, will you persuade your father and Mr Nichol to come in for afternoon tea? Please? It does Donald good to have a chat with like-minded men.' Her voice trembled. 'It helps to take his mind off things.'

'I understand,' Kim said with a gentle smile. 'I shall do my best, but it will depend on Daniel. He is driving Father and me today. I'm hoping to have a ride on the chestnut mare he recommends.'

'We have two. They are full sisters and both beautifully mannered,' Fiona Cummings said. 'I've ridden them both. I am sorry they have to be sold, but even if things were different, we could never keep them all. We are always more satisfied if they are going to a good home though.'

Two mares. Kim immediately thought of Nessie. Mel's first wife had been nervous with horses and had insisted on an older, quiet mount. Kim knew it was what Nessie called a plodder. It was difficult to get her to trot, but she was adequate for riding beside the children. Anyway, Nessie would not be thinking of buying herself a pony now. She was married with a husband's wishes to consider.

'Are you coming, Kim?' Ross called. 'Mr Cummings is taking us to the stables. He has the horses inside and ready for a ride around the paddock. Daniel had phoned before we left to say he was bringing us.'

'Oh, good.' She hurried to her father's side.

'You were having quite a chat with Mrs Cummings,' he remarked curiously, lowering his voice.

'Yes. She would like us to go in for tea, whether or not we buy a horse. She says it's good for her husband to have a chat with other men and relax a little. It is so sad for them both.'

'Aye.' Ross sighed. 'It is. Poor man.'

While Daniel tried out the black stallion called Nero and another grey dappled gelding called Cloud, Kim had a good ride on both of the chestnut mares. They were almost identical and she liked them both.

'Either of these would have suited Nessie perfectly,' Ross remarked, 'but I can't advise her or interfere now she has a husband,' he added ruefully. In the end Kim settled for the one named Chessie.

'I will have them delivered, but I can't send them until the middle of next week,' Donald Cummings said. 'I have a man who drives the lorry for me these days, but he's on holiday.' He sighed heavily. 'I will give you a ring and let you know what day to expect them.'

'I will just pay for the mare now, while we're here,' Ross said.

'Yes, that suits me too,' Daniel said.

'Come into the house then,' Donald Cummings said, and Ross winked at Kim and nodded.

'I reckon I owe you in veterinary services nearly as much as the horse is worth,' Cummings said to Daniel.

'Oh, hardly.' Daniel chuckled. 'Anyway, the veterinary fees belong to the firm. Buying Cloud is my own business.'

'Aye, but I hear Mr Turner has finally persuaded you to become a partner in the firm.'

'Has that got around already?' Daniel asked, his dark eyebrows raised.

'Well, he told me anyway,' Cummings said with a wan smile. 'I've known Mr Turner since I was a nipper with my first pony. Almost as soon as you joined the practice he told Fiona and me you were the man he would like for a partner. "A man who will carry on when I retire," he said. I take it you know how he feels. It's a pity he never had a son to take over the business.'

'He does have a daughter,' Fiona Cummings said. 'A lot of women make good vets, too, but she wasn't interested.'

'No, it's a pity because that nephew of his is just a waste of space. I wouldn't let him near a horse of mine.'

'Is his nephew a vet then?' Daniel asked with a frown. 'We haven't a Turner in the practice, as far as I know.'

'No, he gave up halfway through university. Failed his exams and said he needed a gap year. That's about three years ago. He's still travelling — Australia, I think he is now. His mother was Mr Turner's sister. The lad's name is Coleman.'

'I see.' Daniel nodded.

'Come through and have some tea now,' Mrs Cummings said. Daniel looked at Ross, his brows raised in question. Ross nodded.

It was late afternoon by the time they left the Cummings, and Donald accompanied them to the car. 'I've really enjoyed our afternoon, gents, apart from selling you two of my best horses.'

'I'm afraid I've made you late for milking,' Daniel said apologetically to Ross once they were on their way. 'I didn't think we should take so long.'

'I reckon you've done Donald Cummings a good deed today,' Ross reflected. 'His wife told Kim she hoped we would go in for tea because the chat would do him good, and I believe it did. I don't think he has long on God's good earth.'

'No, I'm afraid you're right,' Daniel said soberly.

'Anyway, there are no problems with any of the cows today so Joe will manage the milking himself. I asked young Mac to stay and help him with washing the parlour and the gathering area. He's proving quite a useful man. He is willing to learn and is always cheerful. I can't be doing with sullen workers.'

Daniel met Kim's eyes in the rear-view mirror. 'What about you, Kim? Will your calves be calling for you?'

'Only the very young ones. I got well prepared before lunch. They are all bedded and their hay nets filled so it won't take me long.'

They had almost reached the road into Rowandene when they met Billy Nairn in the Land Rover. He stopped at once and reversed to speak.

'Mrs Dunn got a telephone call at dinnertime to say her sister-in-law had taken a turn for the worse during the night. She died this morning. I have just taken her into Lockerbie to get the train. She was fair worried about leaving Mr Nichol when you were not at home,' he said to Daniel. 'Aunt Annie told her she will look after him. I-I hope we've done the right thing?' Billy looked anxious. 'She was terribly upset. She says Freda was the last link she had with Aberdeenshire.'

'You certainly did the right thing, Billy. Thank you, and thank your aunt. I shall be home in ten minutes to see to Uncle Fergus. Mrs Dunn always keeps a freezer full of food so tell your aunt not to worry.'

'I'm sorry. That's a bad end to a good day, Daniel,' Ross said. 'I like Dolly Dunn, she's a fine woman, and loyal too.'

'Let us know if there's anything we can do,' Kim said as she jumped out of the car.

'Thanks, Kim, I will, but if Mrs Nairn is willing to make Uncle Fergus a cooked lunch and check that he's all right, I can manage his breakfast and evening meal. He will miss Dolly's company as much as anything and it may be a while before she returns. The house belonged equally to Dolly's husband and his sister so Dolly will inherit now.'

Although Dolly Dunn's sad news dampened their spirits, Fergus seemed to keep quite cheerful with Billy or his Uncle William popping in for brief chats each day. Ross went to visit one afternoon, too, and Kim packed afternoon tea for them, as well as a whole Victoria sponge for the old man to eat at leisure since they'd learned he had a sweet tooth. He declared a bit of cake in the afternoon gave him an energy boost.

* * *

There was great excitement when Nessie and Mel returned from their honeymoon. They were due home on the Saturday evening so Kim invited them all for Sunday lunch. She was sure Nessie wouldn't feel much like cooking on their first day back.

'Oh, Nessie, you do look so happy and blooming with good health. The south of France obviously suited you both.'

'It was wonderful, Kim. Everything was wonderful.' She looked Kim in the eye and they understood each other.

'I'm so pleased for you,' Kim said softly. 'I was sure Mel would be kind and considerate.'

'He is, and he says he had never dreamed he could be so happy and content with life.'

It was during dinner that Ross asked Kim if she had told Nessie about her new pony.

'A pony, Kim? How did that come about?' Nessie asked. 'You were so sad when you had to part with Trusty.'

'I know. This one is coming from the same stables. She's a lovely chestnut mare and very obedient.'

'We went with Daniel,' Ross told her. 'He's buying a grey gelding for himself and is going to stable him here. The stables at Wedderburn Hall are in a bad state of repair,' he explained, turning to Mel, 'and we're not far away along the track at the back. He had fancied a black stallion, but when he tried them both he thought the gelding might be easier managed, especially if he couldn't exercise him every day.'

'The Cummings always had good horses,' Nessie said, 'but I'm surprised at them selling a stallion.'

'Ah, lassie. That's the trouble. They're selling everything, except the house. Donald Cummings is very ill with cancer. It's heartbreaking. He loves his horses and was one of the best horsemen round here.'

'That's awful news,' Nessie said in a shocked voice. 'Are they selling the stables too?'

'Not as stables. Fiona doesn't want to move house when they've done so much to improve it and they've been happy there. They are selling the land and an outbuilding to a private buyer who hopes to get planning permission to build a bungalow and set up kennels.'

'I can't blame Fiona for wanting to stay,' Nessie said. 'They've made the whole place a pleasure to visit, and it's a lovely garden. Have they sold all of their horses?'

'Not yet. It was Daniel who told us. It's not common knowledge, but he is their vet. Kim had a problem deciding which mare to choose when he offered her two, didn't you, lassie?'

'I did. They are full sisters and almost identical with just a year between them. In the end, I chose the younger one. Her name is Chessie.'

Evie was sitting next to Kim and her tiny hand stole into Kim's beneath the table. Kim smiled down at her and Evie looked at the remaining red jelly in the glass bowl then down at her empty plate.

'Would you like some more?' Kim asked quietly.

'Yes, please,' Evie whispered eagerly, and gave a big smile. Kim spooned some onto her plate. 'I think we should pass the rest to Jenny, don't you?' Evie nodded, already spooning up her own. Kim passed the bowl across to Mel to spoon onto Jenny's plate since she was sitting beside him, and the conversation became more general as Nessie described some of the sights they'd seen during the few days they had stayed in Paris.

Later, Ross and Mel made their way into the sitting room while Nessie and Kim gossiped over the clearing up and the two children played with the dolls' house and a game Mel had brought back for them.

'So when do I get to see Chessie, then, Kim?' Nessie asked. 'Mel isn't due at the hospital until Wednesday so I shall not be back here for my work until then either. My extension is finished at Fairvale, but I need to move all my stuff down there before I can begin work.' She pulled a face. 'I'm not looking forward to that part.'

'We'll help you move all your office stuff. You are always so methodical anyway, Nessie. I'm sure it will not be as bad as you think. Mr Cummings is sending both horses down in his lorry on Wednesday when his driver returns from holiday, so come prepared to have a ride.' Kim gave a happy laugh. 'I'm looking forward to riding again.'

Later that evening, when Mel, Nessie and the girls had gone home, Ross announced, 'I believe Mel is going to persuade Nessie to go with him to the Cummings' tomorrow to see if he can buy the other mare, if Donald Cummings can help him sell the old mare Sylvia rode. He admits she is not very good for someone who enjoys riding as much as Nessie.'

'Oh, I am so pleased to hear that! Mel does seem to think the world of Nessie, and she looks so happy.'

'She does. There is a bloom about her which I've never seen before.' Ross chuckled.

***

Mel and Nessie arrived at the Cummings' mid-morning. They felt as though they were still on holiday and had stopped for a leisurely coffee and cake on the way. Unfortunately, they arrived to find an elderly man riding the chestnut mare in the paddock with a view to buying her.

Donald Cummings was looking most unhappy, and when Mel explained their reason for coming, he groaned loudly. 'Dear God, if only you'd come fifteen minutes earlier. I remember you being a first-class rider, Miss McLaren. The chestnut mare would have suited you perfectly.' Mel looked as disappointed as Nessie.

'Nessie is my wife now. If you don't mind me saying so, that man doesn't look comfortable on a horse at all.'

'He isn't. He has hardly ever ridden one. He asked for a quiet, well-broken pony. You wouldn't get a better horse than Fern anywhere. I break and school all my horses myself and she is as gentle as a lamb, but she does like a good old gallop now and again, or at least a decent canter. I need to sell them all, but I can't help hoping he doesn't take Fern. His granddaughter is six years old and desperate to learn to ride. He wants to buy this sweet young pony for her.' He indicated a smart little pony tied to the rail. 'I told him the child will need lessons from a good teacher whichever pony he buys. I gather she was premature and delicate, so she is very precious to the whole family. They will likely buy her everything she sets her heart on.'

'This pony is a lovely wee thing,' Nessie said, running her hands down each leg in turn, then patting her neck. 'What's your name then, little lady?' She nuzzled the pony and the pony responded.

'She enjoys a bit of petting, but she is very obedient. Her name is Snowball but we usually call her Snowy.'

The old man rode towards them across the paddock. All he had done was walk the horse and she was really needing a bit more exercise. The man tumbled off rather than dismounted.

'I don't think this yin will do for me. She's too flighty. She keeps tugging. I was looking for something older and sturdier, not something that wants to run away with me. Have ye nothing more suitable?'

Donald Cummings looked almost relieved, but shook his head. 'I'm sorry, but I only had one elderly gelding and I sold him three weeks ago.' Nessie and Mel looked at each other, their eyes widening.

'Do you think my wife could have a ride?' Mel asked.

'Certainly. I see you came dressed for it.' Donald smiled at Nessie.

She put the pony through her paces and both horse and rider seemed to be enjoying it.

'She's a beauty to ride,' Nessie called as they cantered past the onlookers.

'I have an older horse I would sell if I can buy this one for Nessie,' Mel said. 'She obviously likes it. I reckon the one she rides at present has a trace of Clydesdale in her. She has heavier legs than usual. She might have been good at the hunt at one time, but she's getting older now. Nessie gets frustrated because she is reluctant to do more than a walk or a short trot.'

'Well, man, that's what I'm looking for.' The older man looked accusingly at Donald Cummings.

'I'm sorry, but I don't know anything about the one Mr Sanders has to sell.'

'You're welcome to come down and see her. We're just a few miles from Dumfries.'

'I'll do that, but how would I get her home to my place?'

'If you go to see her tomorrow and decide you want her,' Donald Cummings said, 'I'm sending the lorry down with horses on Wednesday and I'll bring her back to your place for you, for a small fee, of course.'

'That would be champion. I'm still not so sure about this sparky young thing for my granddaughter, though. You sure you have nothing smaller?'

'I'm afraid not,' Donald said, shaking his head.

'I'll go home and have a think about it,' the man said huffily, and went stomping off towards his car. Donald Cummings looked exhausted but invited them in for a bite of lunch.

'Thanks for the offer, but I reckon you're ready for a bit of peace yourself,' Mel said.

'Oh, my wife will never forgive me if I don't take you in. We only have soup and sandwiches at this time of day anyway, so you may as well stay. To tell the truth, I am delighted you came and that you want to buy Fern. Even old Smithers could see what a good mount she is once your wife put her through her paces.'

'I hope he likes our mare when he sees her. She is more like what he needs,' Mel said, following Donald into the big sunny kitchen where his wife welcomed them warmly.

'I reckon Daniel Nichol, our vet, will be wanting commission at this rate.' She chuckled. 'That will be three horses going down to Dumfries.'

The following day, Mr Smithers arrived at Mel's house with his daughter and granddaughter. The child was small for a six-year-old. Certainly she was not as big as Evie who was not quite five. As soon as the old man saw the sturdy mare, he declared, 'That's the very thing I'm looking for, and they're two nice wee ponies ye've got in the paddock. The smaller one is the kind o' thing I was looking for to suit oor wee angel.'

'I could bring her in and give your granddaughter a ride, if you would like to see whether she would really like a pony,' Nessie offered. 'Some children are afraid once they are sitting on their backs. They feel it's too far off the ground.'

'Well, if you're sure it's no trouble,' the child's mother said. 'I'm not so keen myself. It was Father who put the idea into her head and now she has toy ponies and toy stables. She's pony mad.'

Nessie soon had the bridle and saddle on Peggy, Evie's pony. Mel lifted the little girl carefully and held her in the saddle as Nessie walked her slowly along the drive. She clearly had no fear and shuffled away from Mel's restraining hands.

'I don't want you! I can ride it without you!' she declared. Mel smiled patiently.

'We will take you into the paddock first, then if you do fall off at least you will fall on the grass.' The child wriggled impatiently until they reached the paddock and Mel released her, but he walked alongside ready to catch her. There was no doubt she enjoyed it, and she got into a tantrum when Nessie said it was time to come off.

'Will you sell us the pony as well as the mare? The bairn has fair taken a liking to her. What's her name?'

'Peggy, but I'm afraid she belongs to our younger daughter.'

'I want this one, Grandy! I want this one!' the child yelled at the top of her voice.

'You will frighten the horse if you shout like that,' her mother said, rubbing her brow.

'It's pretty clear my granddaughter is smitten. Couldn't you buy that filly we saw at the stables for your wee lassie?' Smithers asked. 'I mean, if she has already learned to ride, she would manage her all right.'

Mel looked startled at the idea. He looked at Nessie, who chewed her lower lip.

'Please, Grandy! I want this pony!'

'Would you be kind to her and groom her every day?' Nessie asked. The little girl scowled, then looked at her mother.

'If she is going to have a pony, I shall see that she looks after it properly. I used to have a pony myself and I must admit I did enjoy her. It's just that Elizabeth is so small yet.'

'Can you give my wife and me a minute to discuss it?' Mel asked, and drew Nessie aside.

'You have always said Evie is a natural on her pony, now you have taught her what to do. Do you think she could manage the one we saw at the stables? It was a smart wee thing, but it is as big as Jenny's.'

'Jenny is a good rider too,' Nessie said quickly. She frowned. 'It's just that Evie sits up there with her little back so straight, and the reins held correctly. I don't know what to say, Mel. Do you think Evie would mind you selling Peggy? I think only you can make this decision.' Mel nodded and went across to the waiting family. 'If you will give me a few minutes, I will phone Mr Cummings to see if he still has the pony we saw and how much he wants for her.'

'Whatever he wants I'll pay you the same for this pony. My angel is taken on it and no other will do.'

So it was all arranged. The horsebox with its load of four ponies arrived at Rowandene in the early afternoon, and shortly afterwards it exchanged the load for the two ponies from Mr Sanders' stables. At first Nessie thought Evie was going to burst into tears when she heard Peggy had gone to a new home for another little girl, but when she saw Snowball, she was delighted. And Jenny was more than happy to keep her own familiar pony.

* * *

Daniel couldn't wait to finish his day's work and get down to Rowandene to see his new mount — or at least he told himself it was only the horse he wanted to see. He made a quick meal for himself and Uncle Fergus, glad that he'd retained the connecting door between his side of the house and the modernised apartment.

'My new horse is arriving at Rowandene today. I think he might be ready for some exercise. Do you mind—' The telephone rang before he finished.

It was Ross McLaren. 'We thought you might be coming to see your horse tonight, Daniel, and maybe give him a ride out.'

'Yes, I'm ready to leave now . . .'

'Well you're more than welcome to bring your uncle down to keep me company for a change while Mrs Dunn is away. Kim is going for a ride down to see Nessie and hear how she likes her pony, so there will only be me at home.' Daniel put his hand over the receiver while he consulted his uncle.

'Yes, thanks very much. He says he would enjoy a chat. Ask Kim to wait for us and I'll ride to the village with her. I hear they've bought a pony for one of the wee girls as well. Donald Cummings phoned to thank me for getting him so many sales.' Daniel chuckled. 'I had to admit the latest two were nothing to do with me, so he is grateful to you too.'

***

It was a beautiful September evening and Kim was waiting with both horses saddled and ready to go. Daniel inspected his purchase then leaped into the saddle, grinning at Kim.

'I'm looking forward to this, but I will let you lead the way and set the pace, at least for now.'

Kim had already phoned Nessie to ask if she could ride down to see them and Nessie was delighted to have the opportunity to show off her own new pony. When Kim and Daniel arrived, the Sanders family had just finished their evening meal and all four of them were getting saddled up ready to ride. Evie was too small to manage herself, but Mel was helping her.

'What did Evie say about you selling her pony and buying her a new one without consulting her?' Kim asked quietly.

'I thought she was going to burst into tears, but when she saw her new white pony and realised he was as big as Jenny's, and she saw I had a new pony, too, she got quite excited. I had a job getting them both in for tea. She seems happy with the changes now and we promised Jenny could have a ride on Snowy, too, if she wanted, but she declined quite happily. We don't mind if you and Daniel want to go off and get a good gallop, but we promised we would all go for a ride when Mel got home.'

'Why don't we all ride through the village down to Fairvale? The paddock is much bigger down there,' Kim suggested. 'We can keep the children safe between us on the way, then Daniel and I could ride home from that end of the village and give the horses a gallop across Burnhead. Is that all right with you?' she asked, turning to look at Daniel.

'You know the area better than I do so I'm in your hands. I'm just happy to have a decent mount again.' He looked at Mel and the girls. 'And it is lovely to have company.'

They all enjoyed the ride and putting the horses through their paces in the Fairvale paddock, but eventually Nessie decided it was time to head for home and bedtime. Daniel and Kim rode companionably side by side, sometimes trotting, cantering where they could, before breaking into a gallop when they reached the long stretch of grass between the river and the wood through Burnhead land.

'I don't know when I have enjoyed an evening so much,' Daniel said as they approached the stables at Rowandene. They chatted easily as they groomed and fed the horses, but as they were leaving the stable, Daniel reached out and drew Kim to him. She looked up in surprise and he bent his head in a lingering kiss on her upturned mouth.

'And that was the perfect end to a perfect evening, at least for me,' he said softly. Kim didn't answer but knew her cheeks were still flushed when they entered the sitting room to collect Daniel's uncle.

'You're very welcome to come any evening when Daniel comes down to exercise his horse,' Ross told him, 'especially while Mrs Dunn is away. When do you expect her home?'

'She hopes to be back at the beginning of next week,' Fergus replied with a sigh. 'Neither of us have any reason to go back to Aberdeen now. Dolly wants to stay long enough to get the cottage ready for the estate agents to sell, to save her going back up again. I hope you will come over to see me again when she returns, Ross.'

* * *

Later that evening, Mel sat up in bed watching his wife undressing. He thought again what a lucky man he was. Nessie was as modest as any young girl, yet she had all the passion and generosity of the spirited and warm-hearted woman she was.

'I wouldn't be surprised if we have another wedding within the year,' he mused.

'Another wedding? One of your doctor colleagues?'

'No, no. I meant Daniel.'

Nessie was about to draw her nightgown over her head. 'Daniel?' she echoed, reappearing.

'Yes, if he gets his way. Anyone can see how he feels about Kim.'

'Kim?' Nessie echoed, popping her head out of her nightie again.

'You'll know whether Kim returns his feelings better than I do.' He chuckled, bounding to the end of the bed and snatching the nightdress. 'You don't need that nightie, my darling.'

'Mel!' she yelped softly, aware of the girls sleeping in the room across the landing.

'Come to bed and we'll have a lovely end to a lovely evening.'

It was considerably later as Nessie lay dreamily in her new husband's arms that she thought about Kim.

'Do you really think Daniel fancies Kim?' she murmured. 'She is the complete opposite to his ex-girlfriend, that Estelle Roon-Kurcher, and I don't think she has quite forgiven him for refusing to make her a joint tenant.'

'I never met the Roon-Kurcher woman, but I doubt he considered her a girlfriend from what he's said about escaping to Africa,' Mel said seriously. 'I'd say he and Kim have a lot in common. I get the impression Ross approves of Daniel too. I wondered whether his suggestion that Daniel should stable his horse at Rowandene was by way of encouragement.'

'I hadn't thought of that,' Nessie said sleepily. 'Whoever Kim marries, I hope she'll be as happy as I am,' she added, snuggling into Mel's arms.

CHAPTER THIRTEEN

Dolly Dunn returned from Aberdeen, so Fergus sent word with Billy to tell Ross he looked forward to resuming their Sunday afternoon chats, and any other day or evening when Ross had an hour to spare. Kim guessed the old man enjoyed her father's company and she felt the meetings were good for them both. It seemed that Dolly was often asked to be hostess and join them over the tea cups, especially when they enjoyed an evening playing cards or dominoes, but Dolly also enjoyed Annie Nairn's company and they never missed meetings at the WRI.

Daniel and Kim often ended up exercising their horses together in the evenings, but sometimes Daniel arrived early in the morning to give Cloud a good ride if he knew he might be on call later in the day. And they enjoyed meeting up with Mel and Nessie and the children on a Saturday or Sunday afternoon.

This Saturday, Daniel was working so they were riding out without him. 'Have you received your invitation to the dinner dance next Saturday, Kim?' Nessie asked. 'I received mine for doing my annual talk about farm accounts and the tax changes affecting farmers. Mel is included this year too—'

she gave a glorious smile to her new husband on horseback at her side — 'but he's in surgery that day. We shall go for the dinner and maybe even manage the speeches and the first dance, but will have to leave after that as Mel will be doing an evening round.'

'Oh, that's a shame,' Kim said. 'I always enjoy the dance. The hotel makes a delicious meal, though, and we shall see you at that. Dad has got his usual invite too.'

'Has Daniel got an invitation?' Mel asked. 'I'd like to think there will be somebody I know.'

'I haven't seen him today but expect he'll have one. I know he gave a talk about his time in South Africa so he has earned an invitation. Like Nessie, my father gets one every year because he usually gets roped in for coaching the dairy classes, or for holding a stock judging for them at Rowandene. Often both. Our invitations only came this morning, though.'

'At least you'll have your lovely bridesmaid's dress to wear,' Nessie said.

Daniel asked about the dinner dance invitation the following morning when they met for a Sunday morning ride.

'Yes, we've all got one, and Mel was asking if you'd be there because he's hoping for a familiar face.'

'I may be a bit late myself as it's my turn to take the small animals' clinic that evening and none of the young vets want to swap. I may take my evening suit with me. I could shower and change at the surgery. That would save time.'

'That would certainly be better than missing the meal anyway,' Kim said, hiding her disappointment that he would not be arriving with them.

* * *

As everyone began to take their seats ready for the waitresses to start serving, Ross opted to wait beside the door to meet Daniel and bring him to his seat. He didn't have to wait too long before he saw him hurrying to the entrance.

'I was lucky to get parked fairly near as someone drew out,' he said breathlessly. 'Are you waiting specially for me, Ross? That is very good of you.'

'There is always a seating plan, so I thought it would be easier if I showed you where we are.' He signalled to one of the drinks waiters. 'We always get a free welcome drink at the beginning,' Ross told him.

'Ah, but I'm driving so I'll stick to fresh orange juice, please. I might have a small glass of wine with the meal. I expect we shall dance it off later.'

'You young ones will.' Ross chuckled. 'Kim drove here but I said I'd drive myself home after the opening dance. My leg has mended well, but it does ache by night. Mel and Nessie will be leaving then, too, but Kim knows nearly everyone who is here so she'll get a lift home.'

'It would be my pleasure to drive Kim home,' Daniel said, as Ross had guessed he might.

There was no twinkle in Ross's gaze for once when he met Daniel's eyes. He gave an imperceptible nod. 'I shall leave that for the pair of you to arrange between you. It is a custom that I always have the first dance with the woman sitting at the end of that far table. Beth was secretary when I was chairman of the club many moons ago,' he said with a faint smile. 'We have always made a point of having the first dance together ever since. She lost her husband a few years ago so she always says she is pleased I remember to get her evening off to a good start. She loves dancing. Kim's the same.' He began to lead Daniel towards their table as the waitresses started bringing out the starters.

'Have you ever considered her as more than a dancing partner after all these years?' Daniel asked with interest.

Ross turned to him, his eyes sparkling merrily. 'No, nothing like that. We have always been good friends. She and her husband were wonderfully supportive when Miriam died. It is good to have sincere friends who share your interests and make you feel at ease but—' he shook his head — 'it needs something more, an extra spark between you, as well as a lot of give and take, for marriage.' Again he met Daniel's eyes steadily.

Was Ross sending him a silent message? Did he know how he felt about Kim? Was it possible he would approve if he could persuade Kim to marry him? Daniel had had a busy and frustrating day, but suddenly felt he was walking on air as they approached their table and he found he was sitting next to Kim and opposite Mel. He was among friends.

It was a delicious meal. Afterwards, there were toasts and the presentation of achievement awards. The speeches were witty, with none of them tediously long.

'Did you really change clothes at the surgery, Daniel?' Nessie asked with a big smile.

'I did. The light was not very good, so I hope I've shaved properly?' He felt his jaw for any bristles.

'No, no.' Nessie laughed. 'You are immaculately groomed and looking more handsome than ever, don't you agree, Kim?'

'Nessie, my love, you are not supposed to admire other men when you are so newly married,' Mel teased. 'Come on, everybody, we don't want to miss the first dance. Everyone is heading for the ballroom, and the waitresses are waiting to clear the tables.'

'You're looking very lovely, Kim,' Daniel said softly. 'Will you be my partner for the first dance? Your father says he has got his already booked.'

'Did he tell you that?' Kim grinned. 'It seems to be a sort of ritual between the people who were in the club at that time — imagine a whole generation ago.'

Daniel took her hand to make certain no one else came to claim her as they followed Mel and Nessie. 'Your father tells me he's not staying for much of the dancing. I hope you'll let me take you home?'

'If you're offering then of course I will,' Kim declared, laughing up at him.

'So can I claim the last dance as well as the first?' Daniel asked. 'It would be more convenient, after all, if we're together. Usually everybody is in a rush to get away.'

'All right, if you're sure you will want another dance after we've had the first.'

He bent his head close to her ear and murmured, 'I would have them all with you if I could get away with it.'

'I'm sure you don't mean that, Daniel Nichol,' Kim said, blushing prettily.

'I do, but I expect you'll have a few duty dances to do as well.'

'One or two,' Kim agreed, 'but there are some I would rather avoid if I can.'

'If I knew who you wanted to avoid I'd be sure to rescue you first,' he assured her.

'Would you really be so gallant?'

'Where you're concerned, I would.'

Kim looked up at him and saw he was serious. 'Well, one of the worst is the man over by the bar with the red face, and he's already speaking loudly. By the middle of the evening he will be demanding that ladies should dance with him although he can barely keep his balance. Another one is that thin fellow near the door with the ginger hair and a face like a weasel.' Kim shuddered. 'He is looking you up and down.'

Daniel looked over her shoulder. 'I'm not certain, but I think he used to be a client with Mr Turner's practice. If it is the family I think it is, the vets no longer have him on their books because he always complained and then refused to pay his bills.'

'Cook is his name.'

'Yes, I'm almost sure that's the family Mr Turner mentioned. Any more you want to avoid?'

'Only one, and I haven't seen him yet, but he's sure to be here. He thinks he is God's gift to all women.'

'So if I'm lucky, does that mean I might claim you for the first and last dance and three more besides?' Daniel asked.

Kim looked up at him and bit her lip. 'Shall we see if you want more after we've danced the first?'

'I know I shall, even if it's just so I can hold you in my arms,' Daniel whispered in her ear and grinned wickedly.

The band was striking up for the first dance by the time they entered the ballroom with a stream of other guests, and Daniel drew her into his arms. Kim felt how well suited they were in height and the way they moved together. Her eyes were shining as the music drew to a close.

'That was wonderful,' she said. 'Where did you learn to dance?'

'I felt it was wonderful too,' he said softly, 'and I don't consider myself anything special on the dance floor. We all had to learn in our last year at school, and then, of course, there were dances at university. You would be the same, I suppose?'

'Yes, we did enjoy the dances.'

'You fit so well into my arms. Ah, I think Mel is coming for a dance with you before they leave. Maybe Nessie will be my partner?'

'I'm sure she will. Nessie loves to dance. She was my first teacher.'

The whole evening was a delight, but after one strenuous reel with one of the past chairmen Kim felt she must remove the velvet bolero, even though she was conscious of the deep vee down the back of her dress.

'Put it round that chair at the back, lassie,' a pleasant, plump woman said, seeing her looking demur. 'We'll keep an eye on it. There's always somebody at this table, except for the last waltz. We all like to get up for that.'

'Thank you,' Kim said. 'I wouldn't like to lose it.'

'No, that would be a pity. It fits you like a glove and the colour suits you too. We were all admiring your dress while you were dancing.'

'Thank you,' Kim said, blushing, glad Daniel was waiting to lead her onto the floor. 'I feel half naked,' she muttered, 'with such a bare back now I've removed my bolero.' Daniel immediately put his arm round her to lead her back to the dance floor and she smiled her thanks.

'It is a beautiful dress and I, for one, appreciate the style.' He grinned at her as he drew her closer and almost immediately began running his fingers gently up and down her spine.

'You have such smooth white skin,' he said, a little huskily. 'Can we stay on the floor for the next dance?'

'I don't see why not. I think I've done all the dances I feel obliged to do.' It was another waltz and the spotlights had been switched off, leaving the softer gleam of the central chandeliers. Daniel drew her closer still and she felt his fingers moving gently up and down her back. He lifted his head a little and held her gaze. She gave a faint gasp and her eyes widened. He smiled down at her and his dark eyes gleamed with a desire she had never seen before.

As the dance drew to a close, Daniel asked if she would like a cold drink. 'I could do with one myself, definitely something non-alcoholic. I have a precious cargo to deliver home.'

'I would like a fresh orange, please,' Kim said, 'but I think I'll go to the ladies now as there's always a queue near the end of the evening and there are only a few more dances.'

'All right, we'll sit this one out and I'll get our drinks. I'll wait for you at that little table in the alcove.'

Kim smiled and nodded.

There were already several ladies waiting and Kim knew by the time she got back to Daniel it would be almost time for the last dance. She always enjoyed that, but she collected her evening cloak on her way back to her seat. It would be safe enough where he was sitting. She also collected her bolero before all the people at that table departed. She slipped it on but left it unbuttoned.

'Ah, Kim,' Daniel teased, 'you're spoiling my fun.' His eyes danced with laughter.

'I know,' she said, 'but I guess you're like most gentlemen and get impatient while the ladies queue for their coats. I am ready to leave after the last dance now.'

'I don't want this evening to end,' Daniel whispered close to her ear as they got up for the last waltz. He held her close and rested his chin on top of her soft hair.

* * *

They were lucky to get out to the car before the long line of people blocked the exit or waited to collect coats. Even so, there was already a stream of cars pulling away and they waited patiently to join the queue.

'Everybody seems to be heading through the town before they go their separate ways.' Daniel sighed. 'I thought we would be among the first away. I suppose we shall have to follow on.'

'There is another way home for us, avoiding the town. It's longer in miles but probably quicker in time with all the traffic, plus the traffic lights, when we hit town.'

'Direct me then and we'll try that.'

'Turn sharp left round the next bend. The tourists come this way in the summer, except they follow the road closer to the coast so they can visit the ruins of the thirteenth-century castle. They have opened a tea room there now and a children's play area. There's the wild fowl centre too. Have you been there yet?'

'No, not yet.'

'The wild geese will be returning any day now. In fact, I heard a small flock arriving early this morning. Isn't it amazing how they find their way over hundreds of miles?'

'It is, and the formation they keep always amazes me,' Daniel agreed. 'Does this road bring us out at the other side of town?'

'No, we miss the town altogether and come into Ryankirk Village from the end where Nessie and Mel will be living very soon.'

'So we shall be almost home then?'

'Yes. We shall have been just as quick as following all those cars through the town, I think.'

'Are you in a hurry to get home, Kim?'

'No, but I thought you might be after a long day at work. It has been a lovely evening.'

'It has.' They were driving by a small wood and without warning, Daniel drew the car onto the wide grass verge beneath the trees. He sighed. 'It has been such a wonderful evening that I don't want it to end, and it is not often I feel like that.'

He turned off the engine and turned to Kim. She could see the gleam of his white teeth in the dim light and knew he was smiling at her. She had been to dances with lots of young men, and had been kissed goodnight often enough. She knew several of them would have liked to prolong the parting, but none of them had ever aroused her in the way that Daniel did with only the touch of his long fingers, his mouth on hers. He drew her gently into his arms and nuzzled her neck, covering her face with quick kisses before his mouth claimed hers again. Kim felt the passion in him and knew her own response was every bit as heated. For the first time in her life she felt like throwing caution and convention to the wind.

Daniel knew her response was all he had ever desired in a woman — and more. 'Ah, Kim, I want you. I need you. You do things to me no one else has ever done.'

Kim smiled against his mouth because they were her own feelings exactly. She had only fastened the top button of her evening cloak and Daniel easily released it, smoothing his hands over the silk of her dress, arousing needs Kim had never known existed.

His fingers found and opened the two small buttons on the back of her dress. They held the two sides of the deep vee together and now there was nothing to hold her dress in place. Daniel gently pushed aside the material from one shoulder and bent his dark head to nuzzle her exposed breast. She gasped as he sucked on her nipple, but her arms tightened around his neck of their own volition. He lifted his head and pulled her evening cloak closer to keep her warm.

'Have you any idea what you do to me, Kim? Do you know how much I want you, all of you?' he asked hoarsely.

'I think I do,' Kim murmured, her lips against his neck, 'because for the first time in my life I feel like forgetting everything and — and letting you love me. But I have to tell you, Daniel,' she added anxiously, 'I am not taking the contraceptive pill . . .' She felt him smile.

'I was not prepared for quite such a tide of desire tonight either,' he said softly, 'and I respect you too much, Kim, to put you at any risk. Besides, I think your father trusts me with his only daughter and I would never willingly break that trust. Will you marry me, Kim? Please, my darling girl? Please say yes. I know how independent you are, but I promise I will never take that away from you.' He could feel Kim's lips smiling against his own.

'You still want me even though I'm bristly as a hedgehog at times?'

'I love you just the way you are. I don't want you to change a thing. I know how to counter the sharp ripostes now, and they will add spice to our life. Besides, Uncle Fergus believes you are as spirited as my mother was and exactly the type of woman I need for a wife, to keep me on my toes, he says. We have so many interests in common, Kim. Please, please say you will be my wife?'

'I will,' Kim said in a whisper, knowing she was making the greatest decision of her life because she never made promises lightly.

'Oh, Kim, my darling girl . . .' It was some time before either of them surfaced to have a sane conversation.

'I shall have to ask for your father's approval, of course,' Daniel said, stroking her face gently.

'I know my father likes you,' Kim told him. 'That makes our lives easier, but we cannot rush things so soon after Nessie moving out. It will make a big change in his life too.'

'Yes, we must do our best to consider him and make sure he is happy with whatever arrangements we make,' Daniel said seriously. 'I have not much to offer by way of a home at present. The rooms Sir Martin Newall occupied have been adequate for me on my own, but I am sure we could make ourselves a comfortable apartment. You can always change the kitchen, and there's a lovely wide staircase to the rooms above. I think we shall both enjoy planning our home together to suit ourselves.'

'I would not be far away from my father either,' Kim reflected.

'He could come for his Sunday dinner every week instead of me inviting myself to Rowandene.' Daniel chuckled. 'Dearest Kim, you don't know how happy you have made me.' He sighed. 'Another kiss and I suppose we had better get ourselves home. Can we tell your father tomorrow?'

'Yes. I will make a special evening meal and you can bring your uncle. You can bring Mrs Dunn, too, if you like. Dad seems to find her pleasant and easy to talk to.'

'Oh, she is. But I think I ought to come after breakfast and get your father's approval first before we tell anyone else.' He gave Kim one final passionate kiss before he started the car.

Kim directed him. 'First left then left again at the end of this short road. We shall be in Ryankirk before you know it,' she said happily. 'I don't think I shall sleep tonight for excitement.'

But as they turned out of the village towards home there was a red glow in the sky ahead.

'Daniel, that looks like a fire ahead of us. Oh, Daniel! There's only Burnhead, Rowandene and Home Farm up our road.'

Daniel put his foot down, a dreadful fear making his blood run cold.

'It's not Burnhead, that's too near. Oh, dear God, please, please don't let it be Rowandene.' She clamped her hand over her mouth, but she wanted to scream. 'My father sleeps so soundly once he gets to bed,' she choked.

'The animals? Kim?'

'The dairy cows are still out at night due to the good weather, but all my young calves . . . Our horses . . . What if it's the house? Oh, dear God, please let my father be safe.'

CHAPTER FOURTEEN

As they drove further up the incline out of the village, Kim gasped.

'I-I don't think it's Rowandene. Daniel, oh God, Daniel, it must be Home Farm.' She clutched his arm briefly. He was driving fast and she didn't want an accident to add to whatever disaster they might find. As they turned onto the track into Rowandene, Kim's eyes widened with horror.

'Drop me at the door! It's the Hall! The Hall is on fire! Drive on up the track. It's rough, but it's quicker. I'll pull on my trousers and boots and follow you. Please, Daniel, be careful. I couldn't bear to lose you.'

Daniel's face was white with anxiety, but he squeezed her hand before driving on the second she slammed the door. He could see lights now and at least two vehicles. His heart was pounding. It seemed as though the whole vast width of the Hall was alight. Two of the vehicles were fire engines. There was also an ambulance and a car.

'Uncle Fergus!' He jumped out of the car and ran towards his uncle's apartment. It was a burnt-out shell, dripping with water from the firemen's hoses. Still a rogue flame kept springing up, and then another, but the firemen were concentrating their attention on the main part of the Hall now.

Daniel ran towards what had been his uncle's downstairs bedroom, but a fireman barred his way.

'Let go of me!' Daniel struggled furiously. 'My uncle! I must reach him! He's an old man . . .'

'There's nobody in there, son. We got them out . . .'

'Are they hurt? Mrs Dunn . . . ?'

'There were no women.' The fireman frowned. 'Charlie, there were no women inside?'

'No, the two women saw the fire when they came back from their evening out at the WRI. They phoned from yon cottage, but the man who is in the ambulance had already phoned us and the first crew was already on its way so we followed on when we heard it was bad.'

He looked gravely at Daniel and shook his head. 'They're giving him oxygen in the ambulance, but there was nothing we could do for the old man. He was dead when we got them out.'

Daniel was barely aware of Kim arriving at his side, or Ross, still shrugging on his anorak.

'Can we look for Mr Nichol in the ambulance?' Ross asked the fireman quietly. The man nodded. 'Aye, there's nothing anybody can do here. The old timbers are so dry. Half the roof was already falling in when the second crew arrived.'

Daniel walked towards the ambulance in a trance, with Ross linking one arm and Kim the other. Apart from the ambulance crew, Dr Chalmers, the local GP, had also been called. He recognised Ross and Kim. They introduced Daniel.

'I am so sorry about your relative, Mr Nichol,' he addressed Daniel. 'I know it will be no consolation right now, but I am almost certain he would have been dead before the fire started. He would not have suffered. I believe it was angina. Apparently, he forgot to take his pills with him when he went to the Nairns for supper. They'll explain about that. There will be a post-mortem, of course, to confirm the exact cause of death. He looks very peaceful. Come into the ambulance and you can see him before they take him to the hospital.'

Daniel followed him. 'The other man? Someone said you were giving oxygen to—'

'Yes, to Bert Lenox, from Home Farm. I understand it was he who called the first fire brigade. He had broken the window and climbed into the bedroom to try to rescue Mr Nichol. The firemen found him struggling to lift the old man through the window, but as I said, I am almost sure he was already dead.'

'Can I see Bert? I must thank him . . .'

'He is sedated now. It would be better if you wait until tomorrow. His wife was here in hysterics and it upset him. Billy Nairn drove Mrs Lenox to her sister's in the next village. The ambulance is about to leave for the hospital as soon as you have seen your uncle.'

Kim knew she loved Daniel with all her heart when she saw his haggard face and the terrible grief in his dark eyes as he stepped down from the ambulance. She wanted to take him in her arms and comfort him like a child.

'You've had a nasty shock, Mr Nichol,' Dr Chalmers said. 'I think I should leave you a sedative, too, so you get a good sleep. That helps all of us get things into perspective. Where will you—'

'Daniel will be staying with us at Rowandene, Dr Chalmers,' Ross interrupted. 'We have plenty of spare rooms — indeed we have a whole apartment spare now Nessie is married.'

'Very well, I will leave the sedative with you, Ross. I left a couple for Mrs Dunn with Annie Nairn. The poor woman is dreadfully upset. She is blaming herself for being away and leaving Mr Nichol on his own.' He shook his head. 'Then there's Willie Nairn thinks he's to blame for not staying with Mr Nichol after he took him home. Apparently, your uncle said he was weary and wanted to go to bed. He insisted Willie went back home. I'm sure no one could have helped, even if they had been there.'

'He could be a bit crotchety when the angina was playing up,' Daniel admitted, 'but I had forgotten Dolly was going to the WRI evening drive. I should have stayed home myself.' He passed a weary hand across his brow.

'As I said, I don't think anyone could have helped,' Dr Chalmers said reassuringly, 'but Mrs Dunn has worked herself up badly.'

'Perhaps it would help to reassure Mrs Dunn if you talked to her, Daniel,' Kim suggested gently.

'That's true. It might ease her mind a little,' Dr Chalmers agreed.

'I will come with you, Daniel. You go home, Father, and put the kettle on for a hot drink. If there's nothing we can do here, we shall not be long. Perhaps we should phone Mr Turner, or whoever is on call, to let them know Daniel won't be in tomorrow.'

'I reckon they'll have heard by morning,' Ross said dejectedly. 'Bad news always travels but I'll leave a message just in case. You two go and speak to Mrs Dunn then get back home and try to get some sleep.'

* * *

William Nairn was glad to see Daniel and Kim. He drew them into his cottage, eager to explain.

'We were sitting at the table ready to eat our meal when Mr Nichol clasped his hand to his chest in pain. He searched his jacket pocket for what he called his magic pills, then he remembered he'd left them in his other jacket when he changed that evening.'

'Yes, his memory is not so good these days,' Daniel agreed.

'He was obviously in great discomfort and said he couldn't eat anything. I offered to go for his pills, but he said he'd rather go home. I drove him back in Billy's Land Rover. He found his pills and I sat him down to take one with a drink of water. He seemed much better in a short time but said he was weary and needed to lie down. I wanted to wait with him until the women returned but he wouldna hear o' it.' William was getting distressed. 'I should have insisted . . .'

'No, William, don't blame yourself. I know as well as anyone Uncle Fergus could be very brusque when he wasn't well. You know that, too, Dolly, don't you?'

'Oh, I do, but I should have been with him. The firemen think the fire started in our wee kitchen and I know he has had turns like it before. Then after a while he decides he'd like something to eat after all. He always puts the grill on to make himself some toast. He would never ask me and he wouldn't use the toaster, but I always heard him in the kitchen and made it for him. Oh, Master Daniel, I-I should never have left him on his own. I expect he forgot about the toast and went to lie down again if the pain came back.'

'Now, Dolly, don't say that,' Daniel pleaded. 'If anybody should have been at home with him, it is me.'

Kim was sitting next to Dolly Dunn and she took the woman's hands in her own to stop her wringing them. 'Dr Chalmers says no one is to blame for Mr Nichol's death,' she said quietly but firmly. 'He is convinced it was the angina. Now we must all hope Bert Lenox recovers quickly from the smoke inhalation.'

'Aye, you're right, lassie,' Annie Nairn said with a note of relief. 'Now, Dolly, I have made up the spare bed for you and put out one o' my goonies. I'll bring you a hot drink and one o' the pills the doctor left. Nothing will seem quite so bad in the morning.'

'I'd forgotten! I haven't even got my own nightgown,' Dolly whimpered in distress. Kim looked at Daniel and mouthed 'Clothes.'

His eyes widened as understanding dawned. 'We're both like orphans, Dolly. My clothes will have been destroyed too,' he said. 'Maybe Annie will take you into town tomorrow to buy what you need. Send the account to me. If you explain about the fire, they will understand. Everybody will have heard by mid-morning.'

'Th-thank you . . .' Dolly murmured brokenly.

'We'll go back now and leave you in peace to try and sleep,' Kim said. 'Daniel will be at Rowandene in Nessie's apartment until further notice if anyone needs him. Mr Turner will transfer the telephone calls I expect, but meanwhile he needs some sleep too. There will be a lot of things to sort out tomorrow.'

'Aye, that's true.' William Nairn nodded. 'Ye were always a sensible lass, Kim. I'm sure you and Ross will help.'

'We shall do our best. Shall we go, Daniel?' Kim thought he looked dreadful and the sooner she got him home and into bed the better.

* * *

Kim was not up as early as usual the following morning and she felt decidedly groggy when she met her father coming across the yard.

'Ah, Kim, I'm pleased ye're up, lassie, although I know you haven't had much sleep. I'm glad I managed to persuade Daniel to take the pill the doctor left, although I expect he'll feel worse for wear when he wakens. Sleep is a good healer, though. I think he'll take his uncle's death badly and will have a lot of things to do when he rises — the death certificate, people to phone, arrangements to make. Billy was here—'

'Oh? Surely there's nothing else wrong? Bert Lenox . . . ?'

'Nothing wrong, but he wants me to go over to Home Farm and tell him what needs doing. Bert has survived the night and is improving. He was only milking five cows and there's three due to calve, or so Billy thinks, but they still have to be attended. I told him I'd follow him over and we'll walk the cows back to here to milk them. It would be easier to milk them along with ours, unless you think Daniel will object?'

'It seems the best thing to me,' Kim pondered. 'After all, someone will have to milk them twice a day and Billy has never milked. I expect he'll manage to feed any young stock if there are any indoors, and he can count and check the sheep. Once Daniel goes back to work, he'll not want to be tied to milking cows twice a day, however few there are.'

'That's what I thought,' Ross said. 'And it's such an old-fashioned set-up at Home Farm. The milking machine still has to be washed after every milking, whether you milk five or a hundred and five, and the cowsheds cleaned. If you can come and help us, we'll get them back here between the three of us.' He whistled for Jess, his old collie.

***

Gradually, things began to fall into place. There was a delay getting the death certificate due to the post-mortem, and in turn, that caused a delay in arranging the funeral. Daniel notified Fergus's elderly solicitor from their old home town in case his uncle had left any specific instructions regarding his funeral.

'I am terribly sorry to hear such news, Daniel,' Mr Dodds said sincerely. 'He never discussed his demise or any arrangements he wanted. I would like to attend his funeral if you will let me know the time and place. He did make a new will after he bought Wedderburn Hall and the surrounding land, but it was mainly to make provision for Mrs Dunn in case she didn't settle down there. It is a good thing we got new quotes for the insurance. It hadn't been reviewed for twenty years. Fergus thought it seemed extortionate having to pay three times the old fee, but he didn't realise what a difference inflation has made to building costs and such like.'

'You're very welcome to attend the funeral, but I'm sorry I can't offer you accommodation,' Daniel said. 'I'm staying with a neighbour. Mrs Dunn is with another friend. It will only be a small funeral. We haven't lived here long enough to make a wide circle of friends. I shall put an intimation in the paper for those who knew him up there, but only *after* the funeral,' he emphasised. He didn't like to tell the elderly lawyer that he didn't want Roon-Kurcher coming down here and trying to interfere. Later, he wished he had spoken bluntly.

'That's all right, my boy. I will book a hotel in the town as soon as you let me know what day. I'm getting too old to drive there and back in the same day and there might be some advice I can offer you. Your uncle still had some investments. He had kept them separate from the money he set aside for you. He used yours to buy Wedderburn Estate.'

'He gave me far more than I could ever have expected when he gave me a home and the best of care, as well as the education I wanted,' Daniel said, and his voice was not quite steady.

* * *

Eventually, Daniel felt he had dealt with all the main arrangements, and had agreed to an urgent request from the insurance assessors to meet with them the day after the funeral.

'Aye, it is a thankless task, attending to all the formalities, Daniel,' Ross said with sympathy. 'I wish we could have done more to help.'

'More to help? Ross, you have proved yourself the best friend a man could have,' Daniel declared sincerely. 'Apart from making me welcome in your home, and Kim feeding and caring for me, I appreciate your understanding and kindness more than I can tell you.'

'Aye, well . . .' Ross said awkwardly. 'It is a beautiful autumn evening and you have not had much chance to get out in the fresh air these last few days. Why don't the pair of you take the horses out for a good ride? Your uncle would not have wanted to deny you such simple pleasures. Indeed, he would not have wanted you to grieve, I'm sure.'

'I know that, but I shall probably always feel guilty for not being there with him. But you're right, I could do with some exercise. What do you say to a ride out, Kim?'

They took the long ride around the Wedderburn Estate, skirting Home Farm, then slowing to a trot as they cut through a woodland track which would bring them out on the other side of Rowandene, and then a good gallop home. In the middle of the wood, Daniel stopped and slid from his saddle, tying both horses to a branch before he turned and held his arms up for Kim to dismount. He held her close and they stood in silence. Kim could feel his heart beating beneath her cheek. She looked up at him. He bent his head and kissed her, a long, gentle kiss, then he cradled her against his chest. 'I do love you, Kim,' he said softly. 'I don't know how I should have got through these past few days without you. I know there hasn't been much time to talk, or be alone, but you have shown your love in a thousand tender ways. I appreciate it more than I can ever tell you.'

'I'm glad you feel that way still, Daniel. I was afraid you might regret the time we dallied after the dance.'

'I shall never regret that, my darling Kim. Your promise to be my wife is the one thing that has kept me going since the fire. I just wish we'd had the opportunity to share our news with your father and Uncle Fergus before this happened. Uncle Fergus put my mother's jewellery in the bank for safe-keeping until such time as I marry. I have never seen it, but I believe there is a ring. If you would rather choose your own engagement ring, then we will go to Edinburgh at the first opportunity, but I'm impatient to tell the world you are my fiancée, even though I know we agreed to wait a year before we marry.'

'Dear Daniel, we know how we feel, with or without a ring. That doesn't trouble me so long as I know in my heart that we belong to each other.'

'There are so many decisions to make.' Daniel sighed. 'When I visited Bert Lenox he told me his wife doesn't want to go back to live at Home Farm. They had been considering retiring anyway. He asked how much notice he would need to give.'

'Poor Bert. He was such a brave man to go into a blazing house.'

'He was. I told him I could never thank him enough for his valiant efforts. I explained what your father has done, taking in the milk cows to Rowandene, and that Billy is attending to the other animals and Mrs Lenox's hens, so he doesn't need to give any notice unless he wants time to consider. Obviously, I shall continue to pay him as usual until he decides what he wants to do. I told him if there is anything I can do to help, I will do it very willingly. Apparently, they have a small cottage in the same village as Mrs Lenox's sister. It has been rented for several years. The tenants left three months ago and Bert and his wife have been debating whether to move in there themselves. This has made up their minds for them, or at least for Mrs Lenox.'

'I hope they enjoy their retirement,' Kim said with a smile. 'I reckon Mrs Lenox will miss the farm and her butter-making more than she realises.'

Daniel drew her into his arms in another warm embrace and gave her a lingering kiss.

'Do you think your father guesses how we feel about each other, Kim?'

'Sometimes I think he has guessed — like tonight when he suggested we ride together.'

'Do you think he will mind?'

'I suppose he has always known I might get married someday, and he already likes you, Daniel. I think he has approved of you from your first meeting — even though I didn't.' She grinned up at him and he seized her mouth in a passionate kiss.

'And now?' he asked softly. 'Do I have your approval now, Dr Kimberly McLaren?'

'Oh yes,' Kim said fervently.

'Good. I suppose we had better head back before the horses become too impatient.'

CHAPTER FIFTEEN

Daniel had felt it essential to notify Mr Dodds of his uncle's death — apart from being the attorney, he and Uncle Fergus had been friends for years — but he had deliberately avoided notifying anyone else up there. So he was incensed when Mr Dodds telephoned to say which hotel he would be staying in, and that Estelle had made the arrangements.

'Miss Roon-Kurcher seems very upset by the news of your uncle's death. She has insisted I should travel down with her and her father, and she has made the reservations for two nights. I had intended only staying the night before the funeral myself, but no doubt I shall be glad of the lift. Miss Estelle tells me you've been very close friends for most of your lives, so she feels it is her duty to attend the funeral and give you her support at such a time.' He hesitated, then cleared his throat nervously. 'I am afraid Mr Roon-Kurcher was extremely annoyed that you had not contacted him directly.'

'I can't see why he should be. I would not expect—' or want, he thought silently — 'anyone to travel such a distance for a small funeral. Uncle Fergus would not have expected it either, I am sure.'

'I am getting the impression that Edward Roon-Kurcher has always anticipated you would become his son-in-law, even though you refused to consider being an auctioneer. I gather he believed you and Estelle would become equal partners in the auction company.'

'My uncle accepted there would never be any possibility of that happening.'

'I see. Well, I'm afraid Mr Roon-Kurcher is very insistent that I arrange a meeting with you at our hotel the evening after the funeral to discuss things.'

'There is nothing to discuss. I have no desire for a meeting at any time, and especially not the evening of my uncle's funeral,' Daniel declared more abruptly than he had intended.

'Oh dear, Daniel. I do hope you will change your mind,' the elderly solicitor said anxiously. 'I can bring one of the younger partners with me if you would rather discuss your uncle's investments with him?'

'I can't see any need for any of this, Mr Dodds. I shall leave all of my uncle's affairs to you, as Uncle Fergus did. I must go now. I am sorry. I shall see you at the funeral on Thursday. Goodbye.'

He almost slammed the phone down in the hall and Kim and her father looked at each other with raised eyebrows.

'Damn. Damn! Damn them to hell!' Daniel muttered, but his words were more audible than he realised.

'It's an upsetting time for the lad,' Ross said sympathetically, 'especially when he's so alone.'

Daniel was raking his fingers through his hair distractedly when he joined them in the kitchen.

'Things not going according to plan, lad?' Ross asked quietly. 'Anything I can do?'

'No, I'm afraid there's nothing anyone can do,' he said wearily.

Kim couldn't bear to see him looking so dejected. She got up and went to stand beside him, her hand on his shoulder. He reached up and clasped her hand with his own, and when he looked up into her face, so close to his own, Kim could not resist dropping a kiss on his brow. For those few seconds they were in a world of their own. Then awareness of their surroundings suddenly struck them. They looked up and saw Ross with raised eyebrows, but there was a faint smile curving his lips.

'Maybe Daniel is not quite as alone in the world as I thought, eh?' he said quizzically. They looked at each other and Kim shrugged.

'We know this is not a good time to discuss things, Dad, but Daniel had intended coming to see you the morning after the dance.' She shrugged again and gave a small grimace.

'What did you want to discuss, Daniel?' Ross asked gravely, but his eyes were bright with anticipation.

'I-I wanted to seek your . . . your approval. I asked Kim if she will marry me, and . . .' Daniel pushed another hand through his rumpled dark hair.

'Daniel, I have thought you a decent man since our first meeting. For my part, I would be happy to welcome you into my family. Does this mean that you and Kim have unravelled any problems there might have been between you when you first came here?'

Daniel gripped Kim's hand, then looked up at her.

'Oh, you know me! I still intend to have my own way over some things, Dad.' Kim smiled wickedly back at Daniel and trailed her fingers gently along his cheek. 'But so long as we have your blessing, I really do want to marry Daniel. We have not mentioned it to anyone else. Nothing would change for a year anyway, especially now.'

'Kim felt you would need time to get used to missing Nessie,' Daniel said, 'but I hope you will never feel you are losing Kim. I have no idea what we shall do now, because of the fire, but I can assure you we shall not be far away and you will always be welcome at our dinner table, and at our fireside.' There was a sincerity about Daniel's words which brought a warmth to Ross's heart.

'I shall welcome you as the son I never had, Daniel. This news will be no surprise to Nessie and Mel, though. They saw it coming.'

'It's strange how other people could be so certain this would happen when I had to muster up all my courage before I dare ask Kim if she would be my wife,' Daniel said, half seriously, but with a lightening of his expression.

'Yes, well she was rather stern with you, wasn't she?' Ross grinned. 'I expect the sparks will fly on occasion when you both want your own way, but so long as there is give and take between you, I reckon you will do fine.'

'Uncle Fergus declared Kim was the girl I should marry when I drove you all home after Nessie and Mel's wedding. He said I needed a woman with intelligence and spirit who would not give me all my own way. I am glad now that I know we had his approval.'

'So what's the trouble with the funeral arrangements that has upset you so much, Daniel? If we're all going to be part of the family, perhaps we can help, though if it is anything confidential...'

'No, no, nothing like that,' Daniel assured him quickly. 'At least not as far as I am concerned. I don't expect it to be a big funeral. I told Mr Dodds, his solicitor, because I wanted to know if he had left any specific instructions regarding his funeral, but he hadn't. Kim, you met Estelle Roon-Kurcher when she came down here, didn't you?'

'Yes.' Kim bit her lip. She had disliked the woman instantly, but she knew Daniel had known her all her life.

'Well, if you thought she was officious and liked her own way, she has nothing on her father.' Daniel's mouth tightened. 'I imagine he would have been something of a bully at school.' He turned to Ross. 'He is an auctioneer and owns the local auction company. I didn't inform them of Uncle's death because, if I am honest, I didn't want them here. I have had enough of him and his daughter. We saw a lot of each other when we were children, but Estelle always liked her own way and could be quite spiteful if she didn't get it. She has not improved because her father has always spoiled her. Anyway, apparently he's furious because I didn't contact him personally. But they are coming anyway. Estelle has arranged it so they're staying not one but two nights.' He looked at Kim. 'I wish to God I had had time to go to the bank and collect my mother's jewellery. Even if you don't like her ring, you could have worn it once, to let them see we really do belong together. Now that Ross knows and approves I could introduce you as my fiancée, and even Estelle would have to believe it if she saw a ring on your finger.'

'They will both see that you have new friends if Dad and I and Mrs Dunn sit beside you at the funeral, at the front.'

'Oh yes, I shall need you beside me, Kim. You, too, Ross, if you don't mind?'

'Of course I don't mind, lad. Ye're nearly part of the family anyway now.'

'I will instruct the funeral director to keep the front seat clear for us. Dolly too. She will be upset, I know. Maybe Nessie and Mel would join us, do you think?' He looked at Ross.

'I am sure they will.' Ross nodded. 'Kim, perhaps you could quietly let Nessie know that you and Daniel are a couple now, even if it's not official yet.'

'It will soon be over, Daniel, and there is not much opportunity to talk at funerals,' Kim said comfortingly.

'Ah yes, but they've asked Mr Dodds to arrange for me to join them for a meal that evening, the day of the funeral!'

'Surely not. Funerals are a terrible strain,' Ross said. 'Could this be their way of trying to express their sympathy?'

'Oh no! Roon-Kurcher has things he wants to discuss. God knows what!' There was no doubting Daniel's anger and frustration. 'I refused, but Mr Dodds is an old man, and he is the piggy in the middle. He thinks I should at least agree to talk with Roon-Kurcher and listen to what he has to say.'

'I see . . .' Ross said, frowning thoughtfully. 'Well, far be it from me to give advice, Daniel. This is only a suggestion. How about eating with us at home and trying to relax for an hour or so, then meeting them later that evening for a short time?'

'I suppose I could agree to that, for Mr Dodds' sake,' Daniel said reluctantly. He looked at Kim. 'I know it's not really fair to ask you, Kim, but I would like them to meet you as my fiancée, if you would come with me?'

Ross looked from one to the other. 'It would be moral support, lassie, if nothing else,' he said quietly.

'They can't eat me alive, I suppose,' Kim said. 'All right, I'll come with you, Daniel, and I'll literally hold your hand, then they can think whatever they like.'

'I still have your mother's rings, Kim, sentimental old fool that I am. You will probably think her engagement ring a bit old-fashioned, and it may be a bit big for you, but it might serve a purpose for the time being. You can have it if you want. Your eyes are the same colour as Miriam's were, and the ring is diamond and emeralds.'

'I don't think you have ever showed me that, Dad.'

'No, probably not. I will bring it down now and you can see what you both think.'

* * *

There were far more people at the funeral than Daniel had expected. Some of them were people he had visited in his work as a vet. Mr Turner and his wife were there, as well as two of the other vets who were not on call or attending the clinic. Many knew William and Annie Nairn, as well as Ross, and wanted to offer their sympathy. Most of them were unaware that the estate was already in Daniel's name, and many speculated about what would happen to it now the old man had died.

Estelle Roon-Kurcher and her father had no hesitation in walking to the front of the church and entering the front pew. Mr Dodds was about to follow more slowly until the funeral director politely asked the Roon-Kurchers to take another seat because the front pew was reserved for family and close friends.

'We're the closest friends he has,' Edward Roon-Kurcher declared, none too quietly.

'I am sorry, sir,' the man insisted firmly, and stood back, indicating that they must move to the seat behind or any other vacant seat if they wished. Mr Dodds moved into the seat behind and Estelle and her father had no option but to follow.

Billy Nairn, watching this and seeing Estelle's furious sulks, glanced at his Uncle William and winked. Annie saw and gave a small frown, but she was secretly pleased Daniel was not with the horrid girl who had wanted to sleep in his bed. She wondered who would sit with Daniel, or if it would just be Dolly. The poor woman was still dreadfully distressed and dreading this service.

When Nessie and Mel came in and entered the front pew, Estelle immediately leaned forward and hissed, 'That pew is reserved for Daniel and the housekeeper.' Mel smiled at her and nodded. 'It's all right. We're close friends.'

'You can't be . . .'

'Daniel was best man at our wedding,' Mel said quietly, and sat down next to his wife, glad Daniel had warned him what he might expect.

Estelle's eyes widened, but they widened even more when Dolly Dunn came in, leaning heavily on Kim's arm, closely followed by Daniel and then that man who was only a farmer. She couldn't remember his name, but she thought he was the girl's father. What right had they to sit with Daniel? She had known him all her life.

She glanced at her father and saw him scowl. He looked disapprovingly at Daniel's choice of companions on such an occasion as this.

During the service, Mr Dodds was moved by the minister's tribute to his old friend. He saw Daniel tense too — and saw his hand move to take the hand of the slender young woman at his side. Her fingers clasped his in support and Mr Dodds' eyes widened as he caught the sparkle of an engagement ring.

This was going to change things — a lot of things!

Silently, he wished he hadn't agreed to travel with the Roon-Kurchers. It was going to be a long journey back to Aberdeen tomorrow morning with a sullen young woman and her furious father. Roon-Kurcher's plans and expectations had been wrecked — seriously wrecked. In a fury he would drive too fast and without attention to anyone else on the road. The drive down had been hard enough to suffer. He wondered if he could find an excuse to stay longer and travel back later on the train. If he said he didn't feel well, they might think they ought to stay with him. He wondered if he could persuade Daniel that they had more business to discuss, or maybe Dolly Dunn — after all, she was mentioned in Fergus's last will . . . Yes, he could ask to see her to tell her of the arrangements Fergus had made for her.

CHAPTER SIXTEEN

Daniel realised how right Ross had been about the after-effects of the funeral. It had been more of a strain than he had expected, and he'd been truly grateful for Ross and Kim's support. He knew Dolly had valued Kim's company and her kind and gentle manner. When they got back to Rowandene after the light meal was over, he felt totally drained. As they were coming away, Roon-Kurcher had waylaid him.

'Are you sure you will not join us for dinner this evening, Danny, my boy?'

'I am quite sure. I shall be there at seven thirty, but whatever you have to discuss, I hope it will not take long.' He knew he'd been terse. He hadn't slept well the past two nights, wondering if he'd done everything his uncle would have expected of him.

Mr Dodds waylaid him again at the door.

'There is not much to explain about the Will, Daniel, but I told Mrs Dunn I shall call on her tomorrow to explain the part that affects her.' He gave a sheepish smile. 'I would prefer to travel home on the train so I'm looking for a reason to stay longer.' Understanding dawned, and Daniel smiled at the elderly lawyer.

'I'll back you up. One Roon-Kurcher can be a bit overpowering, so I imagine two could be exhausting during a long drive.'

'Exactly so,' Mr Dodds said with relief. 'I am glad you appreciate my motive.'

* * *

When Daniel and Kim arrived at the hotel later that evening they were directed towards a small private sitting room. Kim was feeling nervous, but Daniel squeezed her fingers and smiled at her.

'I'm very glad of your support, Kim. We shall not stay any longer than we can help. I can't understand what Edward wants to talk about that he needs a private audience.'

They went in together, hand in hand. Roon-Kurcher was getting to his feet as the door opened, but when he saw Kim he sat down again, staring at her.

'I made it plain we had business to discuss, Daniel. Private business. This is not a time for company.'

'Whatever you want to say you can say in front of my fiancée. Kim knows all there is to know about Wedderburn Hall and Uncle Fergus's wishes. He approved of her as the ideal wife for me.'

Twice Roon-Kurcher opened his mouth and closed it again — a bit like a stranded fish — but it was Estelle who let out a shriek.

'Fiancée? She can't be your fiancée! You were mine before you ever saw her!'

'You should have climbed into his bloody bed!' Roon-Kurcher bellowed at her. 'I warned you not to let him slip through your fingers!' He spluttered, almost incoherent with rage.

'Do take a seat,' Mr Dodds said quietly, looking at Kim with a decided twinkle in his eye. 'Dr Kimberly McLaren, isn't it?'

'That's right,' Kim acknowledged. 'Thank you.' She ignored the single chair close to Mr Roon-Kurcher's, which had obviously been meant for Daniel, and seated herself on a small two-seater settee, sending a pleading glance to Daniel to join her there. He gave an imperceptible nod and crossed the small room to sit beside her, immediately taking her hand in his.

Estelle glared at them. 'You can't do this to us!' she shouted. 'You can't! You can't. Daddy, tell him he can't do this.'

Daniel felt Kim tense. He had had enough. He had bitten back sharp retorts often enough in the past, mainly for his uncle's sake.

'You know damned well I never belonged to you, Estelle. I never encouraged you, and if you want the truth, your tantrums sickened me. Why do you think I went to Africa? Now if you have nothing of importance to discuss, we have had a wasted evening coming here.' He began to rise.

'There are plenty of matters of importance, you insolent whelp!' Roon-Kurcher sounded almost as hysterical as his daughter. 'If you think I am paying your uncle's share in the company to you, you can bloody well think again. I expected you and Estelle to marry — then I would never have needed to repay anything. I knew Fergus would leave it all to you, as he always said he would.'

'I don't know what you're talking about.' Daniel frowned and looked at Mr Dodds. 'Uncle Fergus used his money to buy the Wedderburn Estate. He bought it because he wanted me back in Britain. He knew I had no intention of ever marrying Estelle, or allowing you to arrange my future.'

Kim's fingers tightened on his and he looked down at her. She shook her head. 'Don't let them upset you,' she murmured, almost under her breath.

'What are you whispering about?' Estelle demanded. 'You're just that tenant's bitch of a daughter out to catch the owner of his bloody mansion. Well, I'm glad it has all burned to the ground, and that stupid old man with it!'

'Miss Estelle! Please . . .' Mr Dodds gasped in protest.

Daniel pulled Kim to her feet and glared down at the Roon-Kurchers. 'We're leaving! No one speaks like that to my fiancée,' he growled angrily. 'Kim is worth six of you and your spiteful, selfish ways, so . . .'

'Oh, please, Daniel,' Mr Dodds pleaded, 'please wait and let me explain . . .' Kim squeezed Daniel's fingers and indicated they should hear poor Mr Dodds out. The elderly man breathed a sigh of relief as they both resumed their seats.

'Mr Roon-Kurcher, let me explain. I have arranged to stay longer tomorrow and explain the terms of Fergus Nichol's Will to Daniel and to Mrs Dunn. As yet he knows nothing of his uncle's investments, apart from the money he spent on buying Wedderburn Hall, which he bought in Daniel's own name, with money he had invested for Daniel from his parents' insurances and sale of their home. Daniel is unaware that his uncle owned a third of your auction company, among several other investments.'

'What?' Daniel was incredulous. 'He owned part of the auction company . . .' He was bereft of speech for a moment. Roon-Kurcher had always acted as though he owned half the county, as well as the company. 'No wonder you wanted to bind me to your bloody family!' Daniel stared in angry astonishment and looked from the solicitor to Roon-Kurcher. He expelled his breath. So that was the reason Estelle had come down to Wedderburn Hall — not for the love of his uncle, or of himself. She was like her father. It was all about money.

'It really is time we left,' he said grimly. 'Mr Dodds, I have an appointment with the insurance assessor tomorrow morning at nine thirty. It may take some time, but I shall be free to discuss things with you after that.'

'Maybe it would be better if you come to Rowandene for lunch,' Kim suggested quietly, 'after you have seen Mrs Dunn. Daniel should be back from dealing with the insurance representative by then and you can speak privately in his apartment.'

'Yes, that would be a good idea,' Daniel said. 'Are you sure your father will not mind, Kim?'

'Of course he won't mind.'

'Of course he won't mind,' Estelle mimicked sarcastically. 'Not when his daughter's getting her hands on the landlord and his money,' she sneered. Daniel ignored her and led Kim towards the door.

'We shall see you tomorrow, Mr Dodds. I will drive you into town afterwards to catch your train.'

Neither of the Roon-Kurchers spoke. Mr Dodds accompanied them out into the hotel foyer. 'I am sorry things turned so nasty,' he began apologetically.

Daniel shook his head wearily. 'Hopefully, you can explain everything tomorrow. It has been a long day so we'll say goodnight now.'

On the way home Daniel drew the car to a halt in a quiet layby. He turned to Kim.

'I'm sorry I put you through such a scene with the Roon-Kurchers, Kim. I honestly don't understand what half of that was about, but I thank my lucky stars I escaped their clutches.' He drew her to him and kissed her gently. 'I thank God sincerely that I have found you, my darling Kim,' he murmured against the softness of her neck.

'You're exhausted, Daniel,' Kim said gently. 'Come, let's get you home. My father will give you brandy and hot chocolate — his favourite sedative-cum-sleeping draught.' She chuckled. 'Nothing will seem quite so bad tomorrow.'

* * *

Kim was right. Daniel slept well after Ross's nightcap, so he felt more like himself and ready to deal with the man from the insurance company.

Daniel found him already at the site and looking around.

'Good morning, Mr Nichol.' He greeted Daniel pleasantly. 'My name is Sam McClure, from the claims department. I am so sorry to hear of the death of your uncle. Someone from your solicitor's office contacted me to explain that the post-mortem revealed he had died of heart failure before the fire took hold. We can be assured there is no question of a fraudulent claim in this case. Presumably you will want to start rebuilding as soon as the claim has been approved?'

'Yes, but I have no intention of rebuilding a house the size of the original Hall,' Daniel declared bluntly.

'I see. The insurance had recently been increased considerably. We can't pay out such a sum without knowing you intend to rebuild.'

'I have not had time to consider the finer details, but my fiancée agrees we would probably build a decent-sized four-bedroomed family home. The site itself will cost a considerable sum to clear.'

'I understand there is one end wall that was almost untouched and which could be incorporated into a new building,' Sam McClure said. 'The report from the fire department told us that. I was taking a look before you arrived. Would you consider using the salvaged stone to rebuild the other external walls, or even the front of the building? It must have been a very attractive place in its day, I imagine.'

'I suppose it was,' Daniel nodded, 'but there is not the labour to keep such houses these days. I will give some thought to re-using the stone, so long as it will not cost a fortune to salvage and dress the stones. Do you need to know about that today?'

'No. In any case, you will need plans drawn up and approved. I will process the claim, but the company will not pay out in full until you can prove you intend to build another house to an approved design and standard.'

'I was not thinking of replacing it with a prefabricated bungalow,' Daniel said abruptly.

'In my job we never quite know what people will do if they get the money,' Sam McClure said, 'but you appear to be a man of taste,' he added, eyeing Daniel's smart suit.

'Most of my clothes were destroyed in the fire, as were those of my uncle and the housekeeper. It has been a case of buying something to wear in a hurry, but now the funeral is over I shall buy the necessities for my work as I need them.'

'Speaking of personal items and the housekeeper's possessions, I will put through separate claims and do my best to rush the payment through. You will both need clothes to wear, and no doubt the poor woman lost other things too. Will you ask her to make a list and the approximate value of any jewellery?'

'My uncle had given her a gold wrist watch for her loyal service, but I think she would have worn it that evening when she was out. There may be other things though. My uncle had a gold hunter pocket watch, but it was probably destroyed and I have no way of proving it.'

'It may have been listed in personal items of value when the insurance was reviewed. I will check our records and get an interim payment for personal possessions to you and to the housekeeper as soon as possible.'

'Thank you, I'm sure Mrs Dunn will appreciate that.' He sighed heavily.

'It is a difficult time for everyone in these circumstances. It is worse when people discover they aren't properly insured, or even not insured at all — it's heartbreaking.' He held out his hand to shake Daniel's. 'I shall not take up any more of your time now and will be in touch as soon as possible. Perhaps you would keep me informed of your plans regarding the house?'

'I will,' Daniel promised, and once again he was thankful to know he could rely on Kim and her father for their down-to-earth advice and suggestions. He thought of Estelle and her wildly extravagant ideas, but she had never had to count the pennies, believing she had a wealthy father.

He decided he would call on the Nairns and speak to Dolly before he returned to Rowandene. He had quite forgotten Mr Dodds was calling on her that morning, too, until he arrived and found the elderly solicitor about to leave.

'I'm sorry, I had forgotten we are meeting later this morning, Mr Dodds. If you wait a few more minutes, I will give you a lift down to Rowandene. I called to ask whether Dolly is all right.'

'It is a relief now the funeral is over, Master Daniel, as I'm sure it must be for you. Please thank Dr McLaren for being so kind and supportive to me.'

'I will, Dolly. I intend to arrange a transfer of funds to your bank, so you can replace your personal belongings. I'm afraid I've not been thinking clearly these past few days, but the insurance assessor said they will pay for our clothes and such like, as well as any personal items of value you may have lost, such as your gold watch.'

'Ah, Daniel, none of us have been thinking right,' Dolly said, with the familiarity of having known Daniel since he was young. 'Now Mr Dodds has been to tell me that Mr Nichol left a trust fund in his will for me. I'm to get a small income every month once I reach fifty-five. He has already paid a pension for me every month since I was twenty and he has always been a kind and generous man. I don't think I deserve any more. It should all come to you.'

'Don't say that, Dolly,' Daniel urged. 'You have cared for both of us most of your life up to now.'

'Aye, and I've been happy doing it, and so was my John, bless his soul. Apart from money, I'm not ready to give up working yet. I shall look for another job. I know your Estelle wouldna want me housekeeping for her. I'm sorry to say we have never got on.'

'Dolly! Dolly, you must not rush into anything,' Daniel urged. 'I have so many things to sort out and consider, but I can assure you I shall make sure you have a home.'

'Aye, I don't want to outstay my welcome here when Annie and Willie have proved such good friends,' Dolly said, glancing round at them all. 'I shall have the money from Freda's cottage when it is sold. I should be able to buy a small cottage down here eventually. Mr Dodds is going to ask one of his young men to attend to that for me, and also advise me about carrying on my pension.'

Daniel pushed his fingers through his thick hair and glanced at Mr Dodds. The old solicitor raised a quizzical eyebrow, and then, to Daniel's astonishment, he winked conspiratorially and cleared his throat.

'My advice is not to rush into anything, Mrs Dunn. I suspect you and your friends here have jumped to conclusions regarding Miss Roon-Kurcher.'

'She as good as told me they were going to be married when she came down to stay,' Annie Nairn declared.

'These past few days have not been a time for sharing good news or celebrating,' Daniel said. 'However, Kim's father knows now that I want to marry his daughter. Kim agreed to marry me the night of the dance, but—' he shrugged helplessly — 'you all know how that night ended.'

'Yes . . .' Dolly shuddered and hid her face in her hands.

'Are you telling me you and Kim are to be married?' Annie Nairn asked jubilantly, bouncing out of her chair and rushing to Daniel's side.

'I am, but not for a year yet, especially now with Uncle Fergus's death. Anyway, we want to give Ross time to come to terms with the changes since Nessie's marriage.'

'But that's wonderful news!' Annie carolled. 'So our Billy was right. He said you would never marry a selfish bi— er, a woman like Miss Roon-Kurcher. Kim's a lovely girl, always has been.'

'Yes, she was very kind to me yesterday,' Dolly said, 'and such a comfort when I got so upset. Oh, Daniel, I do wish you happiness.'

Daniel turned to Annie. 'Speaking of Billy, I haven't had time to speak to him properly.'

'That's all right. He drove Mrs Lenox to her sister's the night of the fire. She was so hysterical we couldn't calm her. She still considered her chooks though, and the pigs and young heifers She asked him to see that everything was shut up nice and tight.'

'Chooks?' Daniel asked.

'Poultry, hens mainly, but Mary always had a few ducks and a goose or two running around. A few bantams as well, I think. She wouldn't want the fox to get them. I believe Billy is quite enjoying looking after things.'

'Yes, Ross and Kim assured me Billy had always liked animals and he would look after them well, even if estate management is still his main calling. But speaking of Mrs Lenox, I believe she has set her heart on retiring to a cottage in the same village as her sister, so I don't think they will be back at Home Farm except to remove their furniture. I've promised to help them with that.'

'Oh dear. What about the dairy cows?' Annie asked.

'Once Ross was sure they were all in good health he took them to Rowandene to milk with his own herd. I shall have to sell them eventually as they are a mixture of breeds, and Ross and Kim like to keep their herd pedigree.' He glanced at his watch. 'I think Mr Dodds and I had better be going now if we're to have lunch and catch the afternoon train to Aberdeen.'

They said goodbye and Daniel led Mr Dodds to his car. 'I know Dr McLaren said we would have privacy to talk,' Mr Dodds said en route, 'but I have not a lot more to tell you, Daniel. I will leave you a copy of your uncle's last Will, but there is no other paperwork at present. If you would like to draw the car to a halt now, I can explain the rest, and why Edward Roon-Kurcher got so angry. He is a man used to having his own way.'

'Oh, I know that only too well. His wife is so different. I have often wondered how she came to marry him.'

'Ah, he would pursue her until she had little option. Her father owned the auction company at the time and Edward was training to be an auctioneer. He can be charming when it suits.'

'I didn't know that.'

'The thing is, the auction company went through a bad patch. I think it was after an outbreak of foot and mouth disease.

Fergus was sure things would pick up again eventually so he put in capital in return for shares to the value of a third of the company. Roon-Kurcher owns a third. Six other farmers own the remainder in small amounts of shares. If you had married Estelle her father thought he would never need to repay the money your uncle invested in the company. To tell the truth, I didn't really approve of Fergus leaving his money in the company. I think for a while he also thought you might marry Estelle.'

'I rather wish he hadn't.'

'However, despite my disapproval, most of the auction companies have done well in recent years. Several companies, including Roon-Kurcher's, expanded into property, as well as animal auctions, yet no dividends were actually paid out on your uncle's shares. Roon-Kurcher said they were accumulating value, but his family were living well off the company. And dividends were paid to the six small shareholders. I believe he thought there would never be a day of reckoning because you would become part of the family and the company, and he would control everything. Fergus didn't need the money, but it was not a good way to do business.'

'No, it does sound a bit deceitful on Roon-Kurcher's part. Most likely it was greed,' Daniel muttered.

'The value will have increased with the accumulated dividends. So you will understand why Roon-Kurcher was so furious when he realised he is going to have to pay out quite a large sum of money if you want to take out Fergus's shares. If you want my advice, you will insist on withdrawing them and cutting any ties with the Roon-Kurchers. You may need to agree to repayment over two years, or even three, unless you are in urgent need of the money. And it must be done with a legal agreement. One of our younger partners is very good at handling such matters. He is also excellent at advising on investments — cautious, but reliable. If you like, I can arrange for him to come down and discuss things with you later. Apart from the shares in the auction company, Fergus had a good portfolio presently valued at around a hundred and fifty thousand pounds, plus a life insurance for thirty-five thousand. He always wanted to be certain he would never be a drain on you financially if he needed expensive health care.'

'I can't believe it!' Daniel said, his face pale. 'Uncle Fergus said . . . or at least . . .' He frowned, trying to recall the telephone conversation they had had while he was in Africa, when Uncle Fergus phoned to say he had purchased Wedderburn Estate. 'Maybe I didn't understand properly, but I thought his pension kept him in comfort so he had spent all his spare cash on buying the Wedderburn Estate in my name. I knew then he was anxious to have me back in the UK.'

'Yes, it upset him badly when you went to Africa, but it made him realise you intended to make your own decisions, and live your own life, without the influence of Edward Roon-Kurcher, or his daughter. He respected you for that, but he was very happy when he knew you were coming home. He told me you used your own money to make a very comfortable apartment for himself and his housekeeper, even though he could have easily afforded to pay for it himself. Fergus and I knew each other well. We were at school together since we were ten years old. We lost touch from time to time, but he always contacted me with any legal business and we could always pick up the old threads again.'

'I never knew about the money,' Daniel said. 'I simply can't believe Mr Roon-Kurcher didn't own the whole of the auction company — and half of Aberdeenshire besides,' he added with a touch of bitterness. 'Both he and Stella talked and acted as though they were extremely wealthy — and influential.'

'Well, as the old saying goes, "we should never judge the contents by the label on the jar". It is so true,' Mr Dodds reflected dryly.

'I suppose it is. Now we had better get back and eat our lunch if I am to drive you to the station in time for your train.'

'Indeed, yes. It was a relief not to be travelling back with Edward, the way he would be driving today. I had breakfast in my room so I didn't see them again before they left.'

CHAPTER SEVENTEEN

Daniel and Kim planned to get married in October of the following year, with Nessie agreeing to be matron of honour, and Mel best man at Daniel's request. They held off telling the girls they would be bridesmaids again because a year would seem a lifetime to them. This was just as well because even the best-laid schemes rarely go according to plan.

After some concerted deliberation, Daniel decided he should move into the house at Home Farm rather than continue renting Nessie's apartment.

They were returning from an evening ride when Daniel decided to confess the reason why. 'I can't explain to your father, my love, that having his only daughter sleeping in a room only a few feet away from me every night is too great a temptation.'

They had stopped in what had become their favourite sheltered glade in one of the estate's woods. Kim's passionate response to his touch left Daniel in no doubt that she would find the temptation just as great as he did himself, sooner or later. Then they would both feel guilty at taking advantage of her father's home and his trust. 'As it is, I shall struggle to resist you for a whole year, my darling Kim, but I would be a scoundrel if I took advantage when your father has been so kind and so supportive.'

'I do understand. A year seems ages to wait now we have truly found each other,' Kim agreed. 'But where will you go?'

'Oh, not far away.' Daniel laughed. 'The Lenoxes are definitely moving out of Home Farm and I have promised Mrs Lenox I will have her furniture and possessions moved to her cottage, with Billy and his uncle's help. She would like us to do it before Bert gets out of hospital so she will have things all comfortable and ready for him.'

Daniel explained about the Lenoxes to Ross when they got back to Rowandene. 'So I thought I would move into Home Farm myself and maybe have a few alterations done while I'm in residence, such as a new kitchen and bathroom. Billy seems happy to continue looking after the few animals and the poultry each morning.'

'Aye, he's a good lad, young Billy, but his uncle was always a hard worker and set a good example.'

'Speaking of Annie Nairn, Ross, I have a very big favour to ask you, but you have done so much already I shall understand if you would rather say no.'

'Ask away, lad, and I'll answer honestly. It's the only way to be.'

'I agree.' Daniel nodded. 'And I appreciate you being straight with me.' He looked grim for a moment. 'I've had enough of two-faced deceivers with the Roon-Kurchers. Anyway, the situation is that Dolly Dunn is afraid of spoiling her friendship with the Nairns if she continues to stay with them indefinitely. She is talking about buying herself a small cottage in this area when she gets the money from the sale of the cottage. She doesn't want to go back to Aberdeenshire, but at forty-eight she says she is not ready to retire. I've known Dolly most of my life so I would like to see her happy wherever she is. I, er . . . I wondered how you would feel about her staying in Nessie's apartment when I move out, until she has had time to decide what she wants to do and where she would like to live? I know it can be completely separate and I would pay the rent for her.' Daniel was hurrying on quickly before Ross could give an answer. 'I have no intention of tying Kim down to being a full-time housewife when we marry, so I thought, when we get a house of our own, that Dolly might help us with cooking and cleaning and so on, and maybe work a bit for you, too, if you want her ... Wh-what do you think?'

Ross was silent for a few minutes, considering. 'It is an excellent idea. Yes, Daniel, that is a brilliant suggestion — mainly because I am relieved to know you understand Kim will never be satisfied with being a full-time housewife, even when you have children — and I hope you will have several. I know she has a lot of pride and independence and can be a bit sharp at times — she takes that from me. So it has worried me a bit ...'

'I can understand that, after all her education and success,' Daniel said. 'I shall never underestimate her intelligence either.' He lowered his voice. 'If you can keep a secret until our wedding day, I think I can give you more assurance of my trust and faith in Kim.'

'I can keep a secret,' Ross said, 'but better be quick — I can hear her getting out of the bath.'

'I have no regrets about refusing to include Kim's name as a tenant with yours, even though it did get me off to a bad start.' He grinned, remembering Kim's temper. 'She was fiery from the beginning, but I knew I was attracted to her. I didn't want her living so near if she married someone else, but I would trust her with my life. So I have asked Mr Dodds to transfer the deeds and ownership of Home Farm into Kim's name. I will give it to her as a wedding present. It will be up to Kim whether she farms it along with you or breeds cattle of her own. I shall not interfere unless she asks for my help with anything, but I would like to know she can go on discussing things with you as she has always done.'

'My word! I knew you were a fair and decent man the first time we met, but that's more than generous, Daniel. It shows more understanding of Kim's ambitions and independence than I think I would have shown myself at your age.' His voice was gruff with emotion and for a moment Daniel caught a glimpse of a tear in his eyes. 'Kim's a very lucky lass.'

'I think I'm the lucky one,' Daniel said quietly, and there was no doubting his sincerity.

With Daniel and Kim requiring a team for their own house-building works up at the Hall, Nessie was keen to recommend the building and trades team they had used at Fairvale. Their alterations had gone extremely well. Nessie's office extension even encompassed an extra room than originally planned, so she could employ a part-time assistant to help with her growing business. The building team were all local small businesses — as well as Nessie's own accountancy clients.

Mel also made a tentative suggestion that they might try a young architect he had been treating as a patient, who had been lucky to survive a very bad car accident.

'I am not recommending him out of pity,' Mel said, 'but in my opinion his company have behaved dreadfully and I suspect he would have good reason to claim against them.'

'How so?' Daniel asked.

'He recently won an award. It brought him considerable commendation, but it also brought prestige and good publicity for his employers, a large company in Birmingham. In spite of that, they terminated his contract, even though the accident he was involved in happened during his work for them.'

'Can they get away with that?' Daniel asked in disbelief.

'I'm fairly sure he would have cause to sue the company. I would have felt very bitter,' Mel said. 'But you know, he is amazingly resilient, and so grateful to have survived the internal injuries, and to still have both his legs. It was touch and go with his left leg, I admit. I believe it will heal completely, given time, although he will have a slight limp, and he will not play in his local football team again.'

'That sounds dreadful,' Kim said, 'and terribly unfair to lose his job in those circumstances.'

'I agree,' Mel said. 'We had to keep him in a coma for a while. He didn't fully understand everything that had happened until several weeks later. For instance, his mother died, and at that stage we could not give his cousin and her husband any guarantee that he would recover. Apparently, his mother had been ill for some time so her death was not a surprise. They dealt with the funeral arrangements, but Mike will have to deal with the sale of her house when he is fully recovered.'

'That's a lot to cope with,' Daniel sympathised.

'It is, but I would never recommend anybody's work because I felt sorry for them, or because I admire their courage,' Mel said, 'especially for something as important as a new house. I can tell you he made an excellent job of drawing up the plans for Fairvale, and he thought of solutions and ideas we would never have considered.

'For instance, it was his suggestion to take the extension all the way to the roof and add an en-suite to what is now a lovely master bedroom, at relatively little extra cost. It vexed him because he was unable to supervise the work personally, but I drove him out to consult with the team on site and passed on any queries they had.

'The builder said he was one of the best he had worked for. Since then he has drawn plans for one of the nurses wanting to build on a sun porch. And one of the doctors wanted to build a double garage, but he couldn't get his plans approved. He drove Mike out to see his house and the site and Mike came back and drew an outline plan, turning the building to a different angle. It has passed without trouble.'

'When would he be fit to work if we decided to let him draw plans for us?' Daniel asked.

'The thing holding him back now is being unable to drive himself to sites to inspect the work in progress,' Mel warned. 'If he did plans as you want them, and if you decide to work with the same builder and his team, would either you or Kim be willing to drive him to the Hall at intervals to make regular checks? I'm fairly sure he's more conscientious than a lot of men in his job.'

'We could do that, couldn't we, Kim? The fellow deserves a break, I reckon,' Daniel said. Kim was in full agreement.

'He is hoping to set up in business on his own, using the compensation he will receive from the accident. It was caused by a drunk driver. A child was killed and the mother badly injured.'

'That sounds nasty.' Daniel shuddered. 'It would take a bit of getting over, aside from the physical injuries.'

'I think it has, and he's been glad to have some work to take his mind off things. All the hospital staff like and respect him, both as a man and as a patient. Even when he was in terrible pain he rarely complained. He's not had an opportunity to draw plans for a new house from scratch yet. I suppose it would be a big step forward for him if you do feel you can give him a try?'

'I think we should definitely meet him and see what he suggests,' Kim said.

'We'll get him up to the Hall,' Daniel agreed. 'It's beginning to look less like a ruin now, with the site nearly cleared. We'll tell him what we have in mind and take it from there. We're hoping a year will be plenty of time to build.'

* * *

Both Kim and Daniel were impressed by the young architect when Mel drove him up to the Hall to meet them. They promised to drive him back to the nursing home, where he was staying temporarily, later in the day.

Michael Miller was a tall, fair young man, thinner in face and figure than he had been before the near-fatal accident. He still had his left leg in some sort of brace and leaned heavily on a walking stick. He was obviously sensitive about it because he told them immediately he hoped to dispense with the stick before long but Mr Sanders had advised him to continue using it, especially on uneven ground. The three of them were viewing the cleared site where Wedderburn Hall had once stood. Neat piles of red sandstone were heaped at one end of the long rectangle, leaving the other end clear where Daniel and Kim hoped their new home could be built with a view facing down the glen.

'This is more exciting than I anticipated bricks and mortar could be,' Kim said, 'or should I say stones and mortar?'

'Using the red sandstone will be more expensive than bricks,' Mike acknowledged, 'but the appearance would be far superior. You have so much beautiful stone already. A lot of it will need dressing, of course, so we should consult your builder and consider costs before we finalise the plans. There should be no difficulty getting planning permission when there has been a house on the site so recently. Probably the planners will be more likely to approve it without much delay if it is to be built with the red sandstone local to this area.'

'I agree about the appearance,' Daniel said. 'We are considering using the builder who did Mr Sanders' extension. I believe you approved of their standard of workmanship and their willingness to cooperate with your suggestions?'

'Yes, they were a good team and all took pride in their work.' He moved to the far side of the Land Rover so that he could support himself by leaning against it while resting his sketchpad on the bonnet of the vehicle.

'I will make a few rough sketches so that you can both consider your preferences. I understand you want a minimum of four good-sized bedrooms with two of them en-suite. When we're starting from scratch there's no reason why they shouldn't all have a shower room, without too much extra outlay, if you would like that. It's fortunate that we have the services such as water, electricity, and even septic tanks, already onsite. You want a dining room, a sitting room, a large farmhouse-style kitchen with a utility room for white goods, and a smaller cosy TV room off the kitchen?'

'Yes, please,' Kim said, delighted that he had remembered so much detail already. 'Oh, and a small cloakroom with toilet and washbasin near the back door as well.'

'It might be a good idea to include a shower in there as well, if possible,' Daniel said. 'I'm a vet and sometimes the first place I want to go when I get home is into the shower.'

'I'm glad you told me that. It's much easier if I know what people do with their lives. Perhaps a small office would be useful too? Do you store some of your animal medicines at home, or your equipment?'

'Not a lot, but an office would be handy, wouldn't it, Kim?'

'Yes, I think it would. If we have children,' she said, blushing delightfully, Daniel thought with a smile, 'I wouldn't want animal medicines stored in the kitchen fridge.'

'No indeed,' Mike agreed. 'Then we must try to cover all eventualities. If it turns out too expensive, we can adapt, or cut out any non-essentials. Also, if you think you might want something added at a later date, such as a sunroom or conservatory, then I would include it in a broad outline for your own future consideration, but not in the plans submitted. How does that sound?'

'That makes sense to me,' Kim said, 'but I wouldn't want it to be so expensive that we would be in debt for years and years,' she said anxiously, looking at Daniel.

'I think you've covered everything, Mike, except perhaps a large garage. There are no outhouses left since the fire. At a later date we may want to build stabling for horses. I only wish we could wave a wand and the house would appear exactly as we want it and allow us to get married tomorrow.'

'Is it the house, or the getting married tomorrow, that you most desire?' Mike asked with a grin, glancing up from his sketch pad.

'The getting married tomorrow, of course,' Daniel said with a wink at Kim, bringing a blush to her fair skin at the desire in his eyes.

'I will draw a few sketches of the front exterior and you can tell me what sort of features you prefer. For instance, do you like bay windows, downstairs only or up and down, dormer windows or . . .'

'No, not dormer windows,' Kim said quickly. 'I know a lot of farmhouses in this area have them, but I like a window with a good wide view.'

'That's the sort of thing I need to know,' Mike nodded. 'Do you want a porch or conservatory at the front door, or something stylish like a portico with a stone column on either side?' As he talked, Mike was sketching swiftly and when they looked at his drawings they both exclaimed at his speed and talent.

'That does help us to decide,' Daniel said with appreciation. 'You should have been an artist.'

'I do paint a bit in my spare time, watercolours mainly,' Mike said, continuing to draw various styles and outlines.

'I think we should go home for some lunch now,' Kim said, 'and let you get the weight off your feet for a few hours, Michael. We can discuss your ideas and suggestions there.'

As they drove back down to Rowandene, Mike said, 'I have to move out of the nursing home shortly so I'm hoping I shall be able to drive soon if I buy myself an automatic car. Dr Sanders says your father drives one, Miss McLaren. Does he like it?'

'Oh, call me Kim, please. We feel we know you after hearing Mel talk about you. He admires your courage, as well as your expertise as an architect.'

'Mr Sanders has been a good friend as well as an excellent surgeon. My right leg is gaining strength now I'm allowed to move about more, but the physiotherapist still comes to massage my left leg every second day. She has been wonderful, and very patient.'

'You will meet my father over lunch so you can ask him about the car. I think he likes the automatic so much he will not have any other in future.'

'Where will you stay when you leave the nursing home?' Daniel asked.

'We-ell, that is something I must decide soon, but I need to know I shall be able to get around independently before I look for lodgings.' He sighed heavily. 'My mother died while I was in hospital.'

'Yes, Mel told us that. You have certainly had a bad time,' Daniel said.

'Yes, but fortunately there are four detached houses in a sort of small cul-de-sac and the neighbours have all been there for years. They all get on well so I know they are keeping an eye on things and they'll make sure the house is secure. If I can set up on my own in this area, I shall sell the house. I have done a few small jobs while I was in hospital. There was nothing wrong with my head or my arms, I thank God. Everyone has been amazingly friendly and helpful. If you approve of my plans for your new home, I would definitely stay up here until I see it finished.'

'That will probably be nine months or more,' Daniel said.

'I shall advertise for jobs, so people can contact me.'

Kim introduced him to her father when they went into the kitchen at Rowandene. 'Now you can ask him about the automatic car, Mike,' she said.

'When you've tried one out, and if you think you can get yourself around a bit,' Daniel said, 'I have a spare bedroom or two at Home Farm. I can't promise you any luxuries, and you would need to be able to make your own meals a lot of the time when I'm at work, but you're welcome to try it, if you think you're up for something like that.'

'Now that we have Mrs Dunn to help us, I'm sure she would cook some meals to store in your freezer, Daniel,' Ross suggested. 'She is an excellent cook, but you and I know that already. I'm glad you suggested she stay here at Rowandene.'

'You're right, I hadn't thought of asking Dolly to fill the freezer. Even so, Mike would have a lot of time on his own when I'm away working. I want him to be sure he's doing the right thing.' He looked at Mike.

'I like my own company when drawing up plans. Would there be room in my bedroom for a decent-sized desk or a table?'

'Of course there would.' Daniel chuckled. 'But there are several empty rooms you can use as an office. I'm not intending to set up a comfortable home there. It's just temporary until Kim and I are married. Mel told me you like to keep checks on the different stages during the construction of a building when you've drawn the plans, making sure everything is as it ought to be.'

'That's true. If there are any adjustments to be made, that's the time to do them.'

'And I hear you like to be present when there's a visit from building control and other officials, so Home Farm would be conveniently situated for all of that while you're building a home for us.'

'Are you really going to let me do the plans?' Mike asked eagerly.

'As Mel said,' Daniel replied seriously, 'you ask questions and you listen to what we like. You know the regulations and what is possible or advisable, so we're happy for you to give it a go from beginning to end, if you think you'll stay in this area long enough to see it finished and approved?'

'Wedderburn House will be the first decent-sized project I shall be able to count as all my own work,' Mike said jubilantly. 'In a big company you're just a cog in the wheel and you rarely get credit. There's usually someone above, or in charge of a job, who claims your ideas as their own.' His tone held a hint of resignation but, for the first time, Kim felt there was also a trace of bitterness, too, and she didn't blame him. That was the way it would have been for her doing research with Professor Bradley.

***

Mike did not delay in drawing up the plans and they were approved without quibble at the next month's planning meeting. Unfortunately, the days were getting shorter and very cold. The builder and his mate, Fred, concentrated on getting all the foundations laid and inspected before the hard frost set in. Fred had already prepared a useful heap of reclaimed stones ready to start building the walls, but they all knew hard frost would delay building work.

Daniel decided the house at Home Farm needed some other heating apart from the cooker which kept the kitchen warm. It allowed Mike to get on with drawing plans for two small extensions, since people had seen his work at Fairvale. He settled happily at the big kitchen table when he was on his own. He knew if he could get enough work to earn his living, he could be contented working alone, with his own small business. As soon as he began to recover, he made his mind up that he would never go back to working in a big company.

Daniel made improvements at Home Farm, both in the house and outside, but he did not mention his reasons to Kim, although he consulted her on each idea and followed her suggestions, especially when she told him that if she was the manager at Home Farm, she would ask for one large shed as well as keeping the small stone buildings.

'If there were milk cows here, it would need a parlour and cubicles. A large shed would be versatile for dairy or for beef. What do you think you will do with it now the Lenoxes have left, Daniel? I know Bert, and his wife, too, worked hard in their way, and Bert proved himself very brave in the end, but he really needed someone to tell him what to do rather than be a manager. Dad says Sir Martin had got too old for that sort of thing. The land is basically very good. It is as fertile as Rowandene, but my father says it needs to be properly farmed, with rotations and some of the grass reseeded.'

'We'll make up our minds once we're married and settled in our own house, my dear Kim. Meanwhile, I remember you said the farmyard badly needed cleaning up and concreting.'

'You must admit it was like a sea of mud that day.'

'I know. So that will be another job to keep Nessie's young builder busy, except he can't lay concrete either while it's so frosty.'

'Can we afford all this expense?' Kim asked. 'I would hate any of my ideas to get you into debt. The insurance have not paid up for the house yet, have they?'

'No, but don't worry, Kim, my darling. They have agreed the final sum. It is larger than usual because Wedderburn Hall was a very large house and nothing could be saved, not even the stables, so they will pay in three stages. The final stage comes when the house is completed to their satisfaction, with possible plans prepared for new outbuildings, so that would include stables.'

As yet he hadn't told Kim that he intended using the money from his uncle's shares in the auction company to pay for whatever she would need to do with Home Farm. He wanted it to be his wedding gift to her. Ross had already told him that after the wedding he would give her the choice of the ten best young heifers from his herd if she wanted to start breeding a herd of her own.

Mr Dodds had written to say he had informed all the shareholders in the auction company that Daniel wished to withdraw his shares in the company over two years. They had eventually agreed to settle payment with interest over three years and he had accepted that. It was a relief to think he would never be bothered again by Estelle or her father.

* * *

Kim knew that her father wanted her to have a white wedding with all the trimmings.

'You are his only daughter, Kim,' Nessie reminded her, 'and you're young and pretty. I think you will have to humour Ross over this. He has already persuaded Daniel that it is the sort of wedding you both deserve, with friends old and new to wish you happiness.' Eventually, Kim had agreed. And at the time she thought Nessie had approved wholeheartedly of their plans.

Ross had accumulated quite a lot of money over the years, always with a view to buying Rowandene outright when Sir

Martin died. He did not need to buy the farm now. He could retire in comfort whenever it suited him, but both he and Kim knew he would not retire from his beloved cattle for many years yet. Even so, he was determined no expense would be spared on Kim's wedding day, or on a wedding gift to help her make the most of Daniel's generous gift of Home Farm.

Consequently, Nessie and Kim agreed to have another day's shopping in Edinburgh, this time for a traditional wedding dress for Kim and a long dress for Nessie as matron of honour. They decided to wait until the end of April when the weather would have improved. Kim knew Nessie had been looking forward eagerly to their day together, so she was puzzled, and a little hurt, when April came and went with a great improvement in the weather but a lack of enthusiasm from Nessie for any shopping, or even for discussing what style of dresses Jenny and Evie should wear. Earlier, they had agreed the little girls should have a colour to match Nessie's, if possible, and perhaps help choose their own style with a little guidance. Now Nessie seemed to have lost all interest.

Kim began to wonder if the first fascination of married life had begun to wear off, or even if Mel and Nessie had quarrelled. She decided to pay an unexpected visit to Fairvale on a Sunday afternoon when she knew Mel and Nessie would both be at home.

After the usual warm welcome the conversation became a little strained and Kim couldn't remember ever feeling any awkwardness between herself and Nessie. She looked from one to the other in bewilderment. She heard Mel take a deep breath.

'I think you must tell Kim, Nessie, my love,' he said gently. 'I'm sure she will understand, even though we know she will be disappointed. She needs to know now so she can make other arrangements.' Kim looked from one to the other.

'Oh, Kim, I know I am letting you down terribly on the most important day of your life, but I-I can't be your matron of honour. In fact, I may not even attend your wedding . . .'

'What! Nessie . . . You can't mean that, surely? W-we have been so close all our lives. You have been my second mother and big sister and best friend all in one . . .' Kim felt her eyes fill with tears and tried hard to blink them away. She never cried, but how could Nessie let her down so badly? Had marriage changed her so much?

CHAPTER EIGHTEEN

'We didn't expect it to happen at all,' Mel said gently, 'and if we had, we would certainly have tried to time things better for your wedding, my dear. Nessie doesn't want anyone to know because she thinks she is too old to be having a baby, and people—'

'A baby! Oh, Nessie! You're going to have a baby?' Kim's face was suddenly transformed. Mel had no doubt about the joy she felt for his beloved wife. He sighed with relief. 'But why didn't you tell me that? When is it due? Are you keeping well?'

'Oh, Kim, I should have told you as soon as I knew, b-but I really didn't want to tell anybody. I couldn't believe it when Dr Chalmers confirmed Mel's opinion. People will think I'm a silly old woman to be having babies at my age, especially when we already have two lovely wee girls.' Nessie's voice quavered, which was not like her at all.

Kim crossed to sit beside her and gave her hug. 'People will be pleased for you, as I am now I know,' she said warmly. 'I reckon everyone will be delighted. When is it due?'

'October,' Nessie said reluctantly, her voice little more than a croak. 'A-about the second week.'

'O-oh. I see . . . I understand now . . . We have booked our wedding for the tenth. It will be around your first wedding anniversary too.'

'I know,' Nessie said sheepishly. 'But Kim, I really don't want anyone to know — at least not until I can't hide it. Promise you won't tell anyone.'

Kim couldn't hide a smile. 'You're a respectably married woman, Nessie. You have nothing to be ashamed of,' she said, as though she was the older of the two. 'She hasn't, has she, Mel?'

'Not a thing.' His eyes danced with laughter as he looked at his wife. 'I keep telling her how proud I am of her. See how she's blooming.'

'It is true. You have always had a lovely skin, but there's an aura about you now, Nessie.'

'Just you wait until it's your turn,' Nessie muttered.

'Well, I would like to be married first,' Kim quipped mischievously, then more seriously, 'but this will mean a whole change of arrangements. Mel might not be free to be best man for Daniel. Jenny and Evie . . . Oh no . . .'

'I know. I've spoiled things for everybody,' Nessie mumbled.

'Dear Nessie, it takes two to make babies. You're not to blame,' Mel said, with a wicked glint in his eye.

'I can tell Daniel, can't I?' Kim asked. 'After all, it is his wedding too. And what about Dad? You know he will keep a secret, Nessie, if we ask him to, but I'm sure he will be pleased. Think about Granny McLaren, she was older than you are when she had you.'

'Nessie, dear,' Mel said, 'we must let Kim share our news with the two most important men in her own life.'

'Dad already adores Jenny and Evie, and he's said several times how patient and kind you are with children, Nessie.'

'I suppose you had better tell them,' Nessie agreed, 'but nobody else. Promise. Will you ask one of your university friends to be bridesmaid?'

'Oh, I don't know. I never considered anyone but you. I shall have to think about that, I suppose, but it will not be the same. We so enjoyed our shopping day in Edinburgh before your wedding.'

'You could have a day's shopping with one of them.'

'There were four of us in our flat and we were all the best of friends, but if I choose one, the other two will probably be hurt — and no, I don't want three bridesmaids and two flower girls. If I could, I would just have Jenny and Evie, but I know they're not quite old enough on their own. Oh, Mel, you're a doctor, for goodness' sake! Why didn't you arrange things better than this?'

Mel burst out laughing. 'You should know better than anyone, Kim, what happens when you put the bull in the field with his attractive cows.' Kim blushed, and that made both Nessie and Mel chuckle.

Nessie knew she could never explain to Kim what had happened that day early in February when Mel was in bed — supposedly dying with a man-cold. As soon as the girls had gone off to school she had taken a drink of hot lemon and honey upstairs for him. He had taken two sips, set it on the bedside table and grabbed her wrist, pulling her onto the bed beside him.

'I feel a lot better already,' he told her with laughter in his voice and no sign of a croaky throat. Much later, Nessie told him firmly there was certainly nothing wrong with his performance, even if he did have a bit of a sniffle. Mel had not been keen on her taking the contraceptive pill. He seemed to have vague doubts about its effects on some women. He had said he would take care of that side of things, but that day neither of them had given a thought to such matters. Nessie freely admitted she had enjoyed their passionate lovemaking as much as Mel, and she often teased him that she needed to make up for lost time. She had kept in the best of health and it was Mel himself who mentioned the passing weeks as they reached the end of March and Kim began to mention making a date for their proposed trip to Edinburgh.

When Daniel and Ross heard Nessie and Mel's news they were delighted. Only when Kim mentioned the conflicting date and the possibility that maybe none of them would be able to attend the wedding, even less participate, did they fully understand the implications. They stared at her in dismay.

'I thought all that frost and the delay with the house building was going to be what spoiled our plans,' Daniel said. 'I never thought of anything like this. I'm so sorry, Kim. I know how close you and Nessie have always been.'

'I suppose Nessie wouldn't agree to be matron of honour if you brought the wedding forward?' Ross asked diffidently. 'I know we all felt you should wait a year after your uncle's death, Daniel, and I would never want you to think we don't respect his memory . . .'

'I'm sure Uncle Fergus would be only too happy to know Kim has agreed to be my wife, whatever date we marry. He even told Dolly Dunn she was the girl I ought to marry, and he told me several times I shouldn't wait too long or someone else would snatch her away.' He looked steadily at Kim. 'So if we assume he would approve of an earlier wedding, would Nessie agree to that?'

'We shall have to ask her and Mel how they feel,' Kim suggested.

'Ask them to lunch the first day Mel is free,' Ross said. 'The sooner we know the better, for the sake of changing the hotel booking. What about the beginning of August? That's fully two months before the baby will be due.'

'I doubt the house will be complete by then,' Kim said, 'but so long as we have a kitchen, a bathroom and a bed to sleep in, we would manage.'

'I could take you to South Africa for a month on honeymoon,' Daniel suggested, more than half seriously. 'I would love to show you where I worked and introduce you to some of the people.'

'It seems to me that everything depends on what Nessie and Mel decide,' Ross said. 'Go and telephone them, Kim. Ask when they can come to lunch. Will you be able to make it, Daniel?'

'I'll do my best, even if it has to be a bit of a rush. We can usually swap a clinic or something.'

So it was arranged that they would all meet for lunch at Rowandene in three days' time.

* * *

When Nessie and Mel heard of the proposed change of plan, Nessie demurred and in the same breath Mel promptly agreed.

'Think how disappointed Jenny and Evie will be if they can't be flower girls again,' Mel said. 'Even worse, if none of us can attend the wedding — which could easily happen given the dates.'

'But I shall look like a ship in full sail by then,' Nessie mumbled.

'People will see how happy you are, lass, and the women expect such things,' Ross said.

'If we go to that same shop where we both got our outfits for your wedding, I am sure that clever wee woman will have some ideas about the best style of dress for you, Nessie,' Kim pleaded. 'You know, some brides and bridesmaids are naturally plump and have to wear floaty styles.'

'And I shall buy you the biggest and most beautiful bouquet of flowers to carry,' Daniel added with a teasing grin.

'Oh, you men!' Nessie groaned. 'There wouldn't be any babies if you had to have them.'

'You're probably right there,' Mel agreed. 'We should never survive. We're much too soft.' He winked at Daniel. 'The good Lord knew exactly what he was doing when he made women.'

'I think I read something about doctors in England making a baby in a test tube recently . . .' Ross mused vaguely.

'They have succeeded in fertilising the mother's egg with the father's sperm in a test tube,' Kim said, 'but the mother still has to grow the baby and have it as other mothers do. It has not been born yet. It's not much different to the animal transplants we do in cattle, except that the eggs are fertilised inside the cow before being gathered. That will become more common when it gets a bit cheaper.'

'Men would never survive the months of discomfort and indigestion,' Nessie remarked, but she looked at Kim and bit back a smile. 'All right, we'll go to Edinburgh soon then, and see if I can find something which might be suitable.'

'It suits me very well to bring the wedding forward,' Daniel said with a wide smile at Kim. 'I would not be so happy if anyone suggested postponing it.'

Secretly, Kim agreed, although she would never openly admit it.

***

The owner of the Edinburgh boutique remembered them when they began to explain what they wanted to see. She was delighted they had returned. When she realised it was to choose a wedding dress for Kim this time, she was even keener to give the best possible service. She had a selection of white wedding dresses.

'Never do I have two the same,' she told Kim. She eyed her tall, slim figure and then took them through to another room to show them the styles she thought would most suit her. Ross had insisted he would pay for the dresses for both of them, and had urged Kim to choose something for Nessie which she really liked, however expensive it was. He had always loved his younger sister, even before she could toddle. So it was Kim who explained what they had in mind for Nessie. Madam tactfully brushed aside Nessie's embarrassment and said how lovely it was that they had each helped to make the other's special occasion so happy. Kim said she would like Nessie and the little girls to wear pale blue, if that was possible.

'I have a very clever designer and wonderful seamstress. She usually works from her own home, but luckily, today she is here to see an elderly client. If you will come with me, I shall introduce her and we can hear her ideas. Yes?'

Kim and Nessie nodded and followed the little woman through to what appeared to be a private sitting room, where a middle-aged woman was thumbing through pattern books and swathes of different materials.

'Oh, that is a lovely colour and material,' Kim exclaimed involuntarily as the woman paused in contemplation of a medium blue in very fine crepe. Madam smiled at her enthusiasm and introduced the seamstress as Mrs Massie. The woman got to her feet to shake hands and Kim realised she was very lame and had a built-up boot.

'Please do sit down,' Kim said. 'I didn't mean to interrupt. It was the colour that caught my eye.' Madam explained exactly what they were there for, and Mrs Massie looked up at Nessie and smiled warmly.

'I know how you feel, young lady,' she said. 'Some women seem to want to show off their achievement from the slightest swelling, while others wish to be more discreet. In my pattern book from four years ago there is the very style which I believe would please you.' She was about to get up to bring the book, but Madam laid a hand on her shoulder. 'I will reach it, Louise.'

Mrs Massie found the page she wanted and turned it towards Nessie and Kim.

'This is a most versatile style. It reminds me a little of the gym slips we had to wear when I was a girl at school, but you will see the square neck is flattering to anyone with a flawless skin and slender neck such as you have, Mrs . . . ?'

'Sanders — Nessie Sanders,' Nessie said, smiling at the woman. Kim knew at once that Nessie felt at ease with the tiny, huggable-looking woman.

'Well, Mrs Sanders, the yoke is fitted to the figure to just below the bust line. From there, the front of the dress falls in small pleats. It is very clever because it can look as slim and elegant as you wish and yet allows room to expand without being uncomfortable or obviously bulging, if you follow?'

'Yes, I think I do,' Nessie agreed. 'It will not matter what size I am by August then?'

'No, my dear. And the back is cut in four long, stylish panels, which makes it ideal for an evening dress or for a wedding. Afterwards, it can be shortened and worn perfectly well as a day dress. As I said, it is a most versatile pattern. The only thing is, it does need a good-quality material to hang as elegantly as intended.'

'Is the blue swathe suitable?' Kim asked. 'If you like the colour, Nessie?'

'I love the colour, but isn't that an expensive sample,' Nessie asked. She had noticed the various pattern books arranged in order and she guessed they were arranged by price and quality.

'I'm afraid it is one of the more expensive materials,' Mrs Massie said regretfully. 'It is ideal for this style, but unfortunately it does need rather more material than most patterns.'

'That doesn't matter,' Kim said swiftly. She looked at Madam. 'So long as Nessie will be happy and comfortable. I am so happy that she will be my main attendant. You know it is what my father wants, too, Nessie. He insisted I must buy the best we could get for you.'

'Perhaps if I could take your measurements,' Mrs Massie suggested. 'Then I can make an estimate of the material and the cost.' She looked at Madam. 'I admit I would love to make up this dress, and if it can be in such quality material it will be beautiful.'

'But you wanted the flower girls in the same colour?' Nessie reminded Kim.

'I don't think as deep a blue as this would suit wee girls,' Kim said doubtfully, 'but I don't think they would want white again.' She looked at Madam. 'Would a pale-blue crepe-de-chine go with the deeper blue or should we choose a contrast?'

'I think a pale blue for small girls would be lovely. What do you think, Louise?'

'We will try the colours side by side. I think a miniature version of the same style would be ideal for young children too,' she added with enthusiasm. 'The waist could be drawn in with a silver cord with a tassel on the end for a wedding, and later it could be shortened and worn with a sash made from the hem, or a narrow white belt.'

'That sounds an excellent idea,' Nessie said. 'They would be so pleased to be able to wear the shortened dresses for the school party and similar events. Jenny is inclined to be a bit tubby at present, too, so the style would suit both of us.' Nessie chuckled and Kim realised how tense she had been. She felt a surge of relief.

'If you decide on that style for the children, I could easily draft a pattern for your own seamstress to work from if you send me their measurements,' Louise added. 'It would be my pleasure. I would love to see a photograph of you all on the big day.'

'Oh, we could do that, couldn't we, Kim?' Nessie said. 'It is very kind of you to offer so much help and advice.'

Kim had difficulty choosing a wedding dress. There were so many beautiful ones and she was fortunate to be more or less a standard size.

'It seems such a lot of money to wear only once,' she sighed.

'Both Daniel and Ross will be proud of you, Kim. You look so lovely in most of them. Will you be wearing Granny's veil, as your mother did?'

'I hadn't thought of that,' Kim said. 'I wonder if it will still be white, or if it will look cream. I have almost decided on the plain white satin. It is so beautifully cut and it feels so comfortable.'

'I try not to influence any of my clients,' Madam said, 'but the pure white satin looks so elegant, and with your height you show it to perfection.'

Eventually, with decisions made and arrangements agreed for Kim to collect the dresses later in the month, when Nessie's was finished, they headed for the shoe shop to buy Nessie some shoes with a small but comfortable heel.

'After that we shall go for the finest lunch I can buy you, dear Nessie, then home. I promised Mel I would not let you get overtired or take any risks.'

'I can't believe how much Mel worries, especially considering he's a doctor,' Nessie said, unaware of the dreamy smile which curved her generous mouth.

'But he is an orthopaedic surgeon, not a gynaecologist,' Kim reminded her, 'and even if he does know a lot about other kinds of medicine, it shows how much he cares.'

***

The time seemed to pass all too quickly and the builder and his team did their best to make up for the slow progress during the winter weather. Kim was fairly sure their new home would not be completely finished in time for their wedding, but she had no regrets about bringing the date forward if it meant Nessie, Mel and the children would be part of their day. After her father, Nessie was her nearest relation, and her dearest and oldest friend. Daniel's only relatives were second cousins, and two of them were abroad. One had written to say she would be delighted to come with her husband and two children, and it would be lovely to pick up old threads again and meet Daniel's new bride. They both invited friends from university and most of them seemed keen to attend. All the vets and their partners intended coming, and they were hoping there would be no emergency call outs.

Mr and Mrs Turner were looking forward to the wedding, as their own daughter was to be married in a year's time, and they knew that Ross would do his best to give his only child a splendid day. It would give them an opportunity to check out the hotel. They had already bought a small cottage with a few acres of land as a wedding present, and they had been to see the layout of Daniel and Kim's new home at Wedderburn. Subsequently, they asked Mike Miller to draw up plans for an extension which would double the size of the original cottage.

Kim was surprised and a little worried at the improvements Daniel had made to Home Farm.

'The farm steading is like a brand-new set-up,' she remarked. 'Can we afford to spend so much, as well as build a splendid new house for ourselves?'

'The insurance will fully cover the building of our house, and I want you to have a home you can be proud of.'

'So long as we're together, and we make it a comfortable home, I don't need it to be grandiose.'

'I know that, Kim. It is one of the things I admire about you and your father. Neither of you ever feel the need to put on a false impression.' Unlike the Roon-Kurchers, he thought with contempt, and thanked his lucky stars he had escaped that trap.

'We're ordinary people,' Kim said simply. 'When I criticised Home Farm I never expected you would take any notice of my opinion, Daniel.'

'Don't worry, my darling. You were perfectly right to criticise. I had no idea the place was so neglected and old-fashioned, but then I had never expected Uncle Fergus to buy an estate for me. It is not something I would ever have contemplated owning or looking after. Maybe it was fate, because I met you and soon I shall have the most adorable wife in the whole world.'

'Oh, Daniel. I know you don't mean that.' Kim laughed. 'Wait until the first time we disagree and you tell me I'm prickly as a hedgehog.'

'Yes, but think of the fun we shall have smoothing away the prickles and making wild and passionate love.' He chuckled and drew her into his arms for a lingering kiss. 'I am glad we brought the wedding forward,' he whispered against her ear.

With the wedding but a week away, Kim was truly grateful to both Mrs Scott, for making sure everything about Rowandene house was sparkling clean, and to Dolly Dunn, who had settled into Nessie's apartment as though she had lived there all her life. She had been tireless at baking and cooking to cater for the many kindly people who had come with wedding gifts, and then, in true Scottish tradition, most of the women returned to view a display of all the gifts the couple had received. They enjoyed the chats with other visitors while enjoying the refreshments of tea and coffee, dainty sandwiches, cream scones and a selection of cakes. Kim knew some came from curiosity, but she also knew many attended to sincerely wish the couple every happiness. Even so, it was exhausting, and both Dolly and Kim were pleased to have a day to themselves to relax before the wedding.

CHAPTER NINETEEN

It was a beautiful summer's day and Nessie arrived at Rowandene in good time, bringing Jenny and Evie, with Mrs Bain to help dress the excited little girls. She was closely followed by Nessie's favourite hairdresser in her own car.

'I'm finding it quite hard to reach up to do my own hair properly,' Nessie confided. 'I thought about getting it cut short so it would be easier to manage, but Mel likes it long, and since the doctor confirmed the latest bit of news on Thursday, he insisted he would pay for us to have the hairdresser visit us here when this is such a special day.'

'What bit of news?' Kim asked urgently, spinning round on her swivel stool. 'You are all right, aren't you, Nessie?'

'I'm fine. But the news was a surprise... we're expecting twins! I thought the midwife was doing more listening for heartbeats than usual during my last two routine appointments. She must have mentioned it to the doctor.'

'Oh my goodness. Oh, Nessie! I do hope today will not be too exhausting for you.'

'I feel the same as I did yesterday, and all the weeks that have gone before. Just a few things seem to require more effort than they used to do.'

'The girls will be so pleased when they hear about two new babies!'

'Yes, one for each of them to cuddle. The only thing is, I think Mel will pamper me more than ever now. He wants me to stop working, but there's nothing wrong with my brain and I'm sitting most of the time, except I feel it is important to get fresh air and exercise as I've always done. No riding, of course. I would never take any risks.'

The hairdresser insisted on helping Kim put her dress on so that she would not disarrange her hair, which she had swept up on top of her head in a series of curls with one or two longer ones at the sides.

When Nessie came through, she gasped. 'Dear Kim, you look even lovelier in your dress now than you did in the shop.' Her voice was husky with emotion.

'The tiara and veil sit so beautifully too,' the hairdresser remarked, with a glint of tears in her eyes. 'I do love to see a beautiful bride, and you look so elegant, Kim.'

'Could one of you fasten my necklace please? I should have put it on before my dress.'

'Oh, that is beautiful!' Nessie said. 'It must be new?'

'I'll leave you two alone now,' the hairdresser said tactfully. 'I shall take Mrs Bain with me back to the church and we'll wait at the door until you arrive in case you need anything. You both look so — so special . . . I feel privileged to be here.' She closed the door quietly behind her, but they heard her give an emotional little sniff and blow her nose.

'I have earrings to match the necklace but I didn't want to wear them today in case I lost one with my veil and people hugging. Daniel didn't mind when I decided I would like to wear my mother's engagement ring, and Dad seemed so pleased I liked it. It was a wee bit big so Daniel took it to a jeweller to have it made smaller, and while he was there, he asked if he could make a necklace and earrings to match. He gave them to me last night. He — he said he wanted me to have something extra special from him, especially since he had not bought my ring. He asked me to wear the necklace today as a token of . . . of his love.'

'He couldn't have chosen anything more appropriate, and so lovely too. You have always had lovely eyes, Kim, and they seem even bigger and greener today.'

* * *

The wedding proved to be the biggest and most splendid the village of Ryankirk had seen for many years, and it seemed to Kim that everyone who was not inside the church as guests were outside as well-wishers. Ross was a proud man indeed as he accompanied his only daughter to the church. Both Daniel and Mel were equally proud as the bride and her attendants walked slowly down the aisle towards them.

When the ceremony was over, Daniel kissed his new bride and whispered in her ear, 'I love you, Mrs Nichol.'

'I didn't hear what he said,' Evie said in a loud whisper.

'He said he loves her,' Jenny answered, 'but we knew that.'

There were a few muffled chuckles and many smiles as the congregation stood to watch them all walking out of the church.

There was a dance after the wedding reception. More guests came in the evening, including the return of all the staff from Rowandene who had left to do the milking and feed the animals, and all those who were connected with preparing a home for the young couple, plus a couple of veterinary colleagues of Daniel's who had been called to work during the day. It had been a hot day and, after the first dance with her new husband, and dances with her father and Mel, Kim disappeared to the hotel bedroom with Nessie to change from her wedding gown into a very pretty full-skirted summer dress in primrose yellow. She had a smart white jacket and white accessories laid out on the bed ready to make her escape from the celebrations later. When the time came, Jenny and Evie made sure they had hands full of rose petals to stuff in Daniel's shirt and down Kim's neck. Several other guests followed suit, accompanying them all the way to the limousine waiting to carry them away. Unknown to the guests, the classy vehicle only drove them a few streets away to where Daniel had hidden his car, complete with luggage, in a garage car park amidst lots of other vehicles.

As soon as they were safely inside, Daniel drew Kim into his arms for a lingering kiss.

'It has been a wonderful day. I'm sure you are the most beautiful bride any man could ever have, but now I long to have you all to myself.'

Kim knew he had booked them into the honeymoon suite of a hotel about twenty-five miles away and she sighed with happiness as they drove away.

She had chosen a two-week honeymoon on the Continent instead of a month in Africa. They were simply happy to have time alone together exploring Switzerland and Austria. Some of their accommodation was booked in advance, but they also wanted to have some time to go wherever their fancy took them. Meanwhile, their hotel suite had everything they could desire, including a bowl of fresh fruit and a bottle of champagne on ice, as well as a selection of savoury nibbles and an assortment of fruit juices and other drinks in the small fridge.

'I feel so very fortunate,' Kim whispered when Daniel released her from a long embrace.

'I almost forgot,' Daniel said, drawing an envelope from his inside pocket. 'Here is my wedding present to you.' He grinned at her surprised expression.

'But I have had the most beautiful wedding gift from you.' She clasped her hand to the necklace at her throat.

'Open it, my darling. I can't wait any longer to take you into my arms and into that big bed.'

'I-I don't understand this, Daniel,' Kim stammered, looking up from the letter in her hand. 'It says you bequeath Home Farm to me in its entirety, to demonstrate your absolute trust in me, now and always. It says the solicitor holds the deeds, but they have been transferred into my name and I can farm it as I please. I-I . . . why . . . I don't deserve anything like this.'

'When I refused to include your name as a joint tenant with your father, my darling Kim, I knew you were mad at me and you thought I didn't trust you. I have to confess, even back then, and in spite of our ups and downs and prickly encounters, I fancied you from the day I saw you calving that heifer all on your own. I saw how capable you were, how patient, but you were so damned independent and I longed to climb in the pen and sit behind you with my arms around you, lending you my strength. But you didn't need me. You managed perfectly well yourself.' He began to grin wickedly. 'And then you bent to climb through the feed barrier and presented me with a view of the neatest little derrière . . .'

'Daniel!' Kim blushed.

'It's true. I thought how much I would love to caress those delightful curves in the palms of my hands, and in the next few minutes that is exactly what I shall be doing. I can't wait any longer.'

Kim's blushes deepened. 'Wh-what has that to do with the tenancy, or with Home Farm?'

'I didn't want you to be at Rowandene, living so near to me, and connected by the tenancy to me, not if you had another man for a husband. I wanted you for myself. And now, my darling, you are my wife.'

'Oh, Daniel, I have never wanted any other man, not the way I want you.'

'That's good, because I can't wait any longer to take you to bed.'

He lifted her in his arms and carried her through to the bedroom, kissing every bit of bare skin with an urgent need for more.

THE END

THE JOFFE BOOKS STORY

We began in 2014 when Jasper agreed to publish his mum's much-rejected romance novel and it became a bestseller.

Since then we've grown into the largest independent publisher in the UK. We're extremely proud to publish some of the very best writers in the world, including Joy Ellis, Faith Martin, Caro Ramsay, Helen Forrester, Simon Brett and Robert Goddard. Everyone at Joffe Books loves reading and we never forget that it all begins with the magic of an author telling a story.

We are proud to publish talented first-time authors, as well as established writers whose books we love introducing to a new generation of readers.

We won Trade Publisher of the Year at the Independent Publishing Awards in 2023. We have been shortlisted for Independent Publisher of the Year at the British Book Awards for the last four years, and were shortlisted for the Diversity and Inclusivity Award at the 2022 Independent Publishing Awards. In 2023 we were shortlisted for Publisher of the Year at the RNA Industry Awards.

We built this company with your help, and we love to hear from you, so please email us about absolutely anything bookish at: feedback@joffebooks.com.

If you want to receive free books every Friday and hear about all our new releases, join our mailing list: www.joffebooks.com/freebooks

And when you tell your friends about us, just remember: it's pronounced Joffe as in coffee or toffee!

Milton Keynes UK
Ingram Content Group UK Ltd.
UKHW021949191124
451425UK00011B/86

9 781835 268667